SECOND THOUGHTS

SECOND THOUGHTS

BOBBIE O'KEEFE

FIVE STAR
A part of Gale, Cengage Learning

GALE
CENGAGE Learning™

Detroit • New York • San Francisco • New Haven, Conn • Waterville, Maine • London

GALE
CENGAGE Learning™

Five Star Publishing, a part of Gale, Cengage Learning.

Set in 11 pt. Plantin.

Printed on permanent paper.

LIBRARY OF CONGRESS CATALOGING-IN-PUBLICATION DATA

O'Keefe, Bobbie.
Second thoughts / by Bobbie O'Keefe. — 1st ed.
p. cm.
ISBN-13: 978-1-59414-772-2 (alk. paper)
ISBN-10: 1-59414-772-8 (alk. paper)
1. California—Fiction. I. Title.
PS3615.K43S43 2009
813'.6—dc22 2008053583

First Edition. First Printing: April 2009.
Published in 2009 in conjunction with Tekno Books.

Printed in the United States of America
1 2 3 4 5 6 7 13 12 11 10 09

ACKNOWLEDGEMENTS

Thank you to:

Priscilla, Linda, Julie and Phyllis for their early readings and feedback.

Marcy, Craig, Jim, Sheree, Jeannie and Shirley for their encouragement.

Don Ross for creating and maintaining my website.

Alice Duncan for her "ten-spot" suggestion.

Mary Sue Seymour for offering representation to an unknown.

John Helfers at Tekno Books and Tiffany Schofield at Five Star/ Gale/Cengage.

You've each helped make this dream come true.

This book is dedicated to Richard,
without whom I wouldn't be complete.

Chapter One

Petey dropped his gun and it went off.

Max fell off his chair, and Moose jumped a foot into the air. The bullet ricocheted off the tool box in the corner, struck the edge of the storage cabinet, rebounded from that to the door frame's hinge, creased Petey's ear as it returned to where it had started, then finally lodged itself in the stuffed head of the deer mounted on the wall. It missed Moose's head by an inch and a half.

Too late for the deer; it'd known its first bullet fifty years ago. But Moose was still breathing—once he got his breath back—and undoubtedly he'd prefer to keep it that way. He looked at the deer and its third eyehole.

"Almost killed me," he breathed. "The kid almost killed me."

"And he almost killed himself." With his gaze riveted on Petey, Max got to his feet, righted the wooden kitchen chair but didn't sit on it.

Petey touched his ear, then examined the blood on his fingers. He looked more confused than usual. His eyes moved to the side, and his head turned as he tried to look at his ear. He made a half circle before he gave up.

"My whole gang could've been wiped out with that bullet. Just a single, solitary one. And no one's even shooting at us." Max stared at his hands on the back of the chair, feeling and seeing a tremble settling in as he realized how close he'd been to the initial path of the bullet. He would've been first, then

Petey, and then Moose.

Except if the bullet had hit Max, it would've lodged in Max.

In two strides, he reached Petey and picked the gun up off the floor. He waved it in front of his brother's nose. "You see that thing there? That's a safety, Petey. It's a safety, and you put it on, like this." He paused long enough to demonstrate. "And then it won't go off until you want it to. You got that, Petey? You got it?"

"I'm sorry, Max. I'm real sorry." Petey's voice sounded shaky. His gaze darted around the room, lighting everywhere but on his brother.

Max relented and stuck the weapon in his belt. It wasn't the kid's fault he'd not mentally progressed beyond primary school age. It was just one of those things that happened sometimes. Numerous doctors had come up with possible causes, but nothing that could be treated or reversed. So if the bullet had done any real damage, it would've been his big brother's fault for letting the physically grown man, who was still a child in every other way, have the gun in the first place.

Petey's expression turned even more worried as his gaze followed the gun. "Uh, Max, it goes off real easy," he warned.

Max pulled the weapon back out with forced patience and pointed at the lever. "That's the safety, Petey, remember? When it's on, the gun won't fire."

"Uh," Petey said hesitantly. His gaze flitted over the weapon and its complicated mechanisms. "If you're sure."

"I'm sure, Petey. Positive." Again Max started to stick the pistol inside his belt, then he got another thought.

"Wait a minute." He felt his brow furrow as he looked at Moose. "It won't ring true if each one of us isn't armed." So, after a brief moment, he removed the clip, checked the chamber to make sure it was empty, and then held the gun out to Petey. "No one besides us will know his isn't loaded. Right, Moose?"

"Sounds good to me." Moose blew his breath out in a loud whoosh, then added, "Sounds more than good to me."

But Petey took a quick step backwards. "Uh-uh! I don't trust it. I don't want it back."

"It's not loaded, Petey. It can't go off, so it can't hurt you or anyone else. It's okay."

The gun remained extended toward him. Petey reached for it, then snatched his hand back. "Is the safety on?"

Max closed his eyes for an instant. Then patiently he reset the safety. "Yeah, Petey. It's on."

Petey accepted the gun, still looking dubious, but gamely stuck it inside his own belt as he'd seen his brother do.

Max wet his lips as he stared at Petey. Then he glanced at the table where his own gun lay, then again at Moose. They exchanged a long look. Max returned to the table, wordlessly removed the clip from his weapon as well, and watched his friend also empty his.

He drew in a deep breath. He felt more comfortable with empty guns than with loaded ones, but the feeling he was being forced into an action he didn't want to take was stronger than ever. Any other way, he thought, anything but this. But he'd exhausted every other option.

Damn Hayworth and his greed. But it wasn't even greed, not really, more like jealousness and stupid, underhanded one-upmanship.

He shook off the thought, ignoring his qualms. What was done was done.

He turned back to Petey. "Okay, almost set. Let's have a look at your ear, and then we'll be out the door. That tetanus shot you got last year is gonna come in handy again."

The ear had stopped bleeding and required nothing more than a quick dab of antiseptic. Petey had been lucky. Max didn't want to think about how lucky. Petey followed his brother as far as the bathroom door. Standing in the doorway, he gritted his teeth, closed his eyes, scrunched up his face and clenched his fists while Max applied antiseptic peroxide with a Q-tip.

Finished with the first aid job, Max put the medicine kit away. He returned to the living room and looked at Moose, who still stood next to the deer with its three eyeholes. "So," he said crisply, ignoring his misgivings. "Are we ready?"

Moose shrugged, appearing as unflappable as ever. "Ready as we'll ever be."

Chapter Two

"Annie Connie?"

With her hand poised over the light switch in her nephew's bedroom, Connie Robertson turned and gave him a questioning glance. She'd noticed the generally cheerful five-year-old boy had appeared both mutinous and hurt while he'd prepared for bed. But since he'd said nothing, she'd left it alone. Why borrow trouble?

"How come I have to go to bed first?" he said sullenly. "I'm the oldest, so I should go the last."

So that was it. *Because you're the easiest one to handle*, she thought, but decided not to tell him so. That might make it worse.

"Guess I goofed, Chris." She put apology in her smile. "You're absolutely right, and I should've figured that out for myself. Tell you what, you look at a book till I get the twins down, then I'll come back and tuck you in. Deal?"

His expression turned confused. He apparently hadn't expected such an easy victory and was unprepared to handle it. She crossed to his bookstand and chose *The Adventures of Biscuit.* He could read that one by himself.

"Here you go. Be right back. Promise."

His eyes lit up as he kicked the covers back. He wriggled around until he got his back propped against the wall, then stuck his legs across the bed and reached for the book. His bare feet didn't quite touch the edge of the mattress. Connie couldn't resist pinching the toe nearest her. They exchanged comradely smiles, then she went next door to the twins who'd celebrated their fourteen-month-old birthday yesterday.

Andy looked up and gurgled when she entered the room. Abbie took no notice of her aunt; she was too busy working on her crib. Her blanket and pillow were already on the floor, and only one corner of the sheet remained. This was Connie's third day with the kids, and she'd lost count of how many times she'd remade that bed. *Well, here's another remake.* Put the baby on the floor, close the door to keep the rest of the house safe, and then she'd only have to clean up after her in here.

She went to Andy first—because he was easier to handle—chose a sleeper from the drawer and then pulled his t-shirt off over his head. Giggles erupted. He must've thought that was the funniest thing that had ever happened to him. One pudgy fist closed around her thumb and he tried to eat it. She wiggled her thumb.

"I'm going backwards," she whispered. "I had one down and two to go, and now I've got none down and three to go."

He giggled again, released her thumb, and spit up all over the crib sheet.

Connie leaned her forehead against the top bar of the crib. She was going to have to remake both beds. This was going to be a long night.

An hour later, with the house blissfully silent, her gaze wavered between the stall shower and the bathtub. In and out, or take her time? Stupid question. She rinsed out the tub, activated the stopper, and eyed the assortment of bath aids while the tub filled. Then with a shrug, she poured in a healthy amount of the bright-green Shrek bubble bath, stripped and then put herself in. The ogre had done a pretty good job on three kids, so it'd work for her, too.

"*Ahh.*" She sank lower in the tub. Water lapped at her chin.

Every muscle she had surrendered.

The doorbell rang.

She snapped her eyes open. "Go away," she murmured, barely moving her lips. "Please."

The bell rang again. "Wake up the kids and I'll kill you." She sat up, fastened her gaze on the oatmeal-colored tile. "So help me, I will."

Silence lasted long enough that she started to settle back, then she heard what sounded like a key turning in a lock. She tensed, tighter this time. Kristy and Kevin were in Hawaii. Who else had a key?

The answer occurred to her the same instant she heard the front door opening. "Oh, no, no . . ."

"Kevin? Kristy? Anyone home?"

One other person would have a key. That was his voice, and now she heard his footsteps in the hall, fast approaching the bathroom door. She lunged to her feet, water sloshing. She'd left the door open to be sure she could hear the kids, and now—

"Derek, don't come in here!"

"Oh, you're in the bathroom. I'll wait in the—" When his voice broke off, Connie could almost see his frown. "Kristy?"

"No, it's not Kristy. It's—"

Her foot slipped as she reached for the towel. She grabbed the rack for support, dislodged the towel and it fell into the water.

"Connie? Is that you?" Then he was in the doorway. His face creased into a smile as he looked her up and down. "Yep, that's you, all right."

She sat down so fast water splashed out of the tub. "Derek, will you get out of here!"

"Sure." But he remained still, and his grin kept growing.

"Derek," she growled.

"Okay, I'm gone." He started to step away, then turned back.

"Where are Kevin and Kristy?"

"I'll talk to you later. Will you—"

"Aren't the kids here?"

"Derek—"

"Are you babysitting?"

"Derek!"

"Okay, okay." He held his hands up as if to ward off an attack. "I'll be in the kitchen. Had to drive straight through dinner."

He moved away. Belatedly she realized she should've told him to pull the door closed, but she wasn't about to call him back to do it. Not trusting him, she kept her gaze riveted on the empty doorway for a long moment. Then, letting her guard down a fraction, she stared at the soggy towel sharing the bath water with her. She didn't need this. For crying out loud, what was he even doing here?

He popped back into the doorway. "Sure you don't want me to scrub your back?"

She threw the soap at his grinning face, but he moved too fast and her aim was off. She heard his laugh trailing down the hallway as she watched the soap scum ooze down the buttercup-yellow doorjamb.

He was sitting on one of the tall counter stools when she entered the kitchen. Instead of wearing her shorty kimono over her even shorter nightie, she'd borrowed Kristy's cotton robe in strawberry pink and belted it around her waist. It was too big, but just right for entertaining unexpected—and unwelcome—ex-husbands.

He swiveled toward her. "That was fast."

She caught a whiff of boloney and mustard as he shoved the last of his sandwich into his mouth, and then he watched her musingly as he chewed. "Too bad you were wearing all those bubbles. First time in two years I got to see you like that, and you had to be covered with a coat of soapsuds. Not fair."

She resented the fact he looked so relaxed. He had black wavy hair, collar length, and an errant front curl that wouldn't stay put. It was again adorning the center of his forehead. He gave her another lingering up and down look, and his gaze settled on the hem of the robe spread around her feet. "Kristy's got two or three inches on you."

She made no response.

"And those inches are dragging on the floor."

"What do you want, Derek?"

He sipped from his beer, then held the can up questioningly. "Want one?"

She gave him one shake of her head. "Why are you here?"

He leaned back, resting his elbows on the counter. "Come on, Connie, what are you so uptight about? I've seen you in the tub before. Even shared one with you on more than one occasion." His gaze didn't leave hers, but his eyes took on a far away quality, as if his mind had gone back in time. To a memory he liked.

"What do you want, Derek?" She'd keep asking the same question, in the same no-nonsense, schoolteacher voice until she got an answer.

His eyes once more focused on her, and somehow he managed to turn his silence into pure suggestion. She closed her eyes and gritted her teeth. "Derek, so help me—"

"Okay, okay." He lifted his hands in that defensive gesture again, as if she were the one being difficult. "They must not have warned you to expect me, and I'm early anyway. We're introducing Chris to the art of fishing this weekend. Kevin and me."

That struck a chord, and she frowned. No one had said anything, but she'd noted Derek's name somewhere. "But they're not here. Just the kids and me."

"So I guessed. Like I said, I'm early. They're not expecting me till tomorrow."

"But they won't be home until Thursday."

"That's funny." It was his turn to frown. "I knew about the Hawaii trip," he said absently. "Ten years. How about that." He smiled proudly, as if it were his accomplishment.

Then he glanced at Connie, and his blue-green eyes turned rueful. "We didn't even make five," he said quietly, but didn't sound accusing. She didn't respond. After a short moment, he resumed his first thought. "Anyway, I told him I'd be here on the fourth, and he said they'd be home way before then."

Connie walked to the calendar tacked onto the bulletin board, almost tripping on the hem of the robe. She gathered a handful of fabric and lifted it up for the last couple steps. She scanned the calendar, then tapped the fourteenth with her forefinger, where Derek's name was printed below a penciled drawing of a fish and a pole. The artwork looked like Kristy's. Derek apparently had forgotten whom he'd talked to.

He'd removed himself from the stool to come stand behind her. "Oops. Looks like somebody misunderstood somebody."

He was too close for comfort. Connie took a step away, trying not to be obvious about it. "Well, that settles that. Doesn't matter who made the error. Call next week to reschedule. And as far as tonight is concerned, you can find a motel. Now, if you don't mind, I had a long day with the kids and—"

"A motel? What's wrong with right here?"

"No room. I'm using the master bedroom, and there's no other bed."

"Don't worry. You can keep your bed to yourself. There's an old wooden cot I can set up in Christopher's room. I always bunk with him."

"But—"

"It's somewhere in the garage." He started to walk around her.

"No."

He stopped, turned back to face her. "No?"

"You can't stay here. I don't want you here." Her tone was flat, no apology in it.

His gaze held hers for a long moment. He said evenly, "Well, that's certainly plain enough. Never did have a problem speaking your mind, did you?"

She said nothing.

"Well, you're not winning this one." He continued his move toward the door leading into the garage. "It's late, I'm tired, and I'm going to find the cot and set it up in Christopher's room. You do what you want to do. Goodnight, Connie."

She was left alone in the kitchen, staring coldly at the door he'd left ajar. As she listened to him mumbling while he searched for the cot, she considered locking him in there. It'd serve him right to have to spend the night in the garage. But he had a key in his pocket.

As usual, he'd left her no options. If a disagreement couldn't be settled his way, then he did what he wanted anyway, often leaving her steaming. She liked that fact no better now than when she'd been married to him.

Gathering robe fabric in both hands to lift it off the floor, she stomped to the master bedroom. She couldn't even slam the door like she wanted to because it'd wake up the kids.

Connie awoke to early morning daylight and a quiet house. She wondered how long the silence would last, then a shriek from Christopher broke through the stillness and made her jump.

"Unca Dare!"

She settled down again, giving in to a grudging smile. She might not be ecstatic about her ex-husband's presence, but

Christopher certainly was. Her smile broadened as she remembered how much Derek enjoyed sleeping in on his days off. Served him right.

A muffled response from Derek was interrupted by a horrendous crash that had Connie bounding out of bed. But before she reached her door she realized what had happened, came to an abrupt stop and burst into laughter.

Christopher had jumped on top of his uncle, and the cot had collapsed.

What a rude awakening, she thought with glee, and laughed harder.

But someone could be hurt, and that possibility got her moving again. The bits of conversation she picked up when she opened her door, however, assured her there was more emotional frustration at the other side of the house than injury.

The scrambling chaos finally ceased, and two sets of bare feet padded toward her room. The heavier footfalls sounded like they were limping. The twins simultaneously announced they were awake. Connie grabbed the pink robe, wrapped it around her, and tried to compose herself.

Uncle and nephew arrived at her door and stood side by side.

"I broke Unca Dare's bed," an apologetic Christopher said to the floor.

"You're laughing," Derek said to Connie. He was holding his elbow, but it was clearly his dignity that was fractured. "It's not funny."

One twin hollered something, and the other one answered.

Derek wore a white t-shirt, sleeper boxer shorts in a red and white diamond pattern, and black socks. His legs looked even more bowed and hairy than she remembered. She also remembered that sulky frown. She was working extra hard to keep her own face straight, yet knew she was failing miserably.

"It's not funny," he repeated. The frown cut lines into his forehead.

"Good morning," she managed, then doubled over with giggles. Giving up, she backed into her room, closed the door, collapsed on the bed and let go. She'd almost forgotten how great a really good belly laugh felt.

Chapter Three

At 6:55 a.m., the same moment Connie was enjoying her belly laugh, a security camera was hard at work at a convenience market located two and a half miles away.

It filmed a man entering the store who stood about six-four and appeared to weigh somewhere between two-fifty and two-eighty. He was bearded and wore overalls, but his features and age were indiscernible because he also wore a stocking mask. A run in the stocking, from nose to hairline, made his face appear scarred as well as distorted.

His two companions entered behind him, also wearing nylons, but without runs in them. They weren't bearded, were about five or six inches shorter and maybe a hundred pounds lighter. One wore a jean jacket, and the other one had on a gray sweat-shirt with a blue-plaid shirt collar sticking out of the neck. They were a bit overdressed for Southern California in August, but because of the early hour, they were able to get away with the extra layers of clothing.

The three masked men and the man at the cash register were the only people inside the store. The clerk was too involved in his magazine to look up at first. Using both hands, he spread the centerfold across the counter top and gave it an admiring up-and-down, side-to-side look.

Overalls and Jean Jacket had guns in their hands. They went to the counter and demanded money. The clerk finally looked up, the magazine slid to the floor, and he must have wet his pants because a growing stain discolored his khakis.

Gray Sweatshirt remained at the door with his hands empty as he looked nervously around the store. Jean Jacket stepped back and whispered something in his ear. Nothing happened, and Jean Jacket put his elbow into the belly of the sweatshirt. Gray Sweatshirt reached beneath the pullover, fumbled at his belt, then pulled out a gun. He juggled it, lost it, and it hit the floor with a loud clank.

The clerk jerked around, knocking over a display of sunglasses. With his eyes wide and his glance flitting everywhere, he gripped the counter as if for support. Overalls stepped away, pushing bills in his pocket and wrinkling his nose as if he'd just caught a bad smell, maybe something stronger than urine.

"It's okay," he assured the man. His gentle tone was incongruous with his masked countenance and cold-looking, steel-colored gun. "You're all right. Everything's okay." He picked up the magazine and replaced it on the counter. He even found the man's page for him.

Gray Sweatshirt appeared to be more scared than the clerk. The instant the gun had hit the floor, he'd ducked as if to dodge a bullet. Still crouched, he looked at the floor, at Jean Jacket, at the counter, and then, frowning, he straightened and delicately sniffed the air.

Jean Jacket remained still, his gaze traveling between the gun on the floor and his companion. Overalls swooped up the weapon, pushed Jean Jacket out the door, and grabbed Gray Sweatshirt's arm. Then all three men were gone.

The clerk stood frozen in place for several seconds with his mouth agape and his unblinking stare on the empty doorway. Then finally he must have remembered the alarm button. It was in the same place it always had been, but his mind had apparently drawn a blank. He turned in a circle, as if looking for it, then his gaze settled on something beneath the cash register.

Holding his right wrist in his left hand to keep it steady, he pointed his forefinger at the button and managed to press it.

The camera caught it all on tape, complete with sound. Not high quality sound, but words were discernible. And the same camera had filmed the same three men robbing the same store last night. But it was a different clerk this morning. Though last night's counter tender had also been unnerved, he'd come through the ordeal with a clean pair of pants.

Chapter Four

"Just for you," Connie said, giving each baby a teething biscuit and a rattle. She hoped that would keep them happy until she got herself fed. Their breakfast had been smooth for a change, and faster, thanks to Derek's help. At least he didn't hesitate to jump in where he was needed.

Neither did he hesitate to push himself in where he wasn't wanted.

Christopher was on his second glass of apple juice, sitting next to his aunt at the table and waiting patiently for his breakfast. Derek was in the shower. He'd gotten as much cereal on him as he'd gotten into the baby. Whichever one he'd fed.

She squinted, studying each child in turn. They still looked alike, too young yet for gender to make its mark. She'd just changed their diapers, but they were each wearing yellow sleepers, and she'd forgotten which child she'd placed in which chair.

One of them dropped its rattle. Christopher picked it up. "Here you go, Abbie." She thanked him by beating it on the tray as if trying to dig a posthole with it.

"Uh, Chris, how did you know that was Abbie? How do you tell them apart?"

He looked at each child, as intently as his aunt. "I don't know," he admitted. Then he added, "Maybe it's her nose. It's different from Andy's."

"It is? Oh, I see. It turns up on the end. Andy's got a button nose."

He heard his name and looked up. "Baw, baw, baw."

"Oh, yeah? Tell me more." He dropped his rattle, too. Hoping this wasn't a new game they were learning, she retrieved it for him. When she bent over, she paused, and then angled her neck in order to get a better look at Christopher's feet beneath the table. Yes, the right sneaker was black and the left one navy blue.

"And their hair is different," Chris continued. "See how hers is straight, and he has that little curl right there, just like Unca Dare."

"Yes," she said, straightening up. She smoothed Christopher's hair on his forehead. "You and your daddy have that same curl. Guess it runs in the family." She pointed at his feet. "Uh, Chris."

He looked, nodded. "Breaked a shoelace."

"Broke. Which one?"

"The black one."

"Does the other blue one have a lace in it?"

"Yeah."

"Then go put the other blue one on."

He seemed to think about it, then shrugged. "Sure."

Connie had time to set the table and crack eggs into a bowl before Derek showed up. His limp had disappeared, and there was only a small scrape near his right elbow. His dark hair glistened wetly. He'd shaved but had apparently decided to forego the hair dryer this morning.

His neat gray slacks bore no sign of having recently resided inside a suitcase, and his powder blue polo shirt hung nicely from well-developed shoulders. He always had worn his clothes well. She looked away, annoyed because she'd noticed.

The twins hadn't given her time to get dressed this morning. She was conscious of the borrowed robe and how it hung on her. Not giving the length of it a chance to trip her, she'd hitched it up before belting it, and a fold of fabric hung over the tie belt. Her little red and black kimono would've been okay with the kids, but its hem didn't quite reach her knees, and it fell in a deep vee she couldn't alter no matter how tightly she pulled it around her. No way was she going to show off that cute little number to her ex-husband.

Chris returned, wearing matching blue tennis shoes. The black one now rested in the middle of his bedroom floor, she was sure.

Derek came to stand next to her. "Er, I was going to do that," he said, eyeing the bowl of eggs she was working on.

She glanced sideways, annoyed with him now instead of herself, and feeling better for it. "They're just eggs, Derek. What can I possibly do wrong with scrambled eggs?"

"For one thing, you can get the pan too hot." He removed that skillet from the burner and put another one on it. "And they're better cooked in margarine." Turning back, and without asking permission, he took the fork from her and stirred the egg mixture. "Did you put anything else in here?"

She didn't answer. He gave her a curious look. "No," she snapped.

He looked at Christopher. "Sounds like I'm in the doghouse."

Competing with Abbie's rattle and Andy's jabbering, the kitchen TV was on, broadcasting a news program. Derek's head jerked toward it, and he put one hand out to cover Abbie's and her rattle. She looked up and giggled, then patted his hand with her free one. Though not as noisy, this game was apparently as much fun as the other one.

". . . twice in the last twenty-four hours, and apparently by the same group of three men. The exact figures were not available, but last night's take was estimated to be a small one, and it's thought this morning's loss would be even less. The clerk has—"

Evidently tiring of the one-sided patty-cake game, Abbie's voice joined and then quickly surpassed her brother's. Derek reached for the remote control and punched up the volume, but the program broke for a commercial. He thumbed the mute button and replaced the control on the counter.

"That must've been the convenience store I passed last night, maybe just a couple miles or so from here. Robbery must've just happened because there were flashing lights, big crowd, a lot of commotion." His face was grave as his gaze remained on the TV screen. "That's too close."

Connie wasn't comfortable with the proximity either. She was also puzzled. "But why hit the same place twice? That doesn't make sense. Seems like the motive might be harassment instead of profit."

Christopher reached for the remote control. He'd been watching the screen, paying little attention to the discussion. Sound once again issued from the set.

". . . standing in for Derek O'Reilly. Nate, it's all yours."

Connie watched and listened, then frowned at the TV and at Nate. "Why isn't Rachel on for you, like she usually is? She's better than this guy, whoever he is."

"She's in New York. Nate's the best they could get on such short notice."

She gave him a surprised look. "Short notice? You gave them short notice for a fishing trip?"

He shrugged without returning her gaze. His attention remained on the man who was explaining high pressure and low pressure areas. "I had the time coming, and I'd scheduled the trip a long time ago. Somebody must've gotten their wires crossed."

"It's a news program, and somebody got their wires crossed?"

"He's not as good as you are, Unca Dare. He smiles too much. Makes him look phony."

"Thanks, partner. You're good for the ego." Derek laughed and ran his hand through Christopher's hair.

"And somebody also got his dates crossed," Connie said. "He planned his short-notice fishing trip ten days too early." She realized how peevish she sounded, but she was still resentful about the way he'd pushed himself into the household last night.

With his hand still in Christopher's hair, Derek looked at Connie. "Yeah, uh, I've been thinking about that—"

"And he also got his skillet too hot to cook the eggs. I did that well on my own."

Derek uttered a mild expletive, looked quickly and guiltily at Christopher, then removed the hot skillet from the flame.

"You're running out of room for your skillets," Connie said to his back.

He turned, gave her a look that said she was pushing it, then turned back to replace the original and now cooled skillet atop the burner. This time, he switched the flame off before he again faced her. "May I talk to you for a minute? Then we'll do the eggs."

She frowned. She had a strong suspicion she wasn't going to like this. "I guess so."

"You need to learn to control your enthusiasm," he said wryly. He got the tub of margarine from the refrigerator and put a loaf of bread on the counter. "I may be ten days early, but I don't see why I can't still spend the weekend here as I'd planned."

"Oh, no, you don't."

"That way, Chris and I can still get our fishing in, and—"

"No."

"And I can give you a hand with the kids—"

"No."

"They've got to be quite a handful. And this way I won't lose my vacation time—"

"No."

Derek switched the TV off. "Chris, do you think you could play with the twins in your room or theirs for a few minutes, and let Aunt Connie and me finish our discussion?"

"Sure," Chris said agreeably. Unlike their earlier conversation, he'd been following this one with rapt attention. He pushed himself off his chair and collected a rattle in each hand. He looked up at Derek. "But you're going to win, aren't you, Unca Dare?" He directed an imploring look at Connie. "I want him to stay, Annie Connie. Please?"

Floored, Connie blinked. "Of all the—"

"I didn't set that up," Derek said quickly. "Chris just wants—"

"Talk about stacking the deck."

"I didn't set that up," he repeated with vehemence. "Give me some credit."

She unfastened Andy's tray and got him in the crook of her left arm. She reached for the other highchair and Christopher unhooked the tray for her. She swooped up Abbie, balancing her on her other hip. "I'm going to dress the twins. You do what you want to do." She dodged around the table. "And don't save any breakfast for me. I'm not hungry."

"I think I'm in the doghouse, too, Unca Dare." Christopher's voice sounded like there were tears lurking behind the words.

Connie stopped. Chris wanted to go fishing with his uncle, that was all. Derek was one of his favorite people. She was annoyed with Derek, but punishing Chris. She felt about two inches tall.

She breathed deeply, then turned. "No, Chris, you're not in the doghouse. And I'm sorry I got upset." She took in another long breath. "Of course Uncle Derek can stay, and the two of you can go fishing. Your mom and dad would have no objection, so I don't either."

Christopher didn't look convinced. The tears were still quite close. The babies were heavy, and it was awkward holding both of them. She knelt and put them on their feet. They toddled off in different directions, but she noted that Derek's gaze followed the one who'd wandered behind her. She held her arms out to Chris. "Come here, honey."

His eyes cleared, but he still looked uncertain. He came to her and allowed a hug, then drew back. "Will you eat eggs with us?" He looked hopeful, but hesitant.

The kid drives a hard bargain, she thought. An apology wasn't good enough; she was going to have to prove her change of heart.

"Unca Dare makes scrambled eggs real good," Chris coaxed, as if aware he almost had her. "They're not all dry and crusty and brown on the bottom like yours."

"Uh, Chris," Derek said.

But Connie just laughed. "Really good," she corrected. "And if they're that good, then tell him to make enough for me, too."

Chris rewarded her with a beaming smile. Connie was struck by how much the child resembled Derek. Inwardly, she winced at the strong and sudden tug on her heartstrings.

The twins were napping when Derek and Chris returned from their shopping trip. Connie met them at the door and put her forefinger to her lips in a shushing motion. Derek carried the box containing the new cot into Christopher's room, elaborately tiptoeing. Chris deposited a grocery bag on the counter of the corner bar and followed his uncle, mimicking his walk. One side of the boy's red knit shirt had ridden up to his elbow, which lent a lopsided look to his gait. Connie went back to her magazine.

Derek quickly reappeared. "Wish me luck sleeping on it. I didn't buy it with comfort in mind. I chose the one with the easiest assembly instructions."

"Build it now, Unca Dare?" Christopher entered the room so fast he almost ran into his uncle.

"After dinner, partner. Give me a few minutes." Stooping, he smoothed the boy's shirt down. "Why don't you go practice that computer game you showed me this morning?"

Chris looked disappointed, but he swallowed it. "Okay," he said, and then was out of the room as fast as he'd entered it.

"Great kid." Derek smiled fondly, watching the boy's exit. He shook his head and chuckled. "Endless energy."

"Uh-huh. Except the energy doesn't extend to brushing his teeth, washing his face, or even dressing properly."

"So I've noticed." He opened the liquor cabinet and held up a vodka bottle with a questioning look. She shook her head. He rummaged in the grocery bag and withdrew a jug of her favorite grapefruit juice, then held it up with a second questioning look.

She looked at it, reconsidering, then nodded. "Okay. Thanks."

He left with the ice bucket. She heard the noisy rattle of ice cubes, then he returned, mixed two drinks and crossed the room to hand her one. She sipped, and then looked up in appreciation. "You haven't lost the knack. You can still make an excellent drink without measuring anything."

Connie was sitting in the charcoal-gray recliner with her feet up. He took the end of the gray and white striped sofa, stretched his legs out and crossed his ankles. "Thanks to my years at bartending. I did everything waiting for my big break."

"I remember."

"I smelled something cooking in the kitchen. What is it?"

"Macaroni and cheese."

"Umm. I like the way you make that."

"That's one of the few things I made that you liked. Or would even eat."

He was silent for a moment, and she wondered if he was going to do the gallant thing and refute that statement or the wise thing and let it go.

"That's because it was one of the few things you made that was actually edible," he said mildly.

She'd taken a sip of her drink. She laughed, causing herself to choke, and he grinned.

"It's good to see you again, Connie, and to hear you laugh. It seems strange to be sitting across the room from you like this, yet it feels natural, too."

Connie looked down at her drink, saying nothing. She couldn't have said it better, but she didn't want to turn this into . . .

She frowned to herself, unable to finish the thought. Turn it into what?

"You're just as pretty as I remember," he said. "Still a perfect 'five-foot-two, eyes of blue'. And I notice you let your hair go back to its natural color. You never liked auburn, but red looks good on you." He flashed bright white teeth in a quick grin. "Matches your fiery temperament."

He waited, probably for a reaction. When he got none, he went on. "And you lost some weight. Maybe eight or ten pounds. You couldn't weigh more than a hundred and five right now, tops."

She wore an oversized white t-shirt and loose-fitting navy shorts. The only other garment he'd seen her in was the too big, shapeless robe, yet he'd accurately guessed her weight. Apparently, he'd gotten quite an eyeful last night, despite the bubbles.

He gave her a long, slow-building grin, and she knew he'd read her mind. She returned his gaze, but not the grin.

After a leisurely sip from his drink, he introduced another topic. "Kristy told me you were teaching first grade last year. How'd that go?"

She allowed a smile. "I was apprehensive at first, very much so. I'd never taught kids that young. But I loved it, and I've been assured of the same grade in the fall."

"Good. It's great that you and Kristy maintained your friendship. I'm glad that we . . . well, that our breakup didn't influence your friendship."

She shrugged. "We go back a long way. She's the closest thing to a sister I've got."

He appeared thoughtful as he changed position. Placing his right ankle over his left knee, he stared at his black loafer. "We disappointed them, both Kevin and Kristy."

"We personally didn't disappoint them. But I'm sure the fact that our marriage failed did."

"Yeah." He swirled his drink, then looked up with a half smile and changed the subject again. "How's Barry doing? Met the girl of his dreams yet?"

She laughed. "Which one? There have been so many—girls and dreams both. My brother is a happy and confirmed bachelor. He likes the field way too much to ever settle down with one woman."

"How about you? Have you met anybody . . . interesting?"

She held up the copy of *TV Guide* she'd been reading with Derek's picture on the cover. "The life of a celebrity is an open book. You're doing so well you're being considered for prime time. And, despite the hopes and dreams of many a fair maiden, you remain a confirmed bachelor."

Derek didn't look pleased. Evidently he hadn't grown comfortable with the fame that was now his or the publicity that went along with it. "Uh-huh," he said. "But we weren't talking about me. And you didn't answer my question."

"No, I didn't," she agreed.

They each let the silence stretch. Then he smiled and again went on to something else. She'd never known him to be short on conversation. "Chris and I thought we'd go out tomorrow morning, early, and then play it by ear after that." He waited a beat. "Are you agreeable with that? I might be spending as many as three or four days here."

She shrugged. "You're already here," she said, tone noncommittal.

From the twins' room came a loud thump and a happy squeal. Right on time. She put her glass down and stood. "We'll eat as soon as I get them up. If we wait any longer, my macaroni and cheese will be as dry and crusty and brown on the bottom as my eggs."

Chapter Five

The fast-disappearing sun had turned the sky a light orangey-red, and low-lying clouds had taken on a purplish hue that evening when Moose cruised by the convenience store in his vintage '65 Mustang. The automobile was freshly waxed, royal blue, and the engine purred. This was his second time around the block today, and Max had also driven them by once in his rundown, dark-green pickup. Neither of those vehicles had been used in the actual robberies, however. Each time a different automobile had been *borrowed,* and then returned before the owner realized it was missing. A lot of cars were left unlocked—or the window partially down, which amounted to the same thing—and a person might as well leave a key in the ignition as hide it under the mat or behind the visor.

Moose braked for two kids on bikes racing across the street. Neither boy had looked to either side. The bikes continued at full speed, then stopped at the store's entrance, effectively blocking the doorway, and the kids dashed inside.

"Dang kids," Max muttered. "Don't they have anybody to teach them how to ride a bike? And manners. I'd like to teach them some manners."

Moose drove past the store without comment.

Max stared straight ahead as thoughtfulness replaced his irritation. "So what do you think?"

"Still can't find sign of extra security."

"Hayworth wouldn't pay for it," Max said with a snort. "My

worry was the police might get wise and do it on their own."

Moose signaled for a left turn. "Doesn't look like they did, unless they're smarter than we are. And that's a distinct possibility." He executed the turn, traveled two blocks, then parked in the lot at a medical building. The car's windows were rolled down, and the scent from an orange tree next to the entrance of the premises wafted through the car.

"Yep," Max agreed. "Sure is." He'd nicked himself shaving that morning and absently fingered the cut on his chin. Despite Petey's intellectual limitations, he was more careful when shaving himself than his supposedly smarter brother. Max shot a sideways look at his friend. "You sure you want to go through with this?" He heard the doubt in his voice and figured it showed in his face.

"We've been through this, old buddy." With his gaze on the windshield, Moose let out a sound that was half sigh and half laugh. "I already told you I'm in it. Don't worry about me." Then he glanced across the seat and met Max's eyes. "You want to hit them again today?"

"Tomorrow's soon enough. Three times ought to get the point across. That he either gives the thing back to me, pays me for it, or there's more misery than this that I can heap upon him."

A loud snore from the back interrupted them. Petey sat in the middle of the seat, legs splayed, head back and mouth open. He let out another loud snort, and Max stretched his arm over the seat to gently shake the man's knee. Petey rolled his shoulders, turned his head, closed his mouth, and the snoring ceased.

"He doesn't have to go with us this next time, you know," Moose said, eyeing the sleeping form.

"Yeah, I thought about that, too. But we started out as a group of three and need to continue that way. Got to be consistent. The kid will be all right. But I won't insist he hold the gun if he doesn't want to."

Moose's face creased into a wry, but fond, smile. "The kid. He just turned thirty."

"And still only a kid. That's all he'll ever be." Max faced front. "And Hayworth knew it. He was well aware of that fact, and deliberately took advantage of it."

The other man eyed his friend's profile, then also faced front. He turned the key in the ignition and flicked the headlights on. "After tomorrow's hit, then what?"

"Let him stew for a couple days. Then go pay him a visit."

"Figure out yet how you want to approach him?"

Max knew what was being asked but didn't have an answer, so he replied literally. "Use the door knocker if he's got one. If not, ring the doorbell."

The big man snorted out a laugh as he steered the Mustang into traffic. "Should work."

Chapter Six

A sound awakened Connie. It wasn't yet daybreak, and the dark house was silent except for that grating, low-level buzzing. Then it was abruptly cut off. Glancing sideways at the luminous clock, she scowled. Derek was one of those heavy sleepers who needed to set his alarm at three-thirty in order to get up at five. That peculiarity had both cost her sleep and driven her nuts.

She felt her frown growing as she wondered how to handle this—and resented that she had to deal with it at all since she was no longer married to him. The alarm would continue to blast at ten-minute intervals, he'd continue to press the snooze bar, and the irritating routine would go on and on until someone else put an end to it.

But Christopher shared the room with his uncle, and the child was excited about the fishing trip. He'd get Derek up.

Hopefully, the same way he did yesterday.

Connie turned onto her side and snuggled into the pillow. When the alarm sounded the second time, she turned onto her other side. The third time, she rolled onto her back and stared at the dark ceiling. So maybe Christopher was also a hard waker-upper.

Wearily, and more than a little annoyed, she considered her options. She could put cotton in her ears. She could give up, get up and go make coffee. She could go into Derek's room and pour ice water over him.

The fourth time the alarm went off, a different one followed it that she had to answer. A baby was awake and complaining. Disgusted, she got out of bed.

"I'll kill him. I'll break his fishing pole. I'll hit him with his blasted clock."

Connie struggled into the robe. One sleeve got twisted, and that just made her madder at Derek. She remembered to hitch the garment up over the belt before she tied it. By the time she got to the twins' room, both babies were awake. Andy was fussing, but Abbie was all smiles and giggles and jumping up and down. Connie watched her from the doorway, not nearly as ready to meet the day as the baby girl evidently was. She went to Andy first, cooed softly and rubbed his back. He quieted, and she knew he'd go back to sleep if she could settle Abbie down.

But Abbie didn't want to settle. Completely ignoring her aunt, she continued her morning calisthenics with growing enthusiasm. At least she wasn't fussing to be let out of the crib. Yet. As Connie backed out of the room, Abbie got onto all fours and started pulling the blankets and sheet free from one corner of the bed. Her dismay growing in direct proportion to her niece's energy, Connie called Derek a bad name under her breath.

She went to the room next door.

"Hi, Annie Connie," Christopher said brightly.

Derek snored.

Connie switched the light on, forced a smile for Christopher, then went to Derek's cot and gave him a hard shake. "You've awakened one niece. Two nephews. And one ex-wife. Now, for crying out loud, will you *please . . . get . . . up!*"

She waited. He didn't stir.

"He's asleep," Christopher explained.

She glanced his way but didn't trust herself to speak. Her gaze returned to Derek and she tried to push him off the cot.

He mumbled and pushed back.

The sudden clattering in her ear made her jump. She picked up the clock, resisted the urge to throw it at the wall, and switched it off. Still holding the clock, she looked down at the sleeping man, and it took all her will power not to conk him with it. Instead she replaced it, very carefully, on the chair that served as his nightstand.

Next door, Andy was no longer fussing or sleeping. He was carrying on a spirited conversation with his sister. Defeated, Connie looked at Christopher. "Want breakfast?"

He nodded eagerly.

She motioned toward Derek. "Can you wake him up? I don't care how. Jump on top of him."

He frowned as his gaze traveled from her to his uncle and back again. "But I might break that bed too."

"Go ahead." Then, catching herself, she drew in a deep breath. "Excuse me, Chris."

She waited a beat, searching for patience, and finally found some. "This bed isn't going to break. And I'll take full responsibility anyway. Just wake him up. Somehow. Anyhow."

Chris continued to hesitate, his expression pained as his gaze flitted between his uncle and his aunt. Then his face cleared, as if he'd come to a decision and thereby conquered his worry. "But it's not nice to do that," he explained patiently. "He told me it's not nice to wake somebody else up just 'cause you're awake."

Connie's teeth ground together.

Derek opened one eye. "Can't you two go someplace else to talk? Trying to sleep here." The eye closed and he rolled over.

"See?" Christopher said triumphantly. Then, looking horrified, possibly because his voice was so loud, he put his finger to his lips as if to shush himself and his aunt.

Connie spun around. She gripped the edge of Derek's cot

with both hands and tried to tip it over.

"Annie Connie!"

Derek sat up and stared at her. He looked confused.

She straightened up and stared back. "You just saved your life."

She headed for the kitchen and the coffee pot.

A short while later, Derek came to the kitchen doorway and looked in at her, appearing uncertain of his welcome. "Sorry," he said.

Connie put her elbow on the table and her chin on her fist. She stared at him.

"You think the twins will go back down?" he asked timidly.

"Sure. In two or three hours they'll be ready for an early morning nap—a *very* early morning nap."

"I really am sorry."

Connie drained her cup and then stared at it, wondering if she had time for more caffeine before she had to deal with the twins. She was awake, and yet she wasn't.

Derek came all the way in. He poured coffee for himself, then refilled her cup. "I'll make breakfast. If the babies start clamoring for attention before you're ready for them, I'll take care of them."

"Gee, thanks." Her voice held a definite lack of appreciation.

He laid out breakfast plates. Christopher appeared, and Connie did a double take. His shirt was buttoned correctly and neatly tucked into his pants. His pants were zipped. He wore matching shoes, on the correct feet, and he'd even combed his hair. He looked like a model poster child.

"What happened?" she asked without thinking.

He bared his teeth. "See? I brushed."

"Good," Derek said. "Isn't that good, Aunt Connie?"

"Very good," she said, squinting at the child. Surprises, even good ones, were difficult to absorb when one didn't have enough sleep.

Derek put two perfectly fried eggs onto Connie's plate. Sunny side up, yolk both liquid and intact. Connie tried cooking her eggs like that every Sunday morning and hadn't gotten it right yet. Derek slipped the spatula under the third egg and placed it on Chris's plate, then replaced the skillet on the stove and cracked more eggs into it.

Christopher picked up his fork, and then paused. "Do I have to brush my teeth again after I eat this?" His frown made him look normal again.

"Of course you do," Derek said offhandedly. He pulled the bacon cooker out of the microwave, put the slices on a plate, added a stack of buttered toast and set it on the table. Connie cut into her egg and waited for the inevitable argument, glad it was Derek's problem. He deserved it.

"Okay," Chris said agreeably.

Connie choked on her egg, and her ex-husband helpfully pounded her on the back.

Dawn was breaking when Derek reentered the kitchen. Bright sunlight shone through the window above the sink, creating a warm strip that reached Connie's arm. He stood silently and watched her wash Andy's face. She looked up, thinking he was ready to go and wanted to apologize one last time. She was surprised he wasn't out of here yet. She'd received the impression he was dawdling, but Christopher had taken his cue from his uncle and wasn't chomping at the bit.

"Why don't you go with us?" Derek asked.

"Huh?" She paused, one hand holding the baby's fingers and the other grasping the washcloth. "You want to take the twins and me on a fishing trip?"

Abbie slammed both hands palm down onto her highchair

tray and let out a happy shriek.

Derek laughed. "Good timing, kid." Then, looking back at Connie, he lifted his shoulders. "Why not go? Thanks to me, everyone's already awake. And I've got more than enough food."

She just looked at him. Abbie bounced in her chair, up and down and sideways, as if searching for the best way to tip it over.

"Tuna sandwiches," Derek coaxed, a familiar light in his eyes that drew her toward him, yet warned her to keep her distance. "The way you like them, with lots of chopped pickle. Come on, Connie, it can't be too hard to pack up you and the twins."

At that she broke into a hearty laugh, thinking of all the gear that went along with the two children.

He grinned back, a little sheepishly. "Okay, so there's a lot of stuff. But we can do it, and there's plenty of room in the mini van. You've been here long enough that you're bound to catch cabin fever soon, if you haven't already. You need the break."

"Well," she said dubiously. Although that note of caution was hanging in there, she was tempted. In fact, she was already composing a mental list of supplies and gear for the day. He must be right; she needed the break.

She looked at Andy, who was trying to eat the washcloth, then back at Derek. "You do understand, of course, that neither of the twins has the slightest idea of how to fish."

"That's my girl." His perfect teeth flashed in a fast smile. "I'll toss in free fishing instructions—if you'll get them dressed." He took a few quick steps away. "I'll get the rest of their gear. Chris can help. He knows what they need."

At the garage door, Derek turned back long enough to give Connie a critical look. "And when you're through with them, look for something pretty to dress yourself in. Maybe you could find something that actually fits?"

"You're pushing it, Derek."

He showed her his back. A brief moment later his voice traveled to her from the garage. "Nothing you could come up with will *ever* beat that coat of bubbles."

Chapter Seven

"I can do it," Petey pleaded as he stood outside the mini market. "I know I can. Just give me a chance."

Max's heart filled with misgivings. He hated that Petey was asking for this, a chance to prove he could wield a gun, even an unloaded one, in a holdup. He was grateful their parents hadn't lived to see this. But if either parent still lived, it was doubtful the brothers would've come to this.

He looked at Moose, who simply shrugged. "It's your call," the big man said.

Reluctantly, Max nodded at Petey. He pulled the third gun out of the plastic grocery bag that held their weapons and stockings and handed it over along with a nylon mask. "Go for it."

Petey bounded for the store. Max caught his arm. "The stocking, Petey. The stocking."

"Oh. Yeah." He stretched it out and pulled it on over his head. His brother and Moose followed suit. Each mask now had a tear in it. Petey's was horizontal, running from his left ear to the right corner of his mouth. Max felt torn fibers stretching across his nose and had no idea what he looked like; nor did he care.

The three men stood at the side of the store, between their borrowed car and a dumpster that shielded them from the street. Something smelled rotten inside the dumpster. They wore short-sleeved, button-down shirts today; if not for the masks, they would've looked like a group of friends casually getting together for lunch. Moose's shirt was solid blue with a straight-cut hem, worn loose over khakis so that the gun was hidden inside the waistband of his pants. Black checks for Petey, and he'd tucked his shirt inside his cords; no one was concerned where he'd put his gun because no one thought he'd have one. Max also wore his plain white shirt tucked inside his jeans with the familiar jean jacket over it to conceal his weapon. He suspected the light coat had become his trademark. As serviceable as it was, he was going to have to get rid of it once their adventures came to an end. And he fervently hoped that was going to be sooner rather than later.

Today's vehicle was a light-yellow VW, and the lot was empty except for the bubble buggy, as Petey called it. Max had almost called today's outing off because it had taken an hour to find transportation. People were getting stingy with spare keys.

He held on to Petey's arm while he scanned the area, and when he saw no one he released him. He hoped their luck would hold, and they'd again find no one but the clerk inside the store.

It was a different counter person this time, and there was no one but the clerk, yet Max's heart sank even further. They'd scared the . . . you-know-what . . . out of the last guy, and he'd been a medium-sized, hearty-looking male. This one was shorter, lighter, and female. Max would have backed out, but she'd already seen them.

She was African American, solidly built but not overweight, and her thick black hair was severely swept back into a ponytail. She wore a red sweater over jeans, and gold hoops dangled at her ears. She wasn't the prettiest woman Max had ever seen. Yet there was something about her, a regal bearing maybe, that would make her stand out in a crowd.

Petey wasn't affected by the clerk's gender, if he'd even

noticed. He went to the counter. "I want your money. Give it to me."

She looked at him, at the two men who'd remained at the door, then back at Petey. As she turned her head, light from the overhead fixtures reflected off her earrings. "No," she said.

Max's eyes narrowed. Moose fidgeted.

"No?" Petey echoed.

"No."

Petey appeared to think about that for a second, then he said, "Okay." He put his gun on the counter and turned to leave.

Max dove for the weapon and reached it a split second after the woman got her hand on it. As nervy as she was, her surprise had slowed her down.

Max came up with it and banged it sharply on the counter. Remaining in the slightly bent position that he'd assumed when going for the gun, he pointed the weapon at her with his right hand, and the forefinger of his left hand pointed at the register. He said nothing and neither did she. Slowly he straightened, holding her gaze; the gun was rock steady. The hand pointing at the register jerked once in emphasis.

She waited the space of three long seconds before breaking eye contact. She opened the register, removed some bills, hesitated, then took the rest of the money and handed all of it over.

Wordlessly, Moose appeared at Max's side. Max handed over the bills and motioned for the woman to step out from behind the counter. He figured there had to be an alarm button back there with the cash register, and he didn't want her hitting it before he even got out the door. She stayed put, her coal-black eyes steady as she stared back at him. He drew in a breath, used it to make himself taller, and pointed to the floor where he wanted her to stand. Finally, her gaze still unwavering—but he was relieved to note some wariness in her eyes along with the defiance—she rounded the corner of the counter.

He risked a look behind him. Moose and Petey were gone. With two fingers of his left hand, and the first easy breath he'd taken since he'd entered the place, he saluted the woman. Then he dashed out of there as fast as an Olympic sprinter headed for the finish line.

Chapter Eight

"I don't believe this kid," Derek said as he caught Abbie and hoisted her up. "Every time I turn around, she's got another mouthful of dirt."

Connie hoped her brief sense of guilt didn't show in her smile. Though she hadn't known what the difficulty would be, she'd anticipated problems with Abbie, so had maneuvered to get Andy and leave his sister in her ex-husband's care. Her baby was quite happy playing patty cake and building mounds of gravel and sand. He wasn't interested in new culinary delights, trying to drown himself, or forging new trails in the wilderness.

"Ouch!"

"Careful," Connie warned. "She might decide you taste good, too. First thing Kristy told me was that they have teeth now. Might as well let her have the dirt, if she's already got it." As soon as the last sentence was out of her mouth, she wondered what Abbie's mother would've thought of it.

"She's got it," Derek said tiredly, "and she won't give it up. Let's hope she didn't get anything else in that last handful besides dirt."

He'd chosen an excellent spot for their picnic. A wide bend in the stream gave them ample shore and playing space. Sun shone through the leafy shade, creating a dappling effect on the blue-green water as it glided by, and constantly changing shadows played over the pebbly shore. Although they'd passed numerous parked vehicles on their way here, no other people had joined them on their piece of land.

The two fishermen had caught nothing, mostly because the younger one had quickly discovered he didn't like fishing. Chris kept falling in the water, losing his grip on the pole and then having to traipse after it. He'd eventually taken a short nap with the twins, possibly out of boredom as much as an affect of all that fresh air. Presently he was munching potato chips and skimming pebbles along the water. He was good at both, and it appeared he was enjoying himself more now than he had all day.

"Want to trade kids?" Derek asked hopefully.

Without turning to face him, and feeling more smug now than guilty, she grinned. "No, thanks."

She sat in the sun, enjoying its warmth on her shoulders and back. A slight, cooling breeze made the day's weather as perfect as the spot they'd chosen. She wore a forest-green tank top with braided spaghetti straps over each shoulder, cuffed denim shorts and white sneakers. Her clothes fit without being snug, but exposed more skin than Derek had seen since she'd stood up in the bathtub in all her splendor. He'd made no comment about her outfit, although she'd caught him eyeing her a couple of times.

"About ready to pack it in?" he asked.

She looked his way. "That bad, huh."

He grinned back and came to sit beside her, securing Abbie in his lap. He tried to interest the baby in a squeeze toy, but she ignored it and played with his hand. "Nah," he said easily. "I could always put her back in the playpen. But there's no sense in pushing our luck. What do you think?"

"Sure. It's time," she said, but didn't move. She was surprised at how comfortable she was. It'd been a long time since she'd spent a day with Derek. But, in truth, they'd been too busy with the kids to interact with each other and had mutually foregone trading barbs. They'd actually worked together.

"I enjoyed today, Derek. Thanks."

"Yeah, it was fun. Glad you came with us."

As their gazes held, ambivalence grew, possibly within both of them. It looked like a kiss might be in her near future, and she wasn't fighting it. Her common sense told her to get up and start moving right now. But the other half of her wanted to sit right there, meet that kiss, and return it.

Abbie ducked her head and bit Derek's thumb. He yelped, jerked his hand away and examined it. "She broke the skin." His voice held disbelief.

Connie laughed. Thanking her lucky stars, and Abbie's timing, she got to her feet. She put Andy in the playpen and reached to rescue Abbie from her victim. "They need changing, inside and out. She goes first because she's in worse shape. You and Chris can pack up."

A police cruiser with lights flashing came up fast behind the Mustang. Moose and Max muttered the same expletive, voices in guttural harmony. The game was over. That gutsy clerk must've followed them from the store in her own car, watched them exit the VW in the hospital's underground parking lot and then climb into the Mustang.

Moose slowed and pulled over, hands shaky on the wheel. Fear and self-loathing filled Max. His mind worked furiously, but he could find no way around capture and its consequences. The risk to him was one thing, but the risk to Petey and Moose was unpardonable.

The cruiser flew by. The two men stared after it.

Moose leaned forward and rested his forehead against the steering wheel. Max laid his head back and trailed both hands from forehead to neck. His breathing was shallow. Neither man spoke.

"Uh, guys?" Petey said from the back seat.

"Yeah," Moose said. His voice was hoarse. He looked at the steering wheel, the ignition and the gearshift, and finally figured out how to get the car back into motion.

Derek reached over and punched the volume on the van's radio up a notch.

". . . third time in as many days. There are as yet no leads. The gang of three has been incredibly lucky. An interesting development from today's holdup is that one of the men is not as hardcore as his comrades. He actually handed over his gun to the clerk, but—"

"Huh?" Connie said, and Derek shushed her.

". . . made their escape. More in a few minutes, after this important message. Please stay with us."

Derek frowned, but not at the radio. The van was slowing, and Connie gave him a questioning look. A fast talker on the airwaves was trying to convince her to visit his automotive shop, and she reached across the console to lower the volume. Derek pumped the accelerator, squinted at the fuel gauge, and worked the accelerator again. The vehicle continued to slow and sputter.

"If I didn't know better, I'd swear we were out of gas," he said. The sputtering ceased, the van rolled another couple feet, then came to a stop.

"We are out of gas." His frown deepened as he looked at the fuel gauge, which read half full. He tapped it with his knuckle.

The gauge dropped so fast that Connie blinked. "Huh?"

"Yep. Out of gas. Great."

Connie looked at the empty road. Her concern rose and her heart sank. "Oh, boy," she murmured. More expressive phrases occurred to her, but they weren't fit for the kids' ears.

Derek appeared more annoyed than alarmed. His gaze still on the faulty fuel gauge, he muttered, "Could be worse. How did we manage in situations like this before cell phones?"

He looked at Connie, as if expecting her to produce one out of thin air.

She looked back at him. "Cell phone? I don't have one. You know I never wanted one."

His brows met. "You still don't—"

"Yes, I still manage quite well without a phone attached to my ear, thank you."

"It's not a question of—"

"I was wondering how this was going to be my fault that the vehicle you were driving ran out of gas. It's because I don't have a cell phone. Makes perfect sense. Where's your phone, Derek?"

"As far as this week goes, I'm out of touch, and the only way to truly accomplish that is don't carry the phone around. So I left it in my car. I don't wear it attached to my ear, either, thank you."

"It's in the car you're not driving instead of the one you are driving." She nodded soberly. "Makes perfect sense."

"Annie Connie."

"Just a second, Chris," Derek answered, his eyes not leaving those of his ex-wife. "This is Kristy's van," he said with what sounded like forced patience. "And unlike you, she realizes the importance of a cell phone in case of emergency. There should be one right there in the glove compartment."

Oh, Connie thought. She looked at the glove box but made no move toward it.

"Annie Connie, don't you remember? You took it in the house to see how it worked. Did you put it back?"

Thank you, Chris, she thought. *Thank you very much.*

Derek continued to look at her, she continued to look at the glove box, and then he faced front and stared out the window. "Great."

Connie sat quietly. As her mind searched for a way to redeem herself, she recalled the sights on their drive to the stream this morning. "Maybe it's not too bad," she ventured.

Derek looked at her, at the kids seated behind them, then back at her. "It isn't?"

"We passed a house this morning, maybe only half a mile or so from here. An old green pickup was parked in front. We can ask to use their phone."

Taking another look at the back seat, Derek nodded. "Worth a shot. Okay, we each take a baby on our shoulders, and Chris can take the diaper bag, just in case."

"Wouldn't it be better for you to hike it, and we'll wait here? That'd be faster."

"And leave you and the kids out here alone with three holdup artists running around somewhere?"

Whether it was innocent or not, that statement held sexism, and the implication that he was more capable than she wasn't innocent. She didn't try to hide her annoyance in the stare she leveled at him. "Don't look now, but a streak of macho just showed up." She glanced at Christopher, not wanting to alarm him, but he appeared more interested than alarmed. The darned kid seemed to be enjoying himself. Abbie was humming monotonously, probably on her way to sleep. Andy was jabbering at whatever was outside the window, waving his arms as if conducting an orchestra.

She looked back at Derek. "Not to put you down," she said, her tone proving women could be just as condescending as men when the opportunity arose. "But how much more effective would you be than me against three armed men? One's wit would count for more than one's muscle power, wouldn't you think?"

He gave her a long, equally critical stare, and then opened his car door. "Choose your baby, put him or her on your shoulders, and let's get going."

Max wondered if his heart would ever stop racing. He was glad he wasn't driving because he'd probably run them into a ditch.

Moose wasn't doing a whole lot better. The Mustang unsteadily approached the farmhouse and then jerked to a stop. Everyone remained inside the car, staring straight ahead. Even Petey seemed subdued. The man behind the steering wheel was the first to show life. With a shaky forefinger, he pointed at the plastic bag in Max's lap that contained guns, stockings and money. "Might be our best take yet, and definitely the riskiest. But do you believe that woman? She had balls."

"Yeah, she was something, all right." Max eyed the bag, resisting the urge to fling it away. He couldn't rid himself of the feeling that something in it was going to pop out and bite him. "She took five years off my life, and then that cop who passed us took another five. I'm going to die a young man."

They finally opened car doors and exited. When Petey pushed the seat forward and got out on Max's side, his brother took a double take. *"Shit!"*

Moose jerked his head toward them, then doubled over the car's door, laughing so hard he was reduced to making strangled breathing noises. Petey looked confused by the commotion he'd caused. All he'd done was get out of the car.

"That cop," Max said. "That cop. He was right there. He passed us by, and, and . . ."

Moose got control of himself. "You can take the mask off now, Petey."

Roughly thirty yards away, Derek backed up into Connie and made her stagger. She tightened her grip on Abbie. "Hey, what—"

"They're . . . they must be . . . I don't believe this," he

whispered. He stared as if mesmerized at the Mustang and its occupants. "We stumbled right into them."

"Who?" Connie asked, confused. She'd been behind Derek as they'd approached and had seen nothing but the hood of a car resembling the one that had starred with Steve McQueen in that classic car chase movie. And she'd heard hearty laughter, which shouldn't have bothered anyone.

She and Derek and the kids stood within the shadow of a young oak, adjacent to the yard and at a side angle to the house. When she tried to step aside to look around her ex-husband, his arm went out to halt her.

"Be still," he hissed. "Movement might make them look over here."

"What are you talking about?" Because of his alarm, she also spoke in a whisper.

"The robbers," Christopher breathed. "We found the robbers."

Connie angled her head to look around Derek's shoulder. Three men surrounded an elegant, royal blue Mustang. If they looked this way, there was no way they could miss their visitors. The oak cast ample shadow, but its trunk wasn't nearly big enough to conceal all five of them. Fortunately, two men had their backs to the tree, and the third stood sideways to it. The trio then walked to the house and went inside.

"What makes you think they're the robbers?" Connie asked. Though the men were gone, she still spoke in a whisper.

"The stocking mask was a dead giveaway," Derek said.

Chapter Nine

Three sets of eyes remained riveted on the aging farmhouse that was in bad need of another coat of redwood stain.

Then suddenly Derek and Connie dropped to their knees, as if receiving the same belated command in the same instant. They took the babies from their shoulders and sat them on the ground. One child grabbed a handful of dirt. The other one's head bobbed as if the baby were checking out its new environment. Following their lead, Christopher crouched next to the adults. Music, country rock, broke into the silence. Though it wasn't loud, Connie jumped at the suddenness of the sound.

Her mind raced around their predicament, but she couldn't come up with a really good, really fast next move. They were in the middle of nowhere, and the skinny tree trunk was the only cover in a very wide, very open area. The only good news was they hadn't been seen. Yet.

Following that thought was relief she'd worn the green tank top instead of the orange one. At least she blended into the environment. Then she scrunched up her eyes and ran both hands down her face. She was thinking about how she was dressed?

"Now what?" she whispered. If Derek's mind was no more on target than hers, they were in trouble.

"Main road isn't too far off," he whispered back. "We can backtrack, find some traffic, something. I'm not inclined to ask these guys if we can use their phone."

"Annie Connie."

"Just a second, Chris. But they don't know that we know who they are."

"Unca Dare."

"In a minute, Chris. What difference does that make? We do know who they are."

Christopher was tugging Connie's hand and Derek's elbow. "But—"

In the same instant, their heads snapped around to the young boy, and Connie got the words out first in an exaggerated whisper. "For crying out loud, Chris, what is it?"

In answer he pointed at the baby who was halfway across the yard, already at an equal distance between them and the house.

Connie jumped to her feet.

"What do you think you're doing?" Derek caught her in mid lunge and pulled her back down.

She turned on him, twisting and pulling, and for her efforts she got her other arm captured as well. "The baby, Derek, the baby." She was battling herself to keep her voice down as well as fighting him to get away. "What are you doing! Let go of—"

"I'll go. Settle down and stay with these two."

"Oh, for—Stop it, Derek!"

"You stop it! While we're over here wrestling with each other, that baby is going to knock on the door and say hi. Now quit it."

Connie forced herself to be still. It was the hardest thing she'd ever done. "Then go!" she snapped. "Go!"

Fortunately, the baby wasn't traveling fast. It kept taking time out to bounce and twist to the music. As Derek took off after it, the child turned in a complete circle, its shoulders dipping to each side, then toddled off again. The last dance step had altered the child's course, and it was now headed toward the parked vehicles instead of the house.

Derek sprinted across the yard, scooped up the wanderer into the crook of his left arm, and pivoted to run back. He looked like a football player capturing a fumbled ball.

Behind him, the screen door opened.

"Hey, what—?"

Derek came to an abrupt stop.

Connie had a death grip on each child. Her hold tightened, and both kids squirmed. If the man looked this way . . .

Derek turned. "Uh, hi."

He took a few steps toward the parked vehicles. The man's attention remained on him, which meant it was a little less likely he'd catch sight of Connie and the kids. He was about the same height and weight as Derek but was older and appeared to be in poorer physical shape. Connie couldn't remember the size or appearance of the other two guys. But three against one weren't good odds, regardless of their physical condition.

Another man appeared in the doorway, and Connie's heart sank. He was huge.

"Uh, hi," Derek said to the newcomer.

"Yeah, hi." The first man and the second one exchanged glances. The bigger one shrugged.

The first guy looked back at Derek. "Can I help you with something?"

"I . . . ran out of gas."

"Oh." He looked relieved. "That's all. You want to use the phone?"

"Uh, yeah. Okay. I mean . . . please."

The big man opened the screen door and motioned for Derek to come in. "No problem. Come on in. You got a cute kid. Boy or girl?"

Derek looked down at the baby in his arm. Repositioning the child, he put his hand under its chin and tilted its head to get a better look at its face. It ducked its head, bit his finger and giggled.

He yanked his hand back. "Must be Abbie," he muttered.

The big man frowned. "Must be?" he echoed. But he shrugged it off, probably thinking he'd misunderstood. "Good old-fashioned name and a pretty little baby girl."

Derek and baby followed the big man into the house, and the first guy followed them.

Connie took her first deep breath since Derek had lit out after the baby. Her grip on each child loosened, but only slightly. Then she looked carefully at the baby she held. The twins both wore blue coveralls, but this one had straight hair, no forehead curl, and a turned-up nose. It seemed to be fighting sleep and was losing the battle. She looked questioningly at Chris. "Isn't this Abbie?"

"Uh-huh. Unca Dare can't tell them apart."

She let her breath out in a long whoosh. "As long as he doesn't have to change a diaper, it doesn't make a difference which one he thinks he's got."

She scanned the yard. They had to wait for Derek and Andy, but she didn't like their position. They were like goldfish in a bowl. It was pure luck so far that no one had looked their way. But neither did she want to try to hide behind either of the vehicles. Nothing looked good.

Her gaze settling on the house, she wondered if situating themselves on the side of it, at the front corner beneath the window, would be their best bet. At least they wouldn't be in the wide-open spaces. The window was curtained, so it was doubtful their approach would be detected unless someone inside came right up to the glass. And if anyone did so, she and the kids crouching beneath the tree limbs would show up as clearly as a picture on a postcard anyway. She bit her lip, not wanting to make a move for fear it would be the wrong one, but she had to do something.

"Okay," she said under her breath. Just in case, she mentally ran through the moves she'd learned in the self-defense class she'd taken last year. But the class hadn't covered carrying a baby with a five-year-old child in tow. She'd have to wing that part.

She turned to Chris. "We might be better off closer to the house, right there at the corner. We're not concealed very well here. If we go over there, we might even be able to overhear Uncle Dare and the other men. What do you think, partner?"

He looked at the house, then back at her. "Yes," he said seriously. "I think that's what we should do."

Connie swallowed, acutely aware of just how much she loved this child and his siblings. Fleetingly, she wondered if perhaps she and Chris and the one baby should try to backtrack instead but quickly discarded that thought. The worst thing they could do was become separated. They had to stick together.

And she decided she was going to buy a cell phone at her first opportunity and wear it in her pocket for the rest of her life.

She looked at Abbie. The fresh air and activity had knocked the baby out. She wouldn't be warning anybody of their presence. Connie nodded to Christopher, hefted the baby up, and they made their way across the yard. Chris dutifully tugged the diaper bag along with him.

Hank Williams, Jr. was cut off in mid-note. Connie frowned and paused, not liking the silence. The music would've helped mask sounds she and the two kids might make. But they were halfway there and couldn't stand out here pretending they were invisible. Chris looked up at her, his eyes both trusting and questioning. She breathed deeply, drawing on her courage, and they continued. Then finally they were crouched beneath the window at the front corner of the house. The few minutes their travel must have taken had seemed like an hour.

". . . sure look familiar to me," someone inside the building was saying. "You're positive we haven't met?"

"Yes," Derek's voice said. "I mean, no, we haven't met."

"And your name's Derek. Even that's familiar, but I can't figure out why."

Derek made a noncommittal sound in response.

"Running out of gas with a baby in tow can't be fun," said a deeper voice. Connie assumed that must be the biggest man, and she caught a touch of humor in his tone. That was reassuring, but he still had a mask in his pocket and probably a gun in there, too.

"They call me Moose, Mr. Derek. And that's Max, and that's his brother, Petey. Nice to meet you."

"My pleasure," Derek said. His voice sounded forced. "And, uh, well, since the auto club said it will take close to an hour . . ."

Connie scrunched her face up. An *hour?* He needed a new auto club.

"Abbie and I should start back to the car."

"Won't work, Mr. Derek. You gave them this address, not the location of your car."

Connie closed her eyes and shook her head.

"Yeah, that's right. That's what I did. Uh, well . . ."

"What's that smell?" asked a new voice. Though it was deep enough that it was undeniably adult male, something in it reminded Connie of her first-graders. And Petey was a nickname for a child, not a grown man. She felt lines forming in her forehead as she tried to work out who the men were—more important, what their natures were—from the sounds of their voices alone. Neat trick. "Somebody stinks. Just like yesterday."

"Abbie must've messed her pants," Moose said. A smile in his voice came through loud and clear. "Babies do that."

Derek swore mildly. "Yep, that's what she did, all right."

Moose said, "No diaper bag. You didn't bring anything with you?"

"I brought a bag." Derek sounded relieved. "It's outside. I'll go get it."

"I'll walk with you." That was the first voice again, which probably belonged to Max. He sounded suspicious, and Connie wasn't surprised. Derek was too nervous. His mind was clearly on the group he'd left outside, and his worry showed. And Max might become even more suspicious once he found out Derek didn't know what sex his baby was.

"That's not necessary," Derek said, but Connie didn't think he was going to win this one. She looked around, thinking hard, then pulled the bag apart, put aside a diaper and some moist wipes, and crept to the edge of the house with the carryall, holding the sleeping Abbie on her shoulder. Fervently she wished for something to slow Max down. All she needed was ten seconds. Five.

"You go ahead," Max said. "I need to get something, but I'll be right behind you."

Derek appeared, looking anxiously toward the spot where he'd left Connie and the kids and making go-away motions. Then he faltered, appearing both puzzled and relieved that they weren't there.

Connie stepped out from the side of the house. Derek jumped in surprise, which made his baby laugh. She dropped the bag at his feet and thrust the sleeping Abbie at him. Out of reflex, he accepted the child into his free arm. Connie grabbed the wide-awake Andy and dodged back around the side of the house.

"Uh," Derek said.

The screen door opened. "Oh, you got the bag already. That was quick."

After a short silence, Max said, "Never saw a baby go to sleep so fast. What happened?"

"Must be the fresh air," Derek said lamely.

Abbie made fussing sounds. She probably didn't appreciate being passed around like a football while she was trying to sleep. Her fussing grew fainter as Derek carried her into the house.

Moose said, "Poor little thing. What happened? A minute ago she was all smiles." Then, a short moment later, he said, "Well, I'll be. That diaper is as clean as can be. Could've sworn there was a load in there."

"Yeah," Derek said. He sounded weary, like he was having difficulty keeping up. "I thought so, too. Must've been gas. Babies do that, too."

"You want to watch TV, Mr. Derek, till the auto man gets here?" asked the young yet grownup voice. "Here's the *TV Guide*. You can watch anything you want."

"O'Reilly! Derek O'Reilly. I knew I knew you!" Then the tone turned even more suspicious. "Why didn't you tell us who you were? And that your first name is Derek, not your last, like we thought."

Finishing up the fastest changing job she'd ever done, Connie's hands grew still. She waited anxiously to discover if the fact that Derek's hosts had a celebrity in their midst would turn out to be advantageous or disadvantageous to their guest.

"Well, uh . . ." Her ex-husband was usually quite glib, but he couldn't prove that by his present display of conversational skills.

"And, come to think of it, it says in here you're not married and you don't have kids. Who's that you're holding?"

"I'm divorced. And this is," he paused, sounding uncertain, then finished. "My niece. And you wouldn't believe what happens to too many people once they realize they're talking to a television personality. I'm a lot more comfortable just being me."

"Oh." A short pause, then the voice eased up. "Makes sense."

"Max, go outside with me for a minute?"

Uh-oh, Connie thought. That had been the husky voice, but it no longer sounded like it had humor in it. Once one guy's suspicion had seemed to ease, the other one's got started. She wondered what was wrong. And she also wondered precisely where outside it was these guys wanted to go.

Her gaze flew around the yard, but no cover had popped up anywhere since the last time she'd looked. The only place left to hide was the back of the house. She lifted Andy in one arm, snatched up his soiled diaper in her other hand, and motioned for Christopher to follow her. She hoped Andy would behave himself and not start talking to a leaf. She would've been safer with the sleeping Abbie.

As she rounded the side of the house at a full run she almost collided with the two men who were exiting the back door.

Everybody froze. She looked at them and they looked at her. The three people stood like statues for what seemed like eternity. Chris remained hidden around the corner of the house, but Connie didn't know how that was going to help.

Out of necessity, she took in a breath.

The shorter man came to life. He pointed at the baby. He looked back inside the house, then again at Connie and her ward. "But . . ."

"Twins." The big man's face creased into a smile. "Hey, Max, it's finally making sense."

The smaller guy looked at the bigger guy. "It is?"

"You might as well come on in," the big one said. Moose was an apt name for him. And Max now appeared more dumbfounded than suspicious. "But first," Moose paused and lifted the lid on the garbage can sitting next to the door. "You can throw that dirty diaper in here. And I'll go so far as to guess that baby has a boy's name. Right?"

Connie said nothing. She felt rooted to the spot of ground on which she stood.

Moose said to Max, "They must've seen Petey's mask." Then his gaze returned to Connie. "Come on in. No one's going to hurt anyone, but we still can't let you go. You must be Derek's sister, the twins' mother?"

She shook her head.

That seemed to throw him. "No? Well, we can finish our introductions inside." He stood aside and motioned for her to enter. When she still hesitated, he looked beyond her, scanning the yard. "Er, there's no one else out here?"

Her shoulders sagged as she blew her breath out. "Chris?"

He appeared at the corner of the house. "Hi."

Max appeared taken aback, but Moose merely chuckled. "It just keeps getting better and better."

Though the situation frightened her, Connie realized she didn't fear Moose, despite his size. But she wasn't sure about the other guy. He was too hard to read.

The shorter man's gaze continued to travel back and forth. Connie and Andy, then Chris, then back again, like he was following a tennis ball. He didn't appear pleased with the tennis ball.

"It's a nursery school," he muttered. "They brought a whole school with them. What are we going to do with all these kids?"

Chapter Ten

"So let me see if I've got this straight," Max said. He'd carried a kitchen chair into the family room, and he sat with both feet on the floor and hands on his knees. He appeared to be neither friendly nor hostile. Now that he'd gotten past his initial surprise, he even seemed to be taking in stride the various ages of his uninvited guests.

"You're divorced, from each other." He lifted his hands, ticked the point off on his left forefinger, and then went on to the next item and digit. "The kids belong to Derek's brother and his wife. They're in Hawaii until Thursday. Aunt Connie was babysitting. Uncle Derek showed up and took everybody fishing."

The last point went on his left thumb. He changed hands. "You ran out of gas, packed everybody up and went hiking, and managed to arrive just in time to see Petey's mask. Abbie went to sleep, and Andy went for an unauthorized walk and pooped his pants."

Out of digits, he dropped his hands and stared straight at Connie, who sat next to Derek on the camel-colored sofa with its sagging cushions. "At which time Aunt Connie turned herself into a one-man tag team, running circles around everybody until she ran smack into the people she was trying to run away from."

His attention switched to Derek, who'd been gazing steadily at him. "Did I miss anything?"

"No." Connie bit the word off. She'd tightened up the moment Christopher had opened his mouth. Neither she nor Derek had said a word, but Max now knew everything about them except their social security numbers.

On the straight-backed wooden chair, Max sat taller than anyone else. Moose was next to him, looking comfortable in an upholstered easy chair with Abbie on his lap. Connie wasn't sure how she'd gotten there, but she seemed okay. She appeared fascinated with his ring and watch. Andy was on Connie's lap, wrestling with his shoe.

"Okay, now let's see if we've got the other side of it straight," Derek countered. Once everything and everyone was out in the open, he'd regained his cool and now effectively matched Max's casual yet authoritative manner. It had to be pure facade, and Connie gave him marks for his acting skills.

He stretched his arm along the back of the sofa, fingers brushing her shoulder. Andy eyed his uncle's hand. "You mean us no harm, but we're not free to go. You're armed and will use any means necessary to ensure our cooperation. Julian Hayworth, franchise owner of the convenience store you've robbed three times, stole something from you and you're trying to get it back, again by any means necessary. You hope to accomplish this within a few more days, and we should consider ourselves your *guests* until then, at which time you'll be clearing out for parts unknown, and we'll be allowed to resume our normal lives."

He waited a beat before adding, "Did I miss anything?"

"Nope," Max said, gaze and voice level. "Couldn't have summed it up better."

Andy twisted around to reach for Derek's hand. The child's arm span wasn't quite long enough, so he tried to climb up the front of his aunt.

"May Connie and I talk this over? Privately."

Max gave him a long look. "What's there to talk over? It's not as if you have a decision to make."

Andy got one of Derek's fingers and pulled on it. Derek resisted without looking at the baby. "We still want to talk," he maintained, eyes not leaving those of his host. "And that's not an unreasonable request."

Max's expression told Connie he knew he was being tested. Also evident was his reluctance to be forced into taking a stand. After a short moment, he shrugged, then indicated the front door with one hand and the hall leading to the back door with the other, giving them their choice.

Derek stood and extended his hand to Connie. But Andy plopped back down, tried to turn around, and Connie needed both hands to hold on to him. With his eyes and a nod of his head, Derek indicated the back door where they wouldn't be easily overheard. That was a fact she wished had occurred to her earlier when she'd been trying to guess where Max and Moose were headed.

Once she got a firm grip on Andy, she rose from the sofa, and Max said, "The baby stays here."

She wondered what difference it made, since they still had the other two kids, but she didn't argue. Instead she looked uncertainly between her nephew and Moose. Christopher, no longer involved with disclosing family secrets, was helping Petey set up a toy garage in the corner, on top of and around what looked like a metal tool chest.

The big man patted his unoccupied knee. "Right here. Got two knees, so I can manage two kids. I'm working on figuring out who's who. Then I'll be one up on Uncle Dare."

Derek led the way outside. "So what do you think?" he asked, once she'd passed him and he pulled the door closed behind them. "Max is the one in charge, but what's your take on Moose?" He'd dropped the cool and controlled manner he'd assumed when dealing with Max. He now appeared as anxious and worried as she felt.

"He's content to let Max run it," she said. "But even though Moose seems mellow and good-natured, he's still quite formidable."

"They're going to be separating us and splitting the kids between us, too. That'll be to their advantage. Thanks to Chris, they know we won't be missed until Thursday." Shaking his head, Derek looked toward a wooded area behind the house. "We've got no bargaining power. No way to fight back."

His gaze returned to her. "Petey must be retarded."

She nodded. "Mentally, I think he's somewhere around the same age as Chris. And he has no more harm or violence in him than Chris does, either."

"So I figured. But the other two are enough to worry about."

Again she nodded. "I haven't seen guns, but I believe they've got them."

"They don't need guns. We're kind of outnumbered." He made a sound somewhere between a snort and a laugh. "Depending on how you look at it. Granted, we're five to their three, but four of us are a little on the small side."

She frowned. "Will you be serious, please? We're being kidnapped, and you're making jokes?"

He frowned back. "What makes you think that was a joke?"

By sheer will alone, she managed not to hit him. "We've got two competent adults here, Derek. Two. Are you having trouble counting?"

He looked at the sky for a long moment, then back at her. "Yes, let's be serious here, Connie. What exactly are you going to do? Talk them out of their guns, or arm-wrestle for them?"

"Well, now, there's a thought, Mr. Hotshot. How about you go for the guns while I'm busy arm-wrestling?" Then, needing to rein herself in, she jerked her gaze away. After blowing her breath out in a noisy rush, she muttered to the porch door, "My goodness, but isn't this discussion doing us a whole lot of good?"

She looked back, gave him a hard stare, and then closed the distance between them in order to put her hands flat against his chest. He was nine inches taller, and she had to tilt her head to meet his eyes. "Hey, super hero, we're in this together. If I get us out of here, I promise to take you along. Now, can we go on to something else? Hopefully something a little more productive?"

A hint of a smile curved his lips. "Looking at you right now, I get the feeling you just might be able to pull something off. I stand corrected."

She felt her facial muscles slacken. She dropped her arms and stepped back.

"So that's how to render you speechless," he said wryly. "I'll have to remember that."

Then quickly he sobered and got back to the issue at hand. And she no longer sensed either condescension or confrontation from him. "Speaking of guns," he said, "I think Max has one stuck in the back of his jeans. He wasn't wearing that jacket when I got here, and I think he went to get it and the gun before following me outside."

"You're right," Max said, and Derek's head snapped toward the door.

"Hey, this isn't—"

"I didn't sneak up on you. I announced myself as soon as I opened the door."

Connie wondered how he'd gotten it open without her or Derek hearing it. Possibly because they'd been too busy one-upping each other.

"The truck from the auto club is here," Max continued. "So your time is up. There's a back seat in the cab, so Moose goes with you and Chris, and he's got a gun in the back of his pants, too. Connie and the twins stay with me."

Silently Derek watched Max, and the other man's return gaze was just as unwavering. The way they were sizing each other up made Connie glad they didn't have six-shooters holstered at their hips.

Max broke the loud silence, but not the eye contact. "On your way back, you can detour to that fried chicken place—Moose knows where it is—and pick up dinner. My treat. They have mashed potatoes and stuff there, too, that those two babies can eat."

It seemed to take forever for Derek to cut his attention away from Max, but finally he turned to Connie. His eyes searched hers. The situation could still go either way, she knew: blow up or calm down. She also knew one's wit was way more important right now than one's muscle power, and that there was way too much confrontation between these two. She gave Derek a minute nod of her head, trying to make herself appear steadier than she felt. He held her gaze for another long moment, then took her hand and squeezed it. His eyes said *okay.* Wordlessly, he brushed past Max and entered the house.

Max turned to Connie. "Those babies drink formula or regular milk?"

"Regular milk."

"That I've got. Now you need to rescue Moose from them so he can get going."

Shortly, Connie was kneeling at the front door, holding a hand of each twin as they waved and chanted "Bye-bye" at the departing truck. That was one of the few words in their limited vocabulary, and they'd stand there and repeat it until they found something more interesting to do.

"Aunt Connie," Max said from behind her. "I assume you have a playpen in the car?"

Rising to her feet, she faced him. "Yes."

"We'll set it up in Moose's room. They can sleep with him, and you and Derek can have Petey's room. He can bunk with me."

"But—"

"Ex or not, you've slept with him before. Shouldn't be too uncomfortable. You'll have Chris between you anyway. And in case you're wondering about it, I have one phone and it's in my room, both of which are off limits."

She stared back.

At her silence, he went on. "Tomorrow we'll go grocery shopping and mosey by your place as well—or the kids' place, I guess—and you can pack up what you need." He paused, looking uncertain for the first time. "You've got enough diapers to last till morning?"

The man was thorough; he had a good grasp of everything. She agreed with Derek there was no way, right now, to fight back. So she simply nodded. "I packed extra." With a look off to the side, probably a wry one that matched her thoughts, she added, "Just in case of an emergency."

He watched her for another moment, then directed his attention to Petey. "I'm going to change the sheets on your bed for our guests. You and Aunt Connie put the dishes away that are in the drainer, and she can get used to the kitchen. Be nice to have a cook for a change. Keep an eye on those babies and each other. I don't want anyone—" He stopped and gave Connie a hard look. "*Anyone* going for any more unauthorized walks."

Then he gave Petey a harder look. "She takes even one step out of that kitchen, you call me, you hear?"

Petey's expression turned solemn, as if he realized the importance of his assignment. "Yes, Max. You can count on me." He straightened up to his full height, looking proud.

Max's face softened briefly, then he turned and left.

Petey looked at Connie. "You can cook?" He appeared delighted.

"No."

His face registered disappointment, then confusion. "But Max said you could."

"He's wrong."

"But . . ."

When the twins turned away from the front door and started looking around the room with interest, Petey seemed to lose his train of thought and looked worriedly their way. Then in almost the same instant, both babies zeroed in on the garage in the corner and they headed that way. One moved too fast, teetered and fell on its bottom, then got back up and followed its sibling.

"Uhh . . ." Petey wrung his hands together and lines deepened in his forehead.

Despite herself, Connie smiled. It was like dealing with Christopher. Except Chris wouldn't have been so politely restrained toward his siblings. "Go put your things away. I'll take care of the dishes. I should be able to figure out where everything goes."

A waist-high counter separated the kitchen from the family room, allowing Connie to work with one eye and an ear on the three juveniles in the far corner. For the time being, the twins were content to sit on the floor while Petey explained patiently what each piece was and what its job was.

Searching for the cutlery drawer, she pulled open the one next to the sink, and froze. A gun lay there, partially concealed by a kitchen towel. She looked quickly at Petey, but he was engrossed with his toys.

With one eye on him, she pulled the gun out and held it behind her, then closed the drawer. The weapon was heavy, and it made her think twice about even having it in her hand. Then she discarded the thought of caution. She wasn't in a rational situation, so therefore could not deal with it on a rational basis.

"Petey, will you come here for a minute?" She was surprised at how calm her voice was.

He looked up. "Sure. I got all the little stuff put away. They can't hurt anything."

When he was halfway across the room, she brought the gun around so he could see it. "That's far enough," she said evenly. "Now listen carefully. I want you to call Max, but don't tell him I've got the gun. Can you do that?"

The twins started fussing at one another, and fleetingly Connie recalled that Abbie had been cheated out of her nap, and Andy hadn't even gotten the few minutes his sister had managed to get.

At sight of the gun, Petey drew back, looking tense and anxious. He put his hands out as if to ward off a bullet. "That goes off real easy, Auntie Connie," he warned. Then his face cleared. He lowered his hands. "Oh, good. The safety's on. It won't go off if the safety's on."

Hesitantly she looked at the gun. "The safety?"

"Yeah, it's that little thing right there. Max showed me."

"Where?" Intent upon the gun and its mechanisms, she didn't realize how close he'd come until he loomed almost in her face. She stiffened and brought the weapon up, pointing it straight at him with her elbows at her side. "Don't come any closer," she warned.

"It's okay," he said, and reached for the gun, but all he did was push a lever back, then he stepped away. "There," he said. "Now it will go off, so be real careful." He moved back another pace and put his hands in the air.

When Connie realized her mouth was hanging open, she closed it.

"Should I call Max now?" he asked.

But Max appeared without being summoned. Connie caught the movement at the entrance to the hall and whirled toward it.

He came to an abrupt stop. After a long, tense moment, his gaze rose from the gun to meet hers.

"You don't want to do this, Aunt Connie," he said quietly. He took a step, extending his hand. "Give it to me."

Despite her resolve, she retreated. It seemed her calm had deserted her along with Max's arrival. She held the gun straight out, using both hands, grip so tight her fingers were cramping. "You're right. I don't want to do this, but I will. Don't come any closer."

He stopped. The twins' argument grew louder. But she couldn't take her eyes off Max to check on them.

"You got the safety off." His voice held neither surprise nor alarm.

"Yeah," Petey said. "She didn't know how it worked either. I had to show her."

"So that's how it happened. My own fault. Should've known better than to let her out of my sight."

"I want you to sit down," Connie said. She hated that her voice was so shaky. "Both of you. Right there on the couch. We'll wait for Derek and Chris, then we'll be out of here, and you'll have time to . . . to get a head start . . . to do whatever you need to do." She was babbling but couldn't control that any more than she could control her trembling. She couldn't even hold the gun steady. "I don't want to hurt you, either one of you. Now just sit down."

But Max didn't sit. Instead he took what looked like measured steps, his gaze locked on hers, and he entered the kitchen. Her back came up against the counter. "Stop it! Don't make me do this, Max. Please!"

He was almost close enough to grab the gun, and he wouldn't give it back like Petey had. The trigger was cold and hard. She didn't want to squeeze it, even doubted that she could.

The twins' noise was getting louder. She had to ensure the

children's safety. She had to, but Max wasn't going to back down.

He took another step.

And she squeezed the trigger.

Chapter Eleven

Connie heard a loud click. But nothing happened.

Her gaze broke away from Max, and she looked stupidly down at the gun. She'd tightened her whole body up, waiting for the worst, and now it felt like her muscles had turned into water.

When his hand closed over the gun and he took it from her, she didn't resist.

"I was wondering if you had the guts to pull the trigger," he said. "And now I know." He pulled open the drawer and replaced the gun in it. "That's twice today I did that—underestimated the so-called weaker sex. I'm going to die a very young man if I keep that up."

"Uh, Max, you forgot the safety," Petey warned.

Max paused in the act of closing the drawer. Then patiently he pulled it back out, removed the gun, and reset the safety.

"No bullets," Connie said tonelessly.

He pushed the drawer closed. "Right. Didn't want to take the chance of anyone getting hurt. But I didn't know then that I was the one I'd be saving from getting shot."

Connie stared at the closed drawer. It had taken all the courage she possessed to pull the trigger, and she was now so bone-weary and brain-tired she was having difficulty with coherent thought.

"Sounds like one of those babies might do an injury to the other one," Max said gently. "Maybe you better get over there."

The front door opened and Christopher charged through it. He pulled up short when he caught sight of the twins sitting in the middle of the toy garage. Derek and Moose followed, carrying assorted bags and accompanied by the aroma of fried chicken.

Derek's gaze found Connie.

"The guns aren't loaded," she said dully.

He froze. Moose's head snapped toward Max. Max shrugged. "She got hold of a gun."

Derek gave Connie a worried, searching look. Moose looked thoughtfully wary.

"And she pulled the trigger," Max added. Moose looked even warier.

Derek's gaze traveled back and forth between Connie and Max, and then settled on her. "You okay?"

She nodded. Her wits were returning, one at a time.

The noise in the corner changed. Petey and Christopher were trying to rescue their garage from the twins and having little success. Instead of fighting each other, the babies had joined forces and were resisting the bigger kids. Making resigned faces at each other, Petey and Chris started entertaining the two tots by running toy trucks around them in circles.

Derek unloaded containers onto the table, Moose got plates, and Max counted out cutlery. Connie watched them. Everything she did, even thinking, seemed to be in slow motion.

Derek looked up a couple times, his gaze traveling between Max and Moose. He appeared to be measuring them.

Max turned his way, caught his look, and must've gotten the same impression Connie did. "Uh-huh," he said. "But remember, with or without bullets, nothing else has changed. There are still three of us, one of you, one of her, and three of them. But if you think you can pull something off, you give it your best shot." It didn't appear he'd issued a challenge, however; it was more like a simple statement. He put the handful of cutlery in the middle of the table, and then started placing chairs.

Derek followed Connie into their assigned bedroom. She was spent, ready to drop. She waited for him to pass, closed the door, and then leaned against it. They shared a long look.

"Trying day," she said blandly.

His lips curved. "That is a gem of an understatement."

"If you ever invite me to go fishing again, I won't."

She looked at Christopher. His small form sprawled across the bed. He'd crashed early and had gotten a kick out of going to bed in his underwear instead of pajamas. The situation might be a dilemma for his aunt and uncle, but clearly it was an adventure to him. The twins had also gone down easily, much to Moose's relief, and Connie's. She was operating on automatic pilot.

Remembering what she'd seen in the big man's room, she glanced back at Derek. "It looked like Moose is living out of a suitcase, so this isn't his home."

He nodded, confirming her supposition as fact. "He's on vacation. Said something about the rat race having a definite allure when compared to this holiday." He made a wry face. "Have to agree with him on that one."

"I don't get the impression Max is employed, at least not presently."

"I don't know. From the look of that tool chest, he must be a carpenter. And he's sharp, very sharp. He and Moose appear to be good friends, but Max lacks the . . ." He paused, as if searching for a word, then went on. "Worldliness, I guess, that the big guy has. Max is a very simple, uncomplicated man. But it could be a grievous mistake to underestimate him."

He glanced at the closed door. "The phone I used was in a back bedroom. Have you—"

"Max said there's only one phone. In his room."

Derek gave her an appraising look. "Enough about them. How about you? You seem to be holding up all right. More than all right. If that gun had been loaded, you would've had us out of here."

"I was scared. Still am, but of the situation more than the people. If I hadn't been so obsessed with protecting the kids, I wouldn't have been able to pull the trigger of that gun."

When Derek sat on the edge of the bed, the movement disturbed Christopher. The child rolled onto his stomach, then sprawled out until he covered almost the whole bed.

Connie leaned her head back against the door and stared at the ceiling. "Yeah, I agree Max is sharp. He knew exactly what he was doing. He wanted to know what I was capable of, and he kept pushing until he found out." She stopped and wet her lips, still staring at the ceiling. "Only thing is, I don't know if I flunked the test or passed it."

"How dangerous are they?" Derek said musingly, as if he were asking himself as well as her. "Would they do us deliberate harm?"

"I don't think so. But we're still not going to get out of here until they're ready to let us go." Her gaze lowered to meet his. She gave him a pointed look. "If necessary, they will restrain you, Derek. Take it easy, okay?"

"I can imagine the reception I'd get if I returned to the studio with a black eye and a cut lip," he said wryly.

He massaged his eyes, then rubbed his face. "I've got to get some sleep. My thought processes are about ready to desert me." He looked at Christopher. "We're going to have to rearrange him before either one of us can get in there. It's only a double. Going to be a tight fit for all three of us, but I guess we'll manage."

Connie watched silently as Derek repositioned Chris into the middle of the bed. She was aware of his evasion regarding her warning that he should be careful. He resented controls being placed on him and was apt to fight their captors for that reason just as readily as he would to protect her or the kids.

He stripped to his shorts, quickly and casually, and slipped into bed next to Chris. He placed his hands under his head and looked at Connie. She looked back at him.

"I have no objection to again sharing a bed with you," he said mildly. "But would prefer it to be under different circumstances."

"Uh-huh." She crossed to the bed and sat on the edge of it to remove her shoes. Then, still wearing her tank top and shorts, she slipped in on the other side of Chris.

"That's it?" Derek asked.

"That's it. The two of you might get away with sleeping in your underwear, but I can't."

The lamp was on his side, and he reached to turn it off. She lay still, feeling awkward and uncomfortable while her ex-husband jostled the bed, searching for a comfortable position. Granted, they had a child between them, but she was still sharing a bed with him for the first time in two years.

The mattress finally became still. Then she turned over and searched for her own comfortable position. "And you thought they'd be separating us," she said into the darkness.

Connie got up with Christopher, then gave Derek a good shake. Then she shook him again, using both hands, and kept it up until she saw the color of his eyes. She straightened and turned to leave. He mumbled something that she paid no attention to.

Christopher and Petey were too busy with their toy garage to even look her way. The twins were already up, but Moose had filled bottles for them and they were happy. She hadn't packed cereal, not expecting to have to feed them breakfast on a picnic, so they'd have to take potluck along with everybody else. She checked the contents of the refrigerator and cabinets. Recalling Max's words yesterday, she assumed she'd get to cook breakfast.

She was a woman. Therefore, she could cook. She resented the sexist assumption, which was, in this case, grossly inaccurate. But their captors weren't abusive or violent. Perhaps two out of three wasn't bad.

Although Moose appeared to be good with kids, he evidently wasn't used to them. Derek had gotten up and was helping with the twins, but he hadn't had a whole lot of practice with them either. While he was rescuing one of them from the toilet bowl, the other one took a header off the sofa.

Connie flew out of the kitchen. She gathered the baby up, checking for blood and bruises. Realizing the child was more scared than hurt, she rocked it while still on her feet, humming softly. After a short moment, she figured out that it was Andy.

In the corner, Petey lifted his head and sniffed. "She burned the toast again."

"Yeah." The frown was in Max's voice as well as on his face. "Told her the first time she had to keep a careful eye on the toaster," he muttered. He looked at the smoking pan on the stove. "Guess we can kiss the bacon goodbye, too."

Connie put daggers into her stare. "Maybe you could watch the stupid toaster. And while you're at it, maybe you could also take the stupid pan off the stupid burner." Any adjective could be made scurrilous with enough inflection.

Max's gaze snapped to her.

"I don't know how I'm supposed to watch the toaster, burn the bacon, and take care of two babies at the same time. Now *shut up* . . . and *back off.*" She hadn't raised her voice, but it was backed up with every pound she possessed.

Christopher looked up from the corner, as surprised as Max.

Derek appeared at her side. He silently put Abbie on her feet next to Connie then stalked into the kitchen. Tightlipped, he removed the smoking pan from the stove, then took black toast from the toaster and threw it into the garbage. He searched through the bottom cabinets for another skillet. The look on his face said clearly that nobody should mess with him.

But Connie knew it wasn't she with whom he was upset. If she didn't calm down, he was going to double up his fists on her behalf.

"I'm sorry, Aunt Connie," Moose said, staring up at her and Andy. He looked shamefaced and guilty. "I was right here next to him, and I . . ."

"I know," she said, redirecting her attention to the big man on the sofa. "It's not the first fall he's taken, and it won't be the last." Because Moose appeared to be more hurt than Andy, she smiled and put her hand on the man's shoulder.

Then quickly she grabbed Abbie's arm before she could get away. The child still wore yesterday's coveralls, and both sleeves were soaked to the shoulder. Wearily, Connie shook her head. "Her mother has three baby books, full of the stunts these kids have pulled. She's saving it for their teens, and then she's going to blackmail them. Playing in the toilet will fit nicely in Abbie's book."

She put Andy down—he'd gotten over his scare and was twisting impatiently in her arms—and picked up Abbie. "I've got to wash and change her. There's only one outfit left, and I guess she gets it."

She glanced at the kitchen. Derek had found another pan and was placing strips of bacon in it. She hadn't burned all of it, just most of it. "You'll get a better meal with him cooking, anyway."

Moose's eyes brightened. "He can cook?"

She nodded. "Quite well."

A dreamy look came over him. "Haven't had a decent home-cooked meal since my wife died."

She looked back. "Oh, I—"

He shook his head and waggled his hand, warding off her words. "Five years ago, cancer, no kids." Then, as if hearing himself, he made a rueful face. "I just explained my whole life in six words." His expression, of quiet acceptance and lonely pain, cut straight through to Connie's heart.

Looking embarrassed, he got to his feet. He was so big he absolutely dwarfed Connie. "I'll see if I can give Uncle Dare a hand. Since I haven't been much help with the babies."

Somewhat warily—the aura of temper surrounding Derek was close to palpable—Moose approached the kitchen. Derek glanced up, acknowledging him, then returned his attention to the sizzling bacon. A bowl of eggs sat on the counter.

"Do you know how to make omelets?" Moose asked hopefully.

Derek looked up, nodded. "You want omelets, I'll make them."

Max passed Connie on his way to the kitchen. It seemed he took care to avoid her eyes. "I'll do the toast while you cook the eggs," he told Derek. But it was evident in his manner that he wasn't backing down from anybody but Connie. He gave Derek a look that dared him to say something. Derek didn't.

"With cheese?" Moose asked. There was a little boy's delight in the big man's face.

"Sure." It seemed Derek's mood was easing, degree by degree. "You want to dig out the cheese?"

"It's just slices," Moose said. "But we can cut them up with a knife. And I think we've got an onion," he added, rummaging through the refrigerator. "I can dice it. I know how to do that. And we should have a slice or two of ham left. It's the sandwich kind, but we can cut that up, too."

Connie stood at the entrance to the hall with Abbie in her

arms, watching and listening to the teamwork. She had no doubt that among the three of them, an excellent meal would be produced.

Chapter Twelve

"Since you're the cook," Max said to Derek after breakfast, "you also get to do the grocery shopping." He stooped to put a skillet away in a bottom cabinet. The three men were sharing kitchen cleanup, just as they'd worked together to fix the meal.

Connie had got the twins and Christopher as presentable as possible with their limited supplies. Chris had only frowned at her once, when she'd applied toothpaste to his finger and insisted that he brush his teeth. Then Petey decided he didn't need his toothbrush either, and they'd gone through half a tube before Connie captured it and carried it out of the bathroom.

She sat in the upholstered easy chair, the tube of toothpaste in her lap, one eye and ear on the twins as they attempted to climb the sofa, and the other eye and ear on the trio in the kitchen. Connie doubted either of the babies could get all the way up there on his or her own, yet she didn't trust them not to. Petey and Chris, each with clean teeth and bright smiles, had gone outside with a collection of action figures.

"You go with Moose," Max told Derek, "and—"

"How come I get him again?" Derek asked. "He might be getting tired of me."

"Or vice versa," Moose said mildly.

Max gave Derek a level look. "You get him because you might be able to take me, one on one," he explained candidly. He didn't appear bothered by the thought. "But I don't think you can take him. So you get Moose, and Connie goes with me."

He looked toward the drawer that held the empty gun. "She's formidable enough," he added under his breath.

Connie looked at the tube of toothpaste. She didn't feel very formidable.

Max returned to the day's agenda. "Aunt Connie and I will take the van. The neighbors are used to it and shouldn't notice anything out of the ordinary. We'll go to the kids' house to get what they need. Whatever you want, Uncle Dare, tell her now."

"Just bring my whole suitcase," Derek said, unruffled. "I never unpacked."

Connie nodded, still staring at the toothpaste. She wondered how he could look so crisp when he hadn't even bothered to unpack. Did the clothes make the man, or had he somehow managed to turn that around? "Okay. Where—"

"Under the cot. And bring back the cheese grater and a colander." He paused, then added, "Too bad you can't pack up the microwave."

"What's a colander?" Max asked.

Derek gave him a curious look but didn't respond.

"It drains noodles and stuff," Moose explained. "I asked for lasagna for tonight."

Derek ran his hand over his beard stubble. "And check the bathroom. I don't know if I left my razor in there or if I put it away. And my toothbrush is in there, too. The red one."

Connie made a mental note to bring back all the toothpaste she could find.

"Do you want to take the twins or Chris?" Max asked.

"Chris," Derek said quickly.

Good, Connie thought.

"Then you might as well take Petey, too. And let them choose a treat."

Once plans were concluded, Connie and Max each carried a baby out to the van and fastened them in their seats. Foremost in her mind was the thought of a luxurious shower and a fresh change of clothing once they returned to the farmhouse. Putting the key in the ignition, she realized with a mental start that she was no longer afraid of the situation but had accepted it and their captors. And at some point between last night and this morning, Derek had apparently arrived at the same frame of mind.

As she sat still behind the wheel mulling things over, she became aware of Max watching her. He seemed wary with her inaction, puzzled and suspicious. She shrugged at him, turned the key, got the van in motion, and drove out of there.

She put the babies in their cribs while she packed, furnishing them with toys, and was grateful not to get any complaints. Max kept a close eye on her as she chose their things, but she ignored him. She continued on into the kitchen.

When she pulled open the drawer to get the cheese grater, her gaze fell on the cellular phone. She no longer feared her captors, but neither did she like being a captive. Wondering what her chances were of casually adding the phone to the box of supplies, she glanced at Max. His gaze was also on the instrument, then his eyes coolly met hers and she gave up that idea. She closed the drawer and found the colander in an upper cabinet.

"Oh, that's what it is," Max said. "We used to have one of those. Petey used it at the stream, panning for gold, so I put it in with the fishing gear."

Connie wondered what they used to drain spaghetti, but she didn't ask. Maybe they never cooked it? Even she cooked spaghetti. She bought the sauce in a little deli container in the supermarket, but she boiled the noodles all by herself.

The light on the telephone recorder was blinking, indicating a message. Max gestured for her to attend to it.

"Hi, Connie," Kristy's voice said, disappointment evident in it. "I'm so sorry we missed you. And, oh boy, are we ever missing the kids. Hawaii is as gorgeous as it was ten years ago, and the time on our own is great . . . and yet it's not. We really are missing our little guys. Tell them how much we love them. And, well, we'll see you Thursday. Love . . . and bye."

Connie's eyes misted at the yearning in Kristy's voice. Then she looked at Max. He gave her a matter-of-fact nod. "You'll be back by Thursday, and we'll be long gone." As she continued to watch him, he frowned, then fidgeted. "What?" he asked.

"I'm curious. A whole lot curious. What did Hayworth steal from you that's so important you're risking armed robbery and kidnapping to get it back?"

His gaze left hers to light upon the cabinets, the counter, the window. "Lawn needs mowing."

She leaned against the counter and folded her arms.

"Big yard. Must be nice for the kids." His gaze remained on the window, and hers remained on him. Finally he looked at her, took in a breath and let it out. "A comic book," he said, and the instant he spoke, it seemed that a sizable chip planted itself on his shoulder.

She drew her eyebrows close together. "A comic book?"

"Yeah. A SteelMan comic book."

In the long silence that followed, she pushed her tongue against her lower teeth. That was a bad habit her dentist had warned her about. She bit her bottom lip instead, then said, "I've got to be missing something important here."

"It's a collector's item," he said defiantly, "and worth a lot of money. It was an early one, published in 1940 before the war. My dad bought it when he was just a kid and didn't even know he still had it until he was going through things when his mom died. It was the only thing of value he had, and it was supposed to help me take care of Petey."

Frowning in concentration, Connie studied him. He squirmed

while still standing, then sat on one of the tall stools and rested his elbows on the counter. He looked elaborately around the kitchen. "You about through in here?"

So that was all the information she was going to get. For now.

"Yes, I'm through with the kitchen."

He followed her into Christopher's room. "I'll pack for Chris," she said. "Will you get Derek's suitcase?" She pointed under the cot, then crossed the room to investigate dresser drawers.

She left her own packing for last. In the master bedroom, Kristy had cleared a drawer for Connie and given her a section of the closet. Max waited in the doorway for her, his attention on the picture gallery of the kids hanging on the wall. The twins sounded like they were getting restless. Their jabbering was turning into complaining, and something hit the wall with a thump.

Connie stared at her nightgowns. She'd only brought two with her and didn't have to hold them up to know what they looked like. One didn't even reach mid thigh. The other one was longer but so sheer she needed a slip to wear under it. She left them both in the drawer.

Dinner that evening was another joint effort. While Derek put the casserole together, Moose worked on a salad and Max prepared garlic bread. The apprentice cooks asked about the order of ingredients, how to make homemade salad dressing, and the spreading consistency of margarine versus butter. Connie wondered if any one of the three was aware of how well they worked together.

She tended to the hungry twins, allowing them enough dry Cheerios to sate them until the lasagna was ready, but not enough to harm their appetites. There was a trick to this that

Connie hadn't yet mastered. She thought yearningly about the ease of baby food, but both kids had turned their noses up at that stuff a long time ago.

Petey had dug games out of his closet, and he and Christopher were sprawled on the rug in the family room, involved in an intense session of *Chutes and Ladders.* It'd quickly become evident that they interpreted the rules differently, however, and Connie was hoping she wasn't going to have to referee.

Derek saved her when he placed the steaming casserole on the table. "Chris, it's time to put that away and wash your hands."

"Okay, as soon as I—"

"Now, Chris."

"You, too, Petey," Max said.

Petey and Chris exchanged looks, but neither moved. They were similarly dressed in t-shirts and jeans. Petey's shirt had a picture of Bart Simpson on it, and Christopher's declared that he was the world's greatest kid.

Noting her nephew's resistance, Connie felt perversely satisfied that the uncle and nephew honeymoon had come to an end. She spooned noodles and meat onto two small salad plates, cut everything into little pieces, and then spread it out so it'd cool faster. Once they smelled the food, the babies hurried over, settled themselves on opposite sides of their aunt, and complained about how slow she was.

Derek straightened and looked toward the corner garage. "Chris," he said in a warning tone.

"Petey," Max said. His tone matched Derek's.

Petey and Chris sighed in defeat. "Okay," they said in unison, each voice carrying a shade of longsuffering resignation.

Because it wasn't possible to safely seat the twins at the table, they'd sat on the floor last night, their plates between their feet, and had eaten with their aunt's help. Tonight, however, once the lasagna was sufficiently cooled, she found Moose already on the floor between the two babies. He'd even managed to direct their attention away from their hunger pangs.

"You hold it like this," he told Andy, placing a spoon in his pudgy fist. Abbie stared at hers, and then her brother's, probably trying to decide which one was the best one.

Connie smiled, gave the kids their plates without comment, then heaped salad and lasagna on another dish for Moose. What struck her about the scene was how natural it looked; there was nothing whatsoever ridiculous about the huge moose of a man sitting between the two babies.

Since the men had prepared dinner, she volunteered to do dishes. "Too bad I couldn't have packed up the dishwasher," she muttered. Max offered to help; she washed and he dried.

Derek and Moose found a baseball game on TV, but it was a runaway and they quickly tired of it. They joined Petey and Chris at the corner garage. The two boys must've decided on their own that *Chutes and Ladders* was too contentious.

The twins were napping, and Moose kept peeking in on them. Because of the busy day, they'd missed their afternoon nap and they'd been wired. If they didn't get at least an hour now, it would be murder trying to get them down later for the night. Connie halfway expected Moose to accidentally-on-purpose awaken them, but he was behaving himself.

"Uh, about that comic book," Max said, and Connie jerked her head toward him.

He shrugged, probably because he'd caught her surprise. "I owe you more of an explanation than what I gave you, after what we're putting you through. And you're being really good sports about it, both you and your husband."

"Ex."

"Uh, yeah." He grew quiet, his brow wrinkling. Connie thought he was one of the hardest thinkers she'd ever met.

Then he said, "A couple months back . . . I was, well, indisposed . . ."

He put down the salad bowl he was working on and stared at it. "I don't know why I'm trying to tiptoe around this. The truth is I'm a recovering alcoholic and—"

Connie's gaze flicked to the wine bottle still on the table. She and Derek had drunk a glass with dinner, but she'd noticed Max and Moose had both passed on it.

His gaze followed hers. "I don't get drunk when other people drink," he explained mildly. "Only when I drink."

She felt silly, gave him a look that probably admitted it, and he smiled.

She returned to the crust-caked casserole, and he returned to his story. "I fell off the wagon a couple months back and was arrested for being drunk and disorderly. While I was . . . indisposed, Hayworth approached Petey and offered him ten dollars for the comic book. I was a fool to ever let him know I had it. Mentioned it once when I had more booze in me than brains. Anyway, if he'd paid a decent price for it, I'd accept the loss and figure it was my own fault for, well, whatever. But he took advantage of the situation, and, worse, took advantage of Petey. And that's not right."

"No, it's not." Indignantly, she quit scouring and gave him her complete attention. "He won't give it back?"

"Nope. Won't. So I talked to Moose about it, and together we concocted this—"

"Is Moose, uh . . ."

"Yeah. We met at AA and have been helping each other for a couple years now. He's the best friend I ever had." Once he'd admitted the fact of his alcoholism, he seemed at ease with it. "So we dreamed up this scheme, robbing Hayworth's store to get his attention, then going to him and explaining the situation. That we'd continue to harass him, drive him out of business if we had to, until he either returned the book or paid a proper price for it."

Absently she ran her fingertips over the dish for stubborn crusting she might've missed. "What's a proper price?"

"Well." He hesitated. "I don't really know, but when it first went down, I told him I'd settle for five thousand bucks. So I'll stick to that."

"The police can't help you?"

"It's my word against his. He's got possession. I've got zilch."

"Have you talked to a lawyer?"

"That's how come I know he's got possession and I've got zilch."

She rinsed the dish and gave it to him. "But there must be something you can do." She upended the plastic dishpan to empty it and wrung out the dishcloth. "This is wrong. There's got to be *some* kind of recourse."

"You find some recourse, you be sure and let me know what it is."

That evening, behind their closed bedroom door, Chris again sound asleep, Connie filled Derek in on Max's problem. Her ex-husband's reaction was much the same as hers: initial incredulity giving way to dawning understanding.

"Yeah, that's tough," he said. "And I don't know what they can do about it either. But what they're doing is risky—too risky—and won't work anyway. What's to stop Hayworth from turning them in once he finds out they're behind the robberies?"

"The way I understand it, Petey and Max will be clearing out and could continue to harass him from a distance. And in other ways, not just at the store. And even we don't know anything about Moose. Where he lives, works, even what his real name is."

Derek nodded, then looked relieved. "Yeah, that's right. But

I'll still be surprised if the scheme works. I feel for them. Wish there was some way we could help."

"Well, I was wondering, if, uh . . ."

He looked at her questioningly, then suspiciously. "What? You were wondering what?"

"Well, you're a celebrity, a television personality on a news program. People would listen to you if –"

"Uh-uh. No way. The station would never allow it."

"I'm not asking you to announce it on the air. Just, uh, maybe mention it in an interview, just—"

"I can't do that. Think about it, Connie. I'd be opening myself up to a lawsuit, and possibly the station as well. There's no way I could involve myself in this, at least not publicly."

"But—"

"Forget it, Connie."

"You're not listening, not even allowing me to finish a—" When he opened his mouth she held her hand up to shush him. "Sentence," she finished. "What's your problem anyway? Is it intellectually impossible for you to see more than just your side of something?"

"I heard you," he enunciated precisely. "Quite well. You asked me to risk my job and my career, as well as the station's reputation. Or am I misunderstanding something here?"

She glared at him. It seemed like old times, being at loggerheads with this stubborn and irascible individual. Except that in this case, he had a valid point. She didn't like admitting it, but, yes, he had a point.

"Okay," she said, giving up but not liking it. Shaking her head, she looked at the old-fashioned brass lamp on the bedside table. "Okay, it was a long shot. I just thought that if public opinion was on Max and Petey's side, which it would be, then Hayworth would have to give in. But I hear what you're saying."

She went to Chris and gently pushed and pulled his small body until there was room on either side of him for company. She noted that as Derek watched her, he appeared wary and still ready for battle, as if not aware he'd won the argument. Ignoring him, she removed her socks and shoes and slipped into bed, still in her jeans and pink-striped knit pullover.

He frowned. "You didn't pack anything today to sleep in?"

She turned onto her side, away from him, not appreciating this topic of conversation any more than the last one. Especially since she'd lost the last one. "I wasn't expecting to share a bedroom when I left home. I only brought two nightgowns, and they weren't . . . aren't . . . appropriate."

"I see." It sounded like he was smiling. "And out of deference to Chris, you decided you didn't want to wear either of them."

She didn't like his tone any more than the subject. She rose up onto her elbow, turned, and put as much glare in her stare as she could.

At the look on her face, he tried to straighten his. "Okay, okay. End of subject."

He started to unbuckle his belt, stopped and gave her an overlong look. Then, amusement curving his mouth, he delicately reached to turn the lamp off before undressing himself.

Connie turned back onto her side and had to press her lips together to keep her mouth shut. He was getting to her, and she guessed he knew it. But she was determined not to let him know the degree of her exasperation with him, and the lack of privacy, and especially this dinky little bed she had to share with two members of the aggravating and annoying male species.

Chapter Thirteen

Connie was vaguely aware of Christopher as he climbed over her on his way out of bed, and she took advantage of his absence to snuggle closer to Derek. He was on his side, facing away from her, and she put one arm over him and brought her knees up to slide in behind his, spoon fashion. She fit so perfectly. He stirred, then turned over, dislodging her, but she didn't mind because his arm came over her then, too, and she liked that even better.

His hand fell on her hip, moved to her waist, up to her breast. She wondered absently why she was wearing a bra in bed. She wriggled closer and his arms wrapped nicely around her. She hadn't felt this sexy in a long time. She—

Her eyes snapped open. She broke away and shot out of bed so fast her foot got caught in the sheet and she almost went sprawling.

With her gaze locked on him, she backed away from the bed. He blinked, brow furrowing as if he had trouble focusing. His eyes looked clouded, still confused with sleep. But more than that. She saw want and need, physical and emotional. Then when he focused on her, showing her he was fully awake, his face mirrored her feelings. Not just surprise. Closer to shock. And the desire she'd seen a moment ago was replaced with memory and hurt, probably also very similar to hers.

Her mind flew back to events leading to their divorce. Hurtful, yes, stopping just short of hateful. They'd grown so distant, so cool and indifferent to each other, that they hadn't even engaged in sexual relations for almost that whole last month. She wondered what would've happened if a morning like this had occurred before that final split.

No, don't go there. Stop it. Now.

Forcing her gaze from his, she padded out of the room in bare feet.

Coffee was made; the aroma registered at the back of her mind, and everybody else was up. For a change, Petey and Christopher were watching TV instead of playing with the corner garage. It was a program Connie recommended to parents. Adults who looked and talked like grownups spoke to kids on a kid's level, and both boys were paying rapt attention. They were being told how to make a fort out of cardboard boxes with snippets of teamwork and courtesy woven in here and there.

The twins were happily engaged, one on either side of Moose on the sofa as he read to them, so content they must've already been fed. They were dressed in day clothes: matching tan shorts, a blue t-shirt on one child, and a pink one on the other. Original way to tell them apart.

She walked to the kitchen, found a cup and poured coffee, aware again of that hollow, empty ache in her heart she'd thought she'd finally left behind. At times, especially during that first year, it'd felt as if she'd severed off part of herself. Slowly she'd put herself back together, feeling a little bit more whole in small degrees, one day at a time. Well, surprise, surprise. Here was two years of painstakingly deliberate work wiped out in an instant as if it'd never been.

When she looked up, she realized her feelings must show. Moose gave her a sidelong look, and Max's eyebrows drew together as he watched her over the top of his newspaper.

Trying to clear her face, she rested her elbows on the counter, leaned into it and sipped coffee, and kept her gaze on the two babies who were so enthralled with Moose and their storybook. They pointed at pictures, and in their own language were reading along with Moose.

Before Derek's arrival—how many days ago was it? Only four?—she'd noted that all three kids were missing their parents, and she'd felt grossly inadequate. With the adventure and distraction of the last few days, especially Moose's attention to the twins and the instant bonding between Chris and Petey, the kids' pining for their parents hadn't been as noticeable.

Derek appeared then and started breakfast. He wore jeans, a light-red pullover, and his don't-mess-with-me look. Connie sidled out of the kitchen, getting out of his way. Moose and Max exchanged long looks and shrugs, and then went back to their respective storybook and newspaper, prudently not offering to help with the cooking.

The toast was dark-brown and rock-hard, the bacon undercooked, and the scrambled eggs were dry and crusty and brown on the bottom. Nobody said a word.

After breakfast, Max assigned Petey to kitchen duty. "You've had it too easy for too long. I don't want you to forget how to do things. Chris can help."

Connie went back for her sneakers and carried them to the back yard. She decided to wear the same jeans and top from yesterday, shower later today and change then. She was sitting on the ground next to a pink azalea, tying the second shoelace when she heard the door open. Tensing, she jerked her head up.

She relaxed. "Oh. Hi, Max."

"No way could I sit on the ground like that and tie my shoes. You make me feel old, Aunt Connie."

She got to her feet, feeling surprised with her thoughts, not his speech. "I was going to go for a walk, but it hadn't even occurred to me to talk to you."

He laughed. "Are you telling me we've moved beyond kidnapper and kidnappee?"

She smiled. "Never heard you laugh before. Yeah, looks like we've made some progress in that direction." She glanced around, studying the terrain, then looked back. "Join me?"

"Thought you'd never ask." He indicated a path behind the house. "That stream where you were fishing meanders around back this way. It's not far."

They walked side by side in comfortable silence until Max asked, voice mild, "What happened between you and Derek this morning?"

Her step faltered.

Shrugging, he returned her gaze. "Something happened. He's about ready to blow, and when he does, either you or I will get the full force of it. Before I get both barrels, I should at least know what the problem is."

She resumed walking, and he fell in step. Surprisingly, she didn't resent the question, but the answer wasn't simple. "Well, I, he, uh, we . . ."

"If you can get one whole sentence put together, the rest will probably follow."

She took a deep breath. "Okay. When I woke up this morning, it was like we'd been transported back in time, to a better place when things were good between us. Then harsh reality set in, and I . . . I crashed. We both did."

"Pretty rude awakening."

"Good way to put it."

The farther in on the path they got, the more overgrown the foliage became. "Doesn't look like you guys travel back here very often," she commented.

"Grows in thick in the spring, gets beat back some by fall." He held a branch back so she could pass. "How come you got divorced in the first place?"

She stopped and studied him, feeling the frown come over her face.

He held on to the branch, waiting. "So I'm nosy. You want to talk, fine. If not, then don't."

She shrugged. "Sure, why not? Putting it into words for someone else might make it clearer to me." As she walked ahead, she got a thought and looked back. "Poison oak, poison ivy?"

"Never seen any."

A mass of tree roots was spread over the ground ahead of her, in patient wait for unwary feet. With her gaze on the path and her thoughts in the past, she felt another frown forming. "Derek and I were always, well . . . both of us are . . . well, uh—" Breaking into her speech and stride, she looked back. "We claimed incompatible differences. Would you settle for that?"

He grinned. "That tough, huh?"

She looked back at the path without returning the smile, and her gaze settled absently on a cluster of yellow poppies. She wanted to talk; she was surprised at how strong her desire was to confide. "As you may have noticed, we're both kind of independent and strong-minded—"

When his grin returned, she caught it and gave him a direct look. "Okay, then you know what I mean." She pushed her tongue against her bottom teeth, realized what she was doing and made herself stop. "Okay, let's put it in a nutshell. On a dance floor, one needs to lead and one needs to follow, and that's the way Derek approached marriage. He couldn't leave that pattern on the dance floor where it belonged, and I never learned how to follow after we left the dance floor behind us."

Max nodded. "I get the picture."

"We clashed. Constantly. I felt crowded. And then he got frustrated and bewildered when I pushed back. But we always found a way to work around each other, despite our worst instincts. Then he got his big break, and, well, that was the beginning of the end."

Images, as vivid as snapshots, flashed through her mind and rendered her silent.

Derek's face when he'd brought the news to her . . . his arms around her as he'd lifted her off her feet and swung her around. Celebrating with cold duck, getting sloshed and spending the day in bed making love with wild abandon, and then with soft, gentle precision. Then, too soon, the cold dawn as priorities rose, changed, clashed. His expression harsh with impatience, eyes snapping, refusing to see her side. Then, even worse, those same eyes turning so cool and indifferent. His back as he turned away from her that last time, the door closing behind him. The empty suitcase she'd opened upon the bed and the first blouse she'd folded into it. Her eyes catching her image in the mirror, her expression closed and emotionless . . .

Connie returned to the present. She resumed her hike and her story, sticking to facts and forcing the feelings back behind her where they belonged.

"We're originally from San Diego; I still live there. He worked a lot of jobs, waiting for his break. He is good; you've seen him. But those early years were like limbo. We both knew there are a lot of talented people who never make it." She paused, aware of her pride in Derek and his success. It was bittersweet and always would be.

"Things finally started coming together for him in February. I teach school, and it was the middle of the academic year. He had to go to L.A., and that was a long commute even without traffic." She laughed wryly. "Which never happens. There's always traffic. Anyway, he wanted to move and assumed I'd go with him, right then and there. But I felt a commitment to the kids and wanted to finish out the school year. It didn't seem right to abandon them if it wasn't absolutely necessary, and it didn't seem that crucial to me. We could share weekends, and I'd join him for good in June. I assumed he'd understand that I also had a career and commitments I wanted to honor, but . . ."

"But he didn't."

"No. All he saw was that I was letting him down when he needed me. It was a huge undertaking; he wanted my presence and support, and that was that. That took precedence over everything else."

When she fell silent, Max prompted, "Did you ever get to L.A.?"

"Uh-huh, in June, as promised. But the distance between us by then . . . well, it already seemed too wide to bridge. At first, when he was in L.A. and I was in San Diego, we'd spend the weekends together, and then it became every other weekend, and then I only saw him once in May. Then, when I finally made the move, I had no commitments and plenty of time to devote to him." She paused. "Too much time."

Her gut tightened with remembered tension that had been born out of need and bewilderment, guilt and regret, and was almost as potent now as then.

"Too much time," she repeated as she stepped over a fallen branch. "Which became a problem in itself. I was no longer part of his life. Since I hadn't been involved in the beginning, there were people I didn't know, events happening in which I wasn't included. Demands were made upon him, and he worked irregular hours and was seldom at home. So I felt neglected and unwanted and misunderstood, and he still felt betrayed. There was no middle ground for either one of us."

A sore yearning for what they'd once had swept over her, tugging at her heart and spirit. Forced together these last few days as they'd been, without the past rearing up between them, seemed to have brought the sweetness back and made the loss harder to bear. Then again she forced the emotion back.

In the distance, she heard the sound of rushing water. As she wrapped up the story of the most significant years of her life, she was careful to keep her feelings and voice in check. "Once we finally got together, it seemed we were already past the point of no return. And the distance just kept growing, inch by inch. We stuck it out for almost a year before finally admitting that the marriage was over. And once we did, when we actually talked about calling it quits, it was the first real conversation we'd had in a long time. It really was over."

She rounded a clump of foliage and the stream was before her. It was possibly only a foot or two at its deepest point where it cascaded over a fallen log. At the bank near her feet it lapped gently, creating the peaceful, soothing sound only water can make. She breathed deeply, absorbing it with eyes, ears, and nose. Picture-pretty, constant yet tranquil, fresh clean scent.

"Does that answer your question?" she asked at length, without looking at Max.

She caught his nod, and then he said quietly, "Thank you for trusting me with it."

She'd been right to do so, because she felt better for it. He said nothing more, his gaze on the water, but she got the impression he was looking for a way to get her and Derek back together, just as she'd been searching for a way to get his comic book back. She lifted her gaze to the opposite bank, and then beyond to the tangle of growth and trees. It wasn't going to happen. Reconciliation, nor, in all probability, the return of the comic book.

They heard the kids' commotion before they saw them, then Christopher and Petey bounded out of the trees, followed at a more sedate pace by Derek. He and Max exchanged wary looks, but Derek appeared more subdued than volatile.

"Petey and Moose guessed this was where you were." He

joined them at the water's edge, standing next to Connie and putting her in the middle. His gaze moved upstream and down. "It's pretty here."

Connie regarded him with uncertainty, but if he caught it, he didn't react to it. He spoke around her to Max. "Petey and Chris were trying to talk us into taking them to a movie, but Moose thought you wanted to see Hayworth today."

Max nodded, appearing more resigned than resolved. "Yeah, gotta—" His head snapped toward the water. "Petey!"

Following his gaze, Connie shouted, "Chris, don't—"

Too late. The boys had used rocks as stepping-stones to get to the log, and then tried to walk it, too. They each slipped off the instant they got a foot on it and landed with giant splashes on opposite sides of the limb. The rush of water was swift but fortunately not deep enough to pose a threat. They were stretched out full length, soaked from shoes to hair, but quickly their laughter announced that their bones were still intact.

"Oh, sh—" Derek said, but managed to cut the word off without finishing it. "Kids," he muttered. Then, "Okay, come on out of there," he hollered. "I would've thought you had enough of that on Sunday, Chris."

But apparently it was a whole lot more fun falling into the water with a friend than with a fishing pole. The boys hooted with laughter, splashed each other, and as soon as either one got halfway upright, he fell right back down again.

Connie broke into a grin. Their mood was infectious and she was tempted to join them, but Derek had already ordered them out. It was tough enough dealing with a five-year-old without splitting their forces, so she backed up to lean against a tree, folded her arms and let the men deal with the juveniles. Eventually the waterlogged duo managed to remain upright long enough to make it all the way onto dry land.

"You should've done it," Derek said with a sidelong glance at her.

She gave him a quizzical look. "Done what?"

"You wanted to join them. I would've followed you in, and it would've been fun."

"Uh-huh." Her quick laugh rang out. "And then you would've made doggone sure I ended up more waterlogged than either of those boys."

His slow grin told her she was right. "Like I said, it would've been fun."

"Which would've left me the only dry, sane person around here," Max said complacently. Herding Petey and Chris ahead of him, he said over his shoulder, "I'll walk them back. You guys take your time and enjoy the place. Like you said, it's pretty."

Derek watched thoughtfully until Max was out of sight. "Well, he's certainly mellowed. They've still got the kids, but didn't it occur to him we could find a phone and report them, then return as if nothing had happened?"

"But we're not going to," she said indifferently. Then she gave him a sharp look. "I'm not. You're not either, are you?"

He appeared to study her. "From the expression on your face, if I said yes, I think you'd try to forcibly restrain me."

When she said nothing, he gave a quiet laugh. "Lighten up, Connie. For what it's worth, I'm on their side, too."

"Well . . . good." She looked at her feet, actually shuffled them in the grassy bank. "Well, I guess we should . . ."

"Before we go, I want to apologize for this morning. I didn't have it in mind to take advantage of you. Or the situation. I—"

"Wasn't awake either," she finished for him.

"No. Not until you flew out of bed. That woke me up with a jolt."

She managed a casual shrug. "Well, it happened. But it's not a problem." She turned to leave.

"Yes, it is."

She turned back. "It is?"

"Well, not exactly a problem," he amended. "But I have been wanting to talk to you. For some time now."

A sudden and strong urge to draw in and protect herself kept her silent and watchful. Protect herself from him? From the past? Or the future?

"I was going to ask Kristy for your number and give you a call." Though he generally carried a self-assured air, both his eyes and manner now seemed tentative. He was no more sure of himself at this moment than she was. "What I've been thinking, is that I'd like for us to start seeing each other again. Dating again, if you want to call it that. I've had second thoughts, Connie. Maybe we were too quick to split."

She took a step back and saw him flinch at her move.

"No." She retreated no farther but shook her head. "No. That's over and done with. It's behind us. The marriage, divorce, everything. And it needs to stay there."

Although he heard her out, he didn't respond to her speech. He stooped to pick up a pebble. "Judging from this morning's episode, the spark's still there." He snapped the pebble out over the water as if to slide it, but it sank without skittering. "I'm not exactly asking you for a commitment, but neither do I think it's too late for us. I just want you to think about it."

"It ended, Derek," she said flatly. "We have closure. It hurt enough then and I'm not signing on for more pain now."

Looking back at her, he gave her one slow nod of his head. "I hear you. And an apology isn't good enough, I know, but it's all I've got. I thought it over, time and again, and I realized I was punishing you. You weren't there when I wanted you, and all I could think about was my own situation. Then when you made the final move, I was holding a grudge, just like a little kid. For what it's worth, I'm sorry as hell I did that to you."

She took in a deep breath, let it out slowly. "I drew my own line in the sand and refused to cross it. I should've given you and your needs more consideration. And the truth is that I had an inkling, even then, that I might be sacrificing more than I wanted to. Yet I still didn't back down. We're equally guilty, Derek."

Stooping, he picked up another pebble, tried again to skim it and got more mileage this time. His tight expression testified to how deeply in thought he was, and how strongly he felt. Connie watched him, the man whose name she'd taken and to whom she'd given her heart. She'd legally changed her last name back to Robertson after the divorce, but her heart would never again belong to her alone. And she wouldn't want it to. The love, the union, had been there; she'd never give that up. But as much as she wished that what he was asking for was possible, she knew in her gut it wasn't. How could one go back to the beginning and start the whole world over again?

"What's happened has happened," she said quietly. The firmness she felt she also heard in her voice, and she supposed that it showed in her face. "And I'm as sorry as you are. But it's over. We need to let it go."

"Do we?" His gaze returned to her. The green of his eyes made her think of a pool of water, calm and deep, undisturbed by current. "I'm not so sure about that," he went on. "Maybe that's the mistake we made in the first place. Letting go."

He gave her space to speak, but she didn't. The timbre of his voice deepened. "I've got what I wanted, Connie, as far as my career is concerned. But there's something missing. It took me a while, but I finally figured out that it was you."

Still Connie didn't speak; she simply had no words. Though her resolve hadn't actually lessened, she felt pulled two ways. It was like having two voices warring inside herself: hers and Derek's, with his emotions and needs nearly as strong as her own. If either she or Derek had been capable of putting the other person first three years ago, they wouldn't be where they were now. The realization felt like a knife cutting into her.

"Sure, I've met other women," he confessed, possibly misreading her silence. "But no one I want to look at twice. No one measures up to you. And I don't think you've found anyone either. I would've heard about it from Kristy."

He got another stone, played toss and catch with it, and then again sought her eyes. "You're right that we can't go back to where we were before everything fell down around us. What's happened has happened. But we haven't lost it all, Connie. I don't believe that. Just think about it, okay? That's all I'm asking. Just think about it."

Connie turned slightly away, brought her hands up to massage her forehead and to hide the fact that her poise was deserting her. Her fingers felt shaky, as did her gut. Unsettling question marks had very quickly replaced the semblance of closure she'd worked so hard for and then known for such a short while, and that both surprised her and made her jittery. Yesterday she knew who she was and where she was, and today she wasn't so sure. The man who stood next to her still had the power to unnerve her, to make her want him all over again. And that scared her.

But never had she allowed confusion or nerves to rule her. She glanced up, gave Derek a direct look but was careful to put neither challenge nor committal in it. He returned her steady gaze, and then she turned to lead the way back to the farmhouse. One step at a time.

Chapter Fourteen

"Sure can think of better ways to waste a morning," Max said disgustedly as he trudged into the farmhouse that afternoon.

He stood aside while a morose Petey followed him in. As Max watched him, concern seemed to replace his irritation. He closed the door and caught his brother's arm. "I told you this is not your fault," he said, voice and gaze level. "You didn't know what you were doing, but he did. You are not at fault here. He is. Do you understand that?"

Petey stared at the floor for a long moment, then finally lifted his gaze. He nodded, but his forlorn expression belied the nod. Max waited a beat, squeezed his brother's arm, and then released him.

He caught Christopher's eye. "Chris, why don't you and Petey dismantle your garage over there, and go set it up outside under the tree? That way you can have real dirt instead of pretend dirt for your dump trucks."

Christopher's face brightened, but he directed a questioning look at his friend, awaiting his approval before making a move.

Petey's manner made an abrupt about-face. "Yeah. We won't have to worry about the babies getting into our stuff." His gaze roamed the room and hall, as if looking for little people, and he added in a conspiratorial whisper, "Hurry, before they get in here."

Their enthusiasm grew as they worked, their voices bubbling with excitement, and they kept shushing each other so as not to wake up the little spoilers. As he watched them, Max's expression smoothed itself out.

Once the two were out the door, their arms loaded with miniature garage parts and toy vehicles, the three remaining people looked expectantly at Max. Connie stood at the entrance to the kitchen. Moose had just entered from the hall after checking on the twins, who were napping in his room. Derek was at the window. Max looked at each person in turn, and then lifted his shoulders in a resigned shrug. Connie considered that shrug to be his trademark.

"Wasn't home," he explained succinctly. "Out of town. Back by the weekend."

Four pairs of eyes looked in different directions in various expressions of defeat.

"Zero accomplished," Moose said.

"Zilch," Max agreed. "All that buildup, and now we get to sit around and wait some more."

"And waiting is the only thing you can do," Derek warned. "Don't even think about doing anything else." Three sets of eyes looked at him. He chose to answer Connie's. "That's right. They need to wait, not rob that store again, or do anything else even remotely illegal. They need to sit it out, as difficult as that may be."

She felt her gaze sharpening as she regarded him. "One way or another, they are going to get that comic book back." The extent of her aggression surprised her, and she saw that it'd angered Derek. His mouth set itself in a straight line, and then he turned and stared out the window at Petey and Chris.

"Don't worry about it, Uncle Dare," Max said, face and voice void of expression. "I'm not going to do anything. The truth is I have neither the heart nor will to do anything else."

Connie hated the defeat she saw in him, even more than the defeat she felt in herself.

Max went to the refrigerator and pulled out a can of root beer. The easy-open pop-top wasn't living up to its name; he swore under his breath, changed hands, but still couldn't get it. Connie stood next to him so she took it, got her fingernail under the tab and popped it up, then handed the can back.

He frowned at the can, then her. Lifting her shoulders, she showed him her palms in a questioning attitude. "What?"

Moose covered his mouth, smothering a cough.

Appearing even more dejected, Max shook his head and sipped his soda.

Derek continued to stare silently out the window, not bothering to move the organdy sheers aside. Max crossed the room and joined him. "Petey's going to miss Chris," he said. "Going to miss him real bad."

"Really bad," Connie corrected absently.

Derek's head snapped around. "You correct his grammar, but it's okay for him to commit armed robbery?"

Connie made a bewildered gesture. This was her day for being frowned at.

Derek turned back to the window. "And it's really badly, not really bad. If you're going to correct someone, correct him correctly."

Max and Moose exchanged long looks.

Max cleared his throat. "My timing might be pretty bad here," he paused and looked from Derek to Connie and back again. "Bad or badly?"

Connie massaged the bridge of her nose, and Derek gave him a straight-on look. Max stared blandly back, and Derek gave in with a grudging grin. "Okay, I had that coming. Go on."

"You might as well go home once the babies wake up, and I need to know what your plans are. If you're going to tell all right away, or if you'll hold back until the weekend and give us some time."

"Oh, for . . ." Connie looked at the ceiling. "Damn! Damn! Damn!"

Three heads jerked toward her. She seldom swore—it wasn't a good habit for a schoolteacher to form—but that was the only word that fit. She gave Derek a pleading look. "How could I forget that? I don't believe he . . . it . . . uh, whatever, never even crossed my mind."

His steady expression assured her he hadn't overlooked what she had.

Her sense of defeat grew. She looked at Max, then Moose. "We . . . he . . . well, our . . ."

"What she's trying to say is that we won't be able to hold anything back," Derek explained. "Once Chris opens his mouth—you've already experienced his candor—we can only enlighten and clarify. His father, my brother, is the chief of police."

Max blinked. Moose walked backward until his legs hit the sofa, and he sat down.

"O'Reilly," Max breathed, staring into space. "Kevin O'Reilly. He's the chief of police. Of course he is."

"This just keeps getting better and better." Moose's voice was flat. "If it wasn't so serious, it'd be downright funny."

"The chief of police," Max repeated. "We kidnapped his kids, his brother, and his sister-in-law. The only one we missed was his wife. You think she'll be offended?"

Thoughtfully Max worked his jaw, then he gave Derek a quick look, and then Connie. "Do you know what his name is?" With a nod of his head, he indicated Moose. "Do you know where he works, lives, anything about him except what he looks like? His nickname doesn't matter. Petey and I are the only ones who call him that."

They shook their heads.

Max looked at Moose. "Then you got company, old buddy.

Petey and I will be moving in with you, and we've gotta do it fast." His attention returned to Derek. "When is your brother's flight arriving on Thursday?"

Derek looked at Connie.

"Uh. Late afternoon. Four-thirty, I think."

"Heck of a lot better than dawn," Max said, language surprisingly mild. "But we've still gotta get a move on. Aunt Connie, I hate to ask you this, but . . ."

She nodded knowingly and finished his sentence for him. "You want me to wake up the babies and get out of here, ASAP. After holding us against our will for three days, you're now unceremoniously kicking us out. You don't do things in half measures, do you?"

Max smiled, and then a real chuckle broke through. Derek gave him a curious look, possibly because it was the first time he'd heard the man laugh.

Holding the uncharacteristic smile, his gaze fixed on Connie, Max said, "If I could have a wish granted, it'd be that one day I invite you both to visit me, you would do so because you want to, and you wouldn't leave until you were damn good and ready."

Connie matched his smile. "I'd like that, too," she said quietly.

Then she caught sight of Derek's countenance, and she sobered hers. "But somehow I doubt it. I'll go get the twins."

LAX didn't rank very high on the list of Connie's favorite places. She twisted in her seat at the airline terminal that was overrun with endless people, bustling activity, and overriding announcements.

"Stop fussing," Derek hissed.

"I'm not fussing," she hissed back.

"Then stop fidgeting."

"I'm not fidgeting!"

Christopher looked idly at them, then went back to his

Highlights magazine. Evidently their bickering had become so commonplace their nephew paid little attention. He was busy picking out things that didn't belong in a picnic scene. The magazine had kept him occupied for what had turned into a long wait. Connie was thinking about borrowing it.

Coherent explanation of the past week was impossible. She wasn't looking forward to relating it, any of it; hence the fussing and the fidgeting. And she and Derek had been at odds, even more so than usual, since they'd left the farmhouse. They'd managed to agree on two things: neither of them wanted to attempt to muzzle Chris, and they wanted to stick around for the weekend. But that was the extent of their agreeableness.

She caught herself squirming again and forced herself to sit still. She also forced herself to stop pushing her tongue against her bottom teeth. Unfortunately, she didn't even have a baby to keep her busy. They'd both decided to nap in the van, and neither one had awakened, despite being transferred from car seats into the double stroller and then joining the bustle of the airport.

Her fingers moved to the waistband of her gray slacks and surreptitiously straightened it out. She wished she'd worn something else. These pants had no give, and the white silk blouse was little protection against the air conditioning. She envied Derek his sweatshirt, as ratty as it was.

People had generally steered clear of the group, possibly because of the noise potential of three kids, but a grandmotherly type now took the seat opposite Derek. She glanced idly at him, then gave him a longer, studying look. He'd dressed in old jeans and the well-worn faded blue sweatshirt that Connie coveted, was slouched in his seat, and wore a baseball cap pulled low on his forehead. So far, the simple disguise had worked; no one had looked twice at him. But this grandmother was apparently on the sharp-eyed side.

Fortunately, Andy woke up and stretched, catching the woman's attention. She cooed to him, and he talked right back. Connie smiled, answered questions about age and gender, and concentrated on trying not to fidget.

"Almost an hour late," the woman said, probably catching on to Connie's preoccupation. "But it's finally landed. Are you waiting for someone coming in from Hawaii?"

Connie nodded but didn't elaborate.

Derek said under his breath, "Here we go."

Connie followed his gaze. A horde of people appeared, seeming to race at them from the International gate. Her nervousness growing, she scanned the faces for familiar ones. Christopher stood up, gaze moving excitedly as he searched the crowd, then he took off at a run.

"Chris," Derek admonished, then possibly thought better of it because he smiled, stood, and followed his nephew.

The woman frowningly watched Derek instead of the crowd of arrivals. She knew she knew him, and eventually she'd come up with it. Connie hoped they'd be out of there before she did. She had enough to deal with; one thing more and she might go mad.

Kevin caught Chris and swung him up, gaze moving beyond Derek to Connie. He wore a long-sleeved, blue button-down shirt tucked neatly inside belted Levis. It took Kristy longer to find them, probably because she was shorter, but once she eyed Connie and the twins she made a beeline for them. A black, rounded-neck blouse that hugged her bosom and hips topped her white Capri-length pants. She looked like a fashion statement.

She lifted Andy out of the stroller and hugged him close, reverting to baby talk. Andy was beside himself, clearly not able to find a way to let his mother know how happy he was to see her. Crushing one baby to her, Kristy knelt next to the sleeping

Abbie, smoothed her hair and kissed her forehead, but Abbie continued to snooze.

With moist eyes, her mouth still next to Andy's cheek and her hand on Abby's head, Kristy glanced up at Connie. Connie stared back, wondering at her questioning look, then made a face and helplessly shook her head. She hadn't realized, until that moment, the implication in the fact that she and Derek were there together.

Over Kristy's head, Connie noted that the attention of the woman sitting opposite them remained on Derek. She'd caught her lower lip between her teeth and was slowly nodding her head. She almost had it.

"We'd better get out of here," Connie said.

Kristy glanced behind her, followed the direction of the woman's gaze, and nodded. "Uh-huh."

She gave Andy to Kevin and smilingly watched father and baby. Andy's jabbering spurred up a notch. Excitedly patting his dad's face, he almost squirmed out of his arms. Kevin pointed to his cheek. Andy put pudgy arms around his neck and planted an open-mouthed, juicy kiss on his cheek.

His father grinned at his mother. "He's using his teeth."

Kristy took Christopher's hand. She'd given him one hug already and now gave him another one. Connie pushed the double stroller holding the sleeping Abbie, Derek grabbed the two carry-on bags, and the group was on its way.

"So how did you enjoy your vacation, Chris?" his mother asked. "Looks like you got both Auntie Connie and Uncle Dare. You were lucky."

"Yeah, it was fun. We went fishing and I fell in the water. I ate chips and Abbie ate dirt. We ran out of gas and had to go for a walk, and then we got kidnapped. Annie Connie got to use a gun, but I didn't get to see her do it. It was the most fun vacation I ever went on, but I miss Petey. I miss him real bad."

Chapter Fifteen

His parents managed a full step each before they froze. They looked blankly at Christopher, each other, Connie, and in unison their gazes rose to Derek, who stood behind her.

Edging her way between them, Connie anchored the stroller with her foot and put an arm around each person. She looked sideways at Kristy, twisted her head and glanced up at Kevin, and in return she got identical expressions of unblinking disbelief. Andy, still in his father's arms, continued to jabber and pat his dad's face, vying for his attention. People coming up on them from behind parted as vehicles do around traffic islands and passed on either side. Some showed irritation and others took the jam-up in stride.

"It's true," Connie confirmed. "Every bit of it and more." Her head continued to swivel between them. "But as you can see, we're unharmed, healthy, and relatively happy. It's a long story, and we were hoping we could get home before we have to get into it. Trust us. Let's collect luggage, then we can get ourselves out to the van. Okay?"

Not waiting for concurrence, she pushed the stroller at a fast walk, joining the crowd, and Derek kept pace. Chris and Andy and their parents, the adults slightly glassy-eyed, caught up to them at the luggage carousel.

"Chris said you didn't report it," Kevin said to Derek. He put Andy in the stroller, keeping his gaze on Derek. "This didn't really happen. It's a joke, right?"

"That bag looks familiar," Connie said.

"Uh-huh." Derek grabbed it, took several quick steps and grabbed a matching one. "How many?" he asked.

"One more," Kristy said. She had the look of one trying to add something up that wasn't adding up. "A small one."

"This is not a very funny joke," Kevin said.

"That's because it's not a joke," Derek said. He grabbed the last bag, then exhaled heavily. "Never been through luggage retrieval this fast. Something's finally going right."

He looked pointedly, and critically, at his brother. "You going to take a couple of these bags, or do you want to get one of those carts? I can't manage all five by myself."

Though Kevin sat in the comfortable recliner, he didn't appear comfortable. He stared steadily at his brother. "Why do I have the feeling you're not telling me the truth?"

Connie sat at one end of the gray and white striped sofa. Derek was at the other end. He'd shed the ratty sweatshirt and looked much more presentable in a red knit polo shirt. As he watched his brother, his eyes narrowed fractionally, as if he were debating with himself if he wanted to be insulted or not.

Kevin amended, "Neither of you is lying. I know that. But I also know you're not leveling with me. So far, all you've done, both of you, is wait for Chris to say something, and then you clarify it. You haven't volunteered even one sentence on your own." He paused, with his gaze traveling between them, clearly giving them a chance to speak. When neither did, he went on. "You may not know their last names or where they could be found right now, yet you are withholding information that would lead us to them. Like license plates, for instance? Are you going to tell me you never even thought to check the license plates?"

Connie made a surprised sound that had both men looking at her.

"Well, she didn't," Kevin said, then gave his brother a look with a sharp edge to it.

Connie also looked at the man she'd shared a recent kidnapping with. Had he been as brain-dead as she?

Derek just shrugged. "Yeah, I thought about it, when I drove the van back after we got gas in it. But the Mustang and pickup were at an angle that didn't allow me to see either the front or the back plates. And the next time I got an opportunity to look, it was no longer important that I noted the licenses."

"Uh-huh."

Derek didn't appear to like his brother's tone but didn't comment on it. Apparently giving up on him for the moment, Kevin looked at Connie. She held his gaze, then dropped hers to her lap. "I feel like I got in trouble and was sent to the principal's office."

Derek's chuckle tried to turn itself into a cough. Kevin's countenance grew tighter, and she scrunched up her face. She hadn't intended to make a joke; she'd merely voiced the feeling she had and now wished she could take the words back. "I'm sorry, Kevin. I didn't mean—"

"This is not a joking matter," he said through his teeth. "We're talking about armed robbery and kidnapping. And the two of you are dancing around on the fringes of breaking the law yourselves. Withholding information, obstruction, and whatever else is going on you still haven't told me about."

"I'm sorry," she repeated. Slowly she got to her feet. "But I can't help you. And I'm tired, and I'm going to bed. If we stay with this any longer, we're going to be at each other's throats."

But she didn't complete the move to leave. Her gaze remained on Kevin. "Give us a few days, just a few days, and then we'll talk. Please?"

His eyes didn't waver. "No. Now, Connie. Not in a couple days. You want me to trust you, but you also need to trust me.

You both need to talk to me."

I wish I could, she thought. *If only I could.* With a sense of defeat, an emotion that had grown too familiar this past week, she turned and left.

Kristy stood next to Christopher's bed, her sandy-brown hair pulled back in a ponytail, looking down at him as he slept. She looked good in the strawberry-pink robe. She had inches on Connie in height, bust line and hips, but not in the waist. The belted robe enhanced her measurements instead of hiding them. Connie paused in the doorway, hoping Kristy wasn't in the same *I-want-answers-and-I-want-them-now* mood as her husband.

But when Kristy looked up, her blue-gray eyes were warm and friendly. Connie gave her a smile that she guessed carried her relief, because Kristy said, "He's really giving you the third degree."

Connie nodded without elaborating.

"For one thing, it's his job," Kristy explained, managing not to apologize for her husband, nor put Connie down for being at odds with him. "For another, he's both angry and scared. Having this happen to his own family showed him just how vulnerable and helpless he is. That's an unfamiliar feeling, and not a good one." She looked back down at Christopher. "I don't like it either. But you saw my kids safely through whatever it was that happened, and that's all I need to know. And for that I thank you from the bottom of my heart."

Again Connie nodded. Though she felt greatly out of her depth, she had an inkling of what these two people were going through.

When Kristy next looked up, her expression held a questioning smile that put that issue behind them. "You and Derek finally figure out who's sleeping where?"

Connie laughed. With the change of topic, the tension in the room seemed to evaporate. "I lost the coin toss, which I thought meant I got the sofa. But he said it meant I lost the right to choose, so he chooses that I sleep on the cot, which is the way he wanted it in the first place."

"So the coin toss meant you won the cot, or lost the right to choose the sofa. Hard to lose with those rules." Then she broke into a grin. "Or maybe it's hard to win."

"One or the other. I'd fit better on the couch because I'm not as long as he is, but I give up. That's my bed over there." She paused. "And I see my suitcase is already under it. He's fast."

They were speaking in normal voices, seemingly unmindful of the sleeping child. With an inward smile, Connie realized Christopher truly was as hard a sleeper as his uncle. She recalled animated conversations between herself and Derek in their farmhouse bedroom while Chris snoozed away undisturbed.

Becoming aware that Kristy's expression had changed and that she was being studied, Connie candidly returned her friend's gaze. When Kristy said nothing, Connie lifted her shoulders. "What?"

"I'm wondering how it worked out that Derek was here. Been wondering that since I saw him at the airport."

"Oh. That's easy enough." She crossed to the cot and pulled her suitcase out from under it. "Somehow the dates got mixed up. He thought it was the fourth instead of the fourteenth."

"Uh-uh. We didn't misunderstand dates, either one of us."

Connie was wondering if she should again sleep in her clothes, since she would once more be sharing a bedroom. Perhaps she should invest in a pair of modest pajamas along with a cell phone. She glanced up. "No?"

"Nope. I talked to him the day before we left. He had a photo session on the twelfth, was meeting his agent on the thirteenth, and would be here as soon as possible on the fourteenth. It'd be difficult for either of us to mistake the twelfth and the thirteenth for the second and the third. They don't sound at all alike."

"No, they don't," Connie agreed. Kristy had her full attention.

"Then he asked me which set of grandparents would be babysitting, and I told him you'd be staying with the kids. There was a long silence, then he told me to have a good time, and he hung up."

Her gaze on Kristy, Connie lowered herself to sit on the cot next to her suitcase.

"The only thing that man was fishing for by arriving early was his ex-wife," Kristy added. "And he had to go to an awful lot of trouble to rearrange his calendar in order to do it."

In the silence that followed, Connie stared into space, and Kristy watched her.

"Not too surprising, I guess," Connie said finally. "He told me he wants us to try again. To just start seeing each other again."

"And how do you feel about that, about him? What do you want?"

Connie allowed an even longer silence before answering. Then she said, "I wish I knew." She closed her eyes and shook her head. "I wish I knew."

"That was a rough time. I remember how much you were hurting. Both of you."

Connie nodded, swallowed. "Yeah."

"It must be scary thinking about trying again."

"Rough. And scary. Apt words." Then Connie felt her mood softening as wistfulness slowly settled in. "You know, that day we went fishing, a couple times I found myself . . . conscious of him, I guess is the best way to put it. The way I used to be, before we had a past."

She stopped, and the pensiveness abruptly faded. "A past full of misgivings and misunderstandings. Hurt feelings and hard memories." Purposely she closed off her expression and got to her feet. "Didn't work out then, and it won't work now. We clashed constantly." With resolution she got back on track and returned her attention to the suitcase.

"That you did." Kristy leaned against the closet door and folded her arms. "But it wasn't the fighting that caused the breakup."

Connie's gaze snapped back to her. "What?"

"Face it, kid. You've got a short fuse, and so does he. You're bound to clash. That didn't have anything to do with the breakup. You told me yourself; you never went to bed angry, either one of you, and you never woke up angry. Whatever the problem was, you found a way to deal with it."

"But . . . those last months . . . we didn't even talk to each other, Kris. There was no marriage left."

"Exactly. You weren't talking. You weren't fighting. You weren't communicating. The relationship ceased to exist." She crossed one ankle over the other. "I wouldn't recommend it for everybody—wouldn't work for Kevin and me, for instance—but in your case, conflict enhanced the relationship. It fueled the chemistry."

Connie was silent for a long moment, studying her friend. "Okay, Ms. Freud, then what was the problem?"

"The separation, when he moved and you didn't. Instead of exploding, having a big row over it and clearing the air, you both sulked. You let it simmer, let it steep, and it got so big that neither one of you could deal with it."

Connie was quiet for another long moment. "If this is what you thought, Kris, why on earth didn't you tell me then?"

"I was hurting too, for both of you, and working as hard as I could to remain neutral. I wasn't seeing it very clearly right then either."

Suddenly, Connie collapsed on the cot and put her face in

her hands. "I don't know what to say. Or do. I can't even think straight."

"I'm not surprised." Kristy waited a beat, and then added softly, "Is Derek worth all this stress?"

Connie's head snapped up.

Kristy's gaze was steady. "Is the relationship worth it?"

She crossed the room, and lightly kissed Connie on the forehead. "Those are tough questions, kid. Think about it long and hard. And you know where I am if you need a sounding board. In the meantime, goodnight. And thanks again for taking such good care of my kids."

Although Kevin seemed to lighten up the next day, his guests grew more tense. Since he hadn't been able to break either of them down, it appeared he'd decided to do the next best thing and ignore them.

Max and Petey's house was thirty miles away, and Chris wasn't able to tell his dad how to get there. Police patrols were searching the vicinity; it was only a matter of time before the house was discovered, but Derek and Connie were intent upon squeezing out all the time they could for Max and SteelMan.

The police chief in Kevin insisted that the kidnapping be reported. So, hoping to sneak past the media, the report had been filed in the names of D. Richard O'Reilly and Connie Robertson. So far they'd gotten away with the simple ruse. Since the kids' surnames matched their uncle's, neither had the media caught the connection to the chief of police.

When the phone rang late Saturday morning, host and hostess sat at the kitchen table with after breakfast coffee, and their guests sat on the tall counter stools. The twins were napping, and Christopher was at a play-date with a neighborhood friend.

Connie wasn't comfortable because her feet wouldn't reach the bottom rung on the too-tall stool. As she watched Kevin answer the phone, she wondered why she was here instead of over there at the table where there were four comfortable chairs. But as soon as the thought crossed her mind, the answer followed it: she and Derek were squaring off against his brother.

Kristy had refused to take sides, and Connie was surprised she was at the table and not standing in the middle of the room. Then she remembered Kristy had been there first and Kevin had sat down next to her.

It occurred to Connie that adulthood could be a whole lot like first-grade-hood.

The police chief held the phone to his ear, doing more listening than talking, and glanced occasionally at his guests, who weren't even trying to disguise their interest. Then when he replaced the phone receiver, he just stared at them.

"Well?" Derek asked, probably realizing his brother wasn't going to volunteer anything. Connie didn't blame Kevin for being so closemouthed, but she still would've strangled him if she could.

"Does the name Maxwell ring a bell?" he asked finally.

"Oh," Connie said, trying to cross her legs. She almost slid off the seat, so she continued to let her legs hang. "So that's their name. No, Kevin, it doesn't ring any bells. We told you we didn't know what their last name was."

"Herman and Peter Maxwell. And they have now added attempted extortion to armed robbery and kidnapping. These boys are busy."

"Alleged extortion," Connie corrected. Neither did she like the word *attempted.* Apparently, Max hadn't got the book back or adequate compensation for it.

Kevin gave her an eloquent look that held no appreciation. Then he said, "The big guy, Moose, wasn't in on the *alleged* extortion attempt. We still don't know anything about him, other than that he's big and he wears a beard."

Derek nodded. "And that's all we know. We already told you that."

His brother propped his elbows on the table and made a tent with his fingers. "Amazing what tidbits we pick up here and there, which often enables us to find someone without having his name. For instance, Chris knows he likes extra crispy chicken, lasagna, and cheese omelets. That doesn't help us very much, however. But you know things about him that would lead us to him. At least Connie does."

Derek looked surprised, and Connie blinked. Kevin was right on target, and she wondered how he knew. She glanced sideways at Derek. She hadn't told him about Max and Moose's AA connection, and she wasn't about to mention it to his brother. Confidentiality was a keynote of that organization, but she still feared that tidbit of information might help lead Kevin to Moose.

She looked back at her ex-brother-in-law, but refused to engage in a staring contest, so then lowered her gaze to the counter. "Did you learn anything else in that phone conversation?"

"Connie, can you think of any reason why I should share any information with you?"

She looked up. Answered calmly, "No."

Different emotions warred across his face: surprise at her candor and respect for it, then a renewal of last night's frustration, which was then slowly replaced by resignation. He looked at the window, shook his head, exhaled heavily and then looked back. "Okay, we're going to try it this way and see what happens. Herman and Peter—"

"Max and Petey," the pair at the counter corrected in unison. They looked at each other, then Derek directed a shrug toward Kevin. "We already told you that."

"That's right. The one thing you told me, and I forgot all about it."

Kristy gave her husband a reproving look.

"Anyway," Kevin continued. "They showed up at Julian Hayworth's house this morning—he's the owner of the convenience store they robbed three times, by the way—and demanded five grand or they'd continue to rob and harass him in whatever way they could. Hayworth refused, slammed the door on them and called the police."

Connie felt empty, in heart and gut. She hadn't really expected Max's plan to work and didn't think he'd held much hope of success, either. But until that moment, it wasn't total defeat.

"Charming people you're covering for," Kevin said. "And not especially smart. On top of everything else, Hayworth is also their landlord, so he's got plenty of information on them."

"He is?" blurted two surprised voices.

Kevin glanced sideways at his wife. "How about that. I knew something they didn't."

Derek and Connie looked at each other. Unspoken communication passed between them. She took in a deep breath and let it out. "Okay," she said. "You shared your information, we'll share ours."

"Gee, thanks," Kevin said dryly.

Kristy gave him a look that clearly said *shut up*.

"For starters, it's not Max and Petey who lack charm," Connie stated unequivocally. "It's Hayworth. He stole something from them, and they only want to be compensated for it. And worse than the fact of stealing in itself is the way he did it. Petey is a grown man, but no older mentally and emotionally than Chris. Hayworth knew that, and he took unfair, unjust and immoral advantage. If that isn't illegal, it should be. *He* is the charming person you should be concerned about."

Kevin nodded. "Okay, go on."

"There's nothing else." When she saw his angry disbelief on its way back, she added quickly, "That's the truth. We don't know Moose's name, where he lives, works, or anything. We knew Hayworth owned the convenience store, and that Max wanted to see him this weekend, but that's it. We don't know anything else, Kevin. Honest."

"Another thing you should know," Derek said, "is that we were never in any danger from those men. Not any one of us. Admittedly, I was worried in the beginning, but it quickly became evident there was no danger. Chris knew that before we did, and he's also told you that, in several different ways."

"They didn't even have bullets in their guns," Connie said. "Doesn't that tell you something?"

Kevin gave her his full attention. "And the way you found that out was by pulling the trigger, wasn't it?"

She closed her eyes and breathed deeply, then again met his gaze. "Yes."

"But you're trying to tell me now that you weren't frightened."

"Of course I was scared," she snapped, getting angry and not caring that she was. "I was scared to death. We had two babies and a five-year-old, and Derek and I were not a match for three men, especially when one of them was as big as a moose. I was scared to death," she repeated, "and would've done anything to get those kids out of there."

Kevin's countenance underwent a rapid change. He looked like he would gladly eat his words if she asked him to. He opened his mouth but didn't speak for a long moment. Then he said simply, "I'm sorry."

He looked at his wife. "And I agree with Kristy. We owe you both a debt we'll never be able to repay. You brought our kids through . . . that, and they're none the worse for it." His expression lightened fractionally. "In fact, Chris had the time of his life."

Connie again felt out of her depth. "No apology is necessary. This whole thing has hit you guys hard, and Derek and I haven't been . . . well, very forthright. But we wanted fair play for Max and Petey. They broke the law, and we knew you wouldn't accept that, but we had to give them time. Even though it hasn't worked out for them."

Kevin said, "I still don't understand the why of it. What did Hayworth steal?"

"Oh. Uh, well . . ." Connie's gaze drifted to the hallway.

"Well," Derek agreed. He looked at Connie, then his brother. "It was, uh, well . . ."

There was no way around it. "A comic book," Connie said in a small voice.

Kevin swore under his breath. "So help me, if you two don't stop—"

"Now wait a minute," Kristy said in a warning voice. She looked dubiously between her husband and the people at the counter, as if not sure she should tell Kevin to be civil or their guests to be serious.

"It's true," Derek said. "You wanted us to talk, and we're talking. Now you need to back off and listen."

He waited for his brother's nod before he continued. "He stole a rare SteelMan comic book that's worth at least five grand, probably a lot more. They'd prefer to have the book back, but they'll settle for the money. From the little I know about the subject, I'd think the price tag is a steal in itself, pardon the pun."

Kevin still appeared to be having difficulty, and Kristy looked skeptical as well. "When I think of all the ills in this world," he said, "and then compare them to a lost comic book." His head wagged from side to side. He looked disgusted. "This has got to be one of the stupidest problems I've ever run across."

"Well, there are people who'd disagree with you," Connie said, defensive and defiant at the same time. She'd often seen the mood she felt on the faces of her first-graders, and she was just as stubborn as any one of them ever was. "And you can mark me down as one of them."

Chapter Sixteen

Kevin parked the mini van in front of the farmhouse in approximately the same place it had previously rested. "So this is it," he said to his passengers, and Connie and Derek nodded.

The three people, each wearing jeans but with differing kinds of shirts, as well as varying degrees of curiosity, exited the van. The men wore short sleeves in cool cotton, solid white for Kevin and gray and black pinstripes for Derek, and Connie was a lot less somber in a hot pink pullover.

Though his casual clothing didn't display his profession, Kevin's demeanor did. He looked around, most likely absorbing the layout and committing it to memory. "Off the main road," he murmured. "The stream would be back there, maybe a half-mile or so. We would've found it in another day or two, even without the address."

He looked pointedly at his companions. His unspoken words were, *which we didn't get from you.* But his expression held no antagonism. The incident hadn't been forgotten, but Derek and Connie were apparently forgiven.

They walked to the front door. His companions exchanged amused looks when Kevin knocked. Connie reached around him to try the doorknob, but he nudged her hand away.

He knocked again, and Connie stepped back. If he needed to follow procedure, then let him get on with it. Her glance passed over the young oak where she and Derek and the kids had attempted to hide themselves, and then her gaze flew back.

No movement. Nothing. She wasn't sure what she'd seen in that first look, but she'd seen something. Not wanting to draw Kevin's attention to the tree, she snapped her head forward. Fortunately, he hadn't been watching her, and she worked hard at appearing nonchalant in case he did glance her way.

Derek might've caught her reaction, because he looked casually from her to the oak, then back again, but apparently he saw nothing there. Though he continued to watch her, she didn't meet his gaze.

When the door opened from inside, paralysis seemed to strike all three people on the porch.

"Hi," Petey said. He wore the familiar Bart Simpson t-shirt, and he appeared friendly, yet apprehensive, as his gaze fell first on Kevin, the stranger. Then his eyes found Connie and his face lit up. He gave her an exuberant hug, forcing the air out of her, and then he gave Derek an equally forceful embrace.

When his attention returned to Kevin, he tilted his head and his brow furrowed. "Are you Chris's daddy? You look like Uncle Dare, but you look like Chris, too. I'll bet you're his dad."

"What—" Connie started, stopped, swallowed, and then finished. "What are you doing here?"

Petey bit his lip as he regarded her and her question. Then he hung his head as if ashamed. "I got lost."

And his brother was looking for him. He was hiding over there behind that tree. As concern gave way to frustration, Connie recalled that on their way to the farmhouse, Kevin had entered the last two intersections on a caution light. If he'd been a more law-abiding citizen, he would've stopped like he was supposed to, and Max might've had time to find his brother and get him out of here.

"How did you get lost?" Derek asked.

Petey appeared to be concentrating on his feet. "I went to the bathroom," he mumbled.

Connie squinted. "You . . . what?"

"It was all my fault." Petey seemed near tears.

Derek put a hand on his arm and said gently, "What was your fault?"

"I gave SteelMan to Mr. Hayworth. And now he won't give it back."

"Where's your brother?" Kevin asked, voice as mild as Derek's. He must've realized he was dealing with a child, just as they'd told him. But now he had the proof right in front of him. "Did he go to see Mr. Hayworth again?"

Connie barely managed not to yell *stop it!* at Kevin. Derek's face grew tight and tension was evident in his body language. They were equally helpless to protect the Maxwell brothers.

"I left Max at the restaurant," Petey said. "Long time ago. I don't know where he is right now." He looked up. "Gee, I wish you'd brought Chris with you. I miss him real bad."

"He misses you, too," Kevin said. "He talks about you a lot."

"Are you going to take him fishing? He wants to go fishing with you. He said it was fun doing things with Uncle Dare, but it was more fun with his daddy."

Derek's expression lightened fractionally, and he exchanged half smiles with Connie.

"I told Chris how lucky he is," Petey continued. "My dad died a long time ago." He frowned. "Sometimes it's hard for me to remember him, but Max does and tells me about him." Then he brightened. "And Max takes me places, just like my daddy would have. We go fishing sometimes. He fishes and I pan for gold. Chris wanted me to teach him how to look for gold, but we didn't have time. Will you teach him how if I don't get to see him again?"

Kevin nodded and gave the guileless man a small smile.

Petey smacked his forehead. "Max keeps telling me about my manners. I didn't even ask you to come in." He stepped back to give them room. "Nothing to eat or drink, though. We took everything, except for some furniture. Moose didn't have room for all of it. I sure hope Max finds me soon, because I'm hungry. I didn't get to eat anything at the restaurant."

Kevin stepped inside. His gaze scanned the room then returned to Petey. His manner was mild, but his eyes were alert. "If you're lost, then you don't know how to find your way to Moose's house. Is that right?"

"Yeah. I don't know how to get there. It's too far away."

Connie breathed easier. But that fact would merely prolong the situation, not solve it.

"And I got so confused, I couldn't even remember the phone number," Petey went on, looking miserable. Then relief crossed his face. "I sure am glad you found me. I don't know what I would've done if you hadn't come for me."

A veil seemed to lower over Kevin's features.

"I still don't understand how you got lost in the first place," Derek said. "Tell me what happened at the restaurant." He sat on the sofa and motioned for Petey to join him.

Connie and Kevin remained standing. The house was stuffy from being closed up, and too warm. Connie wished she still had a change of clothes here so she could get out of the overly warm top. What had possessed her to wear ribbed knit? She was either too cold because of air conditioning, or too warm without it.

Petey sat down, staring intently into space as he tried to get his thoughts in order. "It's hard to remember exactly. I wasn't feeling too good. I was feeling real bad."

Derek nodded encouragingly. "That's okay. Take your time."

Kevin was standing near the stuffed head of a deer mounted on the wall. He moved closer, his attention seemingly caught by a small, black hole between the eyes of the deer. He squinted at it, then touched it with the fingernail on his right pinkie.

"I did that," Petey said, and again hung his head. "I shot the deer."

Three heads snapped his way. "You killed the deer?" Kevin asked.

"I didn't kill it. It died before I was born. I just shot it."

Three sets of eyes stared at him. Connie guessed she appeared as dumbfounded as her companions.

Then Petey tugged gingerly at his ear. "I shot me, too."

Derek shook it off first. "Never mind that. Tell us what happened this morning. We need to know how you got lost."

"Well," Petey started. He drew in a deep breath and blew it out. "Okay. I told you Mr. Hayworth wouldn't give the book back and wouldn't pay us for it, either. He was real mean, and called me stupid, and Max got mad. Mr. Hayworth stepped back real quick, like he knew Max was mad, and then he slammed the door on us. He shouted, loud enough we could hear him through the door, and said he wasn't scared of us and told us to get out of there because he was calling the cops."

He looked seriously at the floor. "Max swore. He called Mr. Hayworth a real bad name. Max doesn't like for people to swear in front of me, so I knew he was real angry when he did it. But we had to leave, 'cause the police were coming. Anyway, Max didn't say anything in the truck, and he got over being mad, and then he started being sad. And he looked worried. That's when I started to cry, because I knew it was my fault."

"Why was it your fault?" Kevin interrupted.

Petey looked surprised at the question. "I told you. I gave SteelMan away."

"Tell us how it happened that you gave the book away," Derek said.

"Oh. Well, that was when Max wasn't doing too good. He was drinking what he called the hard stuff. He used to do that a lot, then he stopped, and then he started again. For one day and one whole night, he didn't come home. I was real scared. Then Moose came and picked me up and took me to his house. But before Moose got here, Mr. Hayworth came and wanted to see the comic book and asked if he could buy it. I told him he'd have to talk to Max. But then he said he'd pay me ten dollars for it, and that was a lot more than what our daddy had paid for it, and I'd be making a whole lot of money. Max had lost his job, and we didn't have much money then, so I said okay."

Kevin's face had hardened along with everyone else's. "Did Max ask Mr. Hayworth to give the book back when he came home?"

"He tried, but Mr. Hayworth wouldn't do it. Max talked to Moose about it, too, and he talked to the police, and then we went to see a man in a big office with a secretary and everything. Max never blamed me, but I knew I'd done something wrong."

Petey turned back to Derek. In Max's absence, it seemed Petey had adopted Derek as his surrogate guardian. "Then, this morning, when I started to cry, Max turned all cheery and tried to make me feel better. He said we deserved to treat ourselves to a fancy brunch, even if we did have to take second best."

Derek looked puzzled. "Second best?"

"Yeah. We wouldn't be able to find anybody that could cook as good as you."

Kevin chuckled. "Another fan." He crossed to the window and looked outside. One hand parted the curtain. Connie tensed, mind racing as she tried to figure out how to get him away from there without arousing his suspicion.

Don't move, Max, she tried to communicate telepathically. *Don't even breathe.*

Petey resumed his story. "But before the food came, I had to go to the bathroom. Then I saw the back door, and thought I should go talk to Mr. Hayworth by myself because it was between me and him in the first place. That's how it all got started. I didn't tell Max because I was afraid he wouldn't let me. But then I got lost. And the worse thing was I'd forgotten to go to the bathroom and I still had to go, real bad. So I went behind a tree." He made a face, as if expecting a scolding. "But I made sure nobody was looking."

Derek smiled. "Sometimes emergencies like that happen." Then he added, "It was lucky you remembered how to get here."

"It was the only place I knew to go, and I had to walk for a long time. When the door was locked, I didn't know what to do, but then I remembered that Max had hid a key under the rock next to that pretty pink flower in the back yard. Then I just sat here and waited." His gaze dropped to his lap. His face reddened. "Except for when I had to go to the bathroom again. That's why it took me so long to answer the door."

Kevin turned from the window. He looked long and hard at Petey.

Petey glanced up, met his eyes, and then quickly looked away, as if nervous or pained. His gaze flitted from Derek to Connie, then down at his hands as he held them in his lap. "Did I do something wrong?"

Kevin's face lacked expression. Derek's eyes narrowed as he studied his brother. His hand gripped Petey's shoulder, as if to reassure him. Connie realized she was holding her breath and let it out sparingly.

Kevin turned aside. Not meeting anyone's eyes, he dug into his pocket and came up with keys. "If no one has an objection, I think I'll take care of that grocery list Kristy gave me and leave the three of you on your own for a while." He strode to the door and opened it. He paused, keeping his back to them. "Shouldn't take me much more than an hour or so."

The door closed behind him.

Derek and Connie looked at the closed door for a long time before they looked at each other. Her eyes were moist. They heard the van's engine start and then listened silently as the sound receded.

"Did I do something wrong?" Petey repeated.

"No," Derek said softly.

The door opened.

"Max!" Petey shouted, jumping up and running to his brother. "I knew you'd find me." Then he sobered and jerked to a quick stop before he reached him. "I'm sorry I ran away and got lost. Please don't be mad."

Max let his breath out in a rush. "No, Petey, I'm not mad. Just don't ever do anything like that again. It turned out okay. But it almost didn't." Max clasped his arms around him, drawing him close.

His gaze found Connie, then Derek. "Helpless is not a good feeling. I don't know how you did it, and I can't thank you enough for doing it. I wasn't even sure Petey was here until he opened the door." He shook his head. "And there wasn't a damn thing I could do but stand there and try to will that tree to grow big enough to hide me."

Slowly Derek got to his feet. "We didn't do anything." Then he added softly, "Except pray."

"Petey," Max said, holding him at arms' length. "You and Chris left one of your play trucks out there under that tree. Go get it, and then I'll show you where I left the pickup."

"Gee, thanks, Max. I'm glad you found it."

Connie watched him leave, then flew to Max and wrapped her arms tightly around him. He seemed taken aback but returned her embrace. She stepped back and gripped his elbows. "So help me, you're going to give me ulcers. You get Petey and his truck and then get the hell out of here. I don't want to see either one of you around here ever again."

A touch of sadness was in his smile. "That's exactly what I intend to do, Aunt Connie."

Once Connie released him, she became aware of reaction setting in. She felt shaky, and suddenly she wanted to go to the bathroom. Bad.

"Then you're giving up," Derek said.

"What else can I do?" Max asked, still with that sad smile. "Hayworth hasn't won—he's a loser and always will be. Never will that man be a winner. But I've already risked too much. I can't bear to think of Petey in any kind of confinement, and who would take care of him if I went to prison? Not to mention the risk to Moose." He shrugged, appearing more resigned than defeated. "I gave it my best shot, but it didn't pan out."

He extended his hand to Derek. "Thanks, Uncle Dare. It was good meeting you." He took Connie's hand, then bent to kiss her cheek. "You too," he said. "You both take care."

Then he was gone.

As they stared at the empty doorway, Derek put his arm around Connie's shoulders. Neither spoke. Then the urge to urinate grew so strong she had to excuse herself. She did what she had to do, and had a good cry in there, too. She washed the tears away, dried her face, and rejoined Derek. But from the commiserating look he gave her, she guessed the crying jag had left traces.

When Kevin returned for them, no one asked questions, and no one offered explanations.

Abbie was breaking in a new tooth, and she didn't need a vocabulary to explain what cranky meant. She hadn't been sleeping well, neither had anyone else, and she was no happier in the daytime.

She and Derek were playing with a plastic egg that broke apart in the middle. While kneeling on the floor in front of her, her uncle put the two pieces in separate pockets of her frilly blouse. She made an enraged comment, and he quickly fished out the pieces and gave them to her.

Connie grinned as she set her suitcase near the door. "That little tyrant certainly has whipped you into shape."

He looked up. "Seems to me I've also seen Auntie Connie back down a time or two," he countered.

The teething process wasn't affecting Andy as badly as it did his sister. He was sitting on the floor amidst his toys, happily playing with an empty shoebox. Abbie stopped next to him and dropped the plastic egg pieces. An argument over the shoebox lid seemed imminent. Connie watched, waiting for war to erupt, but Abbie turned aside and complained her way into the hall, searching for her mother.

Connie heard them meet up, the mother's soothing words, and then the baby's protests muffling themselves on her mom's shoulder. When she became aware that Derek's gaze was still on her, she was surprised at the shyness that threatened to overcome her.

She looked back. "Well. That was some fishing trip you took us on."

He sent her a grin, looking comfortable with one knee still resting on the floor. "This gift of understatement of yours is a newly acquired skill."

"I'm glad you're sticking around. Chris is ecstatic he's got both you and his dad. He told me you're going to that new Sears today, to check out their sports department. Sounds manly."

His grin deepened. "Now who's being sexist?" He stood and dusted his hands together. "I still have another week of vacation, and I figured I'd spend it here mending fences."

"I doubt that'll be a problem." She looked at her suitcase, then back up. "I've always respected Kevin, now even more so. It took an extraordinary person to do what he did."

"I'm very much aware of that." Slowly he crossed the room.

"I was planning on calling you next week, but I'll just talk to you now instead. There's a charity benefit coming up this summer that I promised to attend. And I need a date."

She said nothing. He'd stopped a full arm's length away, giving her plenty of space. And Kristy was also giving them ample room, Connie noted.

"You could spend the weekend," Derek added, but not crowding her with the invitation. Instead, she got the impression he was deliberately holding back, giving her time and room and anything else she might want. "You'd have your own bedroom, of course, but I don't want to rush you. If you're not comfortable with that arrangement, there's an excellent hotel nearby."

Here we go, she thought. Did she really want to do this? Did she honestly *not* want to? She swallowed hard. "Sounds like this could be a first date, except it's the second time around." Even her voice sounded shy.

His mouth curved. "Both comments fit." Then he grew quiet and his face smoothed out. She'd never before seen him hold himself in check like that.

Finally she spoke again. "We have to move slowly." Her voice was very quiet and very serious. "Very slowly."

He broke into another grin, this one wide and relieved. He was a good-looking man, but when he smiled, his face was transformed into matinee-idol handsomeness. "You can move as slowly as you want to. As long as we're moving, we're making progress."

He stepped closer, then leaned in to lightly, very lightly, brush his lips across hers. As kisses go, this was as chaste as one could get. Their lips barely lingered long enough to make contact, but the contact carried a jolt of electricity.

Chapter Seventeen

Impatiently, Connie drummed her fingers on the steering wheel. This was the third time she'd sat through this red light. She wanted to use an ATM before getting on the freeway to start her trip home, preferably at a branch of her own bank, but empty parking spaces were nonexistent. This time she stayed on the thoroughfare instead of turning onto her bank's street. She'd hit the first ATM she saw with a parking place anywhere near it.

Two blocks later, she found a bank, a space for the car, and a line at the ATM. Idly, she glanced at the window. The inside of the bank appeared as busy as the outside. At the desk nearest the window, an elderly man was concluding his business. The man behind the desk stood, they shook hands, and the elderly customer exited the building.

Connie stepped inside and took the seat the man had vacated. The name plaque on the desk identified the bank representative as Raymond L. Tidwell, Investment Counselor.

Mr. Tidwell looked up. The automatic smile disappeared. "Uh-oh."

Connie smiled. "Hi, Moose."

His sigh was deep and drawn out. "Hello, Aunt Connie."

The woman seated behind the next desk glanced at them. Her chestnut hair held a touch of gray, her nails were a bright blood red, and her pale green dress fit like a glove, which unfortunately emphasized the ten or so extra pounds she carried. "Aunt Connie? You've got to be kidding. She's at least ten years younger than you." Her voice carried the lilting trace of a southern accent.

Her nameplate identified her as Darlene Marsh, Assistant Manager. Darlene wasn't exactly possessive toward Moose, but there was something about her appraisal of Connie that suggested a relationship—or the wish for one—with Raymond Tidwell.

Connie tried to make herself look romantically harmless. "I'm not really his aunt, but it is a family endearment. We met through my niece and nephews."

Apparently finding nothing in Connie's manner to be concerned about, Darlene gave the smile back, then returned her attention to the file on her desk.

Connie settled comfortably in the chair, returned her attention to Moose, and gave him what she supposed was a wicked grin. He wore a steel gray suit and a deep blue shirt set off by a pinstriped tie, quite a difference from the casual jeans and shirts of the farmhouse. Purposely and sweetly, she used his own pet phrase. "My, my. It just keeps getting better and better, doesn't it?"

He said nothing. He resembled a man awaiting sentence.

She checked her watch. "When do they let you out for lunch?"

"Now," Darlene said, looking up. "His lunch break started just this instant."

"Great." Connie pushed her chair back and stood. "Perfect timing."

"Uh," Moose said.

Darlene waved him away. "Get out of here, Ray. Go treat your aunt to lunch." She critically eyed Connie's snug navy slacks. "Buy her something fattening."

"They've had two days," Connie said, picking at the limp plate of lettuce that had been described as a salad. "So I hope they're long gone."

Without comment, Moose took another bite out of his giant, juicy hamburger. He hadn't livened up a whole lot but had managed two whole sentences. "Just a salad? You'll never find a better hamburger than they make here."

Her fork didn't find anything it wanted to attach itself to. Their hamburgers might be okay, but their salads left much to be desired. "You know where they are, don't you?"

"Why are you asking? Are you in need of a pen pal?"

She pushed her plate away and eyed his basket of fries. "Just curious, I guess." The hamburger didn't turn her on, but the curly fries looked delicious. "But just in case Hayworth changes his mind or somehow someone could get that book away from him, you'd be able to then get it to Max. Right?"

"No comment to the second part. And to the first part, the only way that book could be recovered from Hayworth is by stealing it back. Forget it, Aunt Connie."

That was the longest speech so far, and he'd demolished the hamburger. Apparently, the food had fueled his communicational skills. He took a long swig of Coke, then wiped his hands on the flimsy napkin. It was a tiny one, considering those big hands and all the hamburger juice on them.

She hadn't needed her napkin, so pushed it his way. She pointed at the fries he hadn't touched. "May I?"

Obligingly he pushed the basket toward her. "Darlene says go ahead."

She tasted one. "Umm. They are good." She settled in for a feast, meaning that she now needed a napkin. Rubbing the salty grease between thumb and fingers, she looked for a dispenser. He helped himself to fresh napkins on a nearby table and passed them to her.

"Thanks. Are you and Darlene . . . uh—"

"That's none of your business, Aunt Connie."

"Of course it's not." She ate another French fry. "Can she cook?"

He grinned. Lunch had done him a world of good. "I hope so."

"You hope so?" She watched him as she munched. "How long is it going to take you to get yourself invited to dinner? You're bound to cook better together than you do on your own. It'd be . . . less lonely."

He gave her a careful look, as if wondering how to interpret that statement. Blandly she stared back. He glanced away, and his face appeared strained with the effort of keeping it straight. "Aunt Connie," he said, as if scolding a child.

She finished the fries and drained her glass of water. If she'd known she was having French fries for lunch, she would've ordered a Coke to go with them. "Just as a matter of curiosity—"

"You've got a lot of that, I notice."

"Why did you and Max rob the convenience store in the first place? Why not just go to Hayworth's house, steal the book and be done with it?"

"That would've pointed the finger directly and immediately at Max. We'd hoped to work behind the scenes to influence Hayworth, show him what we were capable of, and ultimately force him to hand over the book in self-defense."

"Your plan didn't work very well."

His slow grin turned into a deep chuckle. "Has anyone ever told you that you have a flair for understatement?"

"Actually, yes. So I take it that Hayworth keeps the book at home?"

He shrugged, appearing tired of the whole thing. "Yeah, but so did Max. If it were mine, I'd put it in a safe deposit box. Max kept it in a drawer, in a plastic bag. At least Hayworth keeps it in a safe." Then he frowned, exhibiting his lack of respect for lackadaisical security measures. "But it's a cheap combination kind that even I could probably break into."

Connie had been rotating her water glass, making wet circles on the Formica tabletop. She looked up. "Oh, yeah? You're full of surprises. You've had experience in such things?"

"No. But I used to have a drinking buddy who did. He told me how to play with the dial until the thing itself gives you the combination."

The circles from Connie's water glass were growing larger. She studied the emerging pattern. "Could you tell me how to do that?"

After a long silence, she looked up to find Moose watching her steadily with a notable lack of expression.

"Wow," he said. "Do I ever have a big mouth." He worked his way out of the booth and stood. "And a small brain."

She stood also. "Wait a minute. I just—"

"I'm going back to work, Aunt Connie. You go home."

"What are you thinking? You're jumping to conclusions. For crying out loud—"

Moose took hold of her arms. He was more than a foot taller, and she felt like a small child. He said, sounding like a stern parent, "It's not what I'm thinking, it's what you're thinking. Now you stop it right now. I warn you, Aunt Connie, I'll call your brother-in-law if I have to."

Her gaze moved to the side of him. "Speaking of whom," she said in an undertone.

He froze. Then his eyes closed, his hands dropped, and his head hung. "You're kidding." He looked like a timid bear in a business suit.

"I wish I were."

She was amazed at her stupidity. Chris had told her they were going to the new Sears today, and it was right next door.

He and his dad and uncle now stood at the counter, waiting to order their meal, right in front of the only door leading outside.

Well, there was one more exit, two steps away from her. It was clearly marked, in big red letters: *Emergency exit. Alarm will sound.* The situation was dire enough she gave that door an instant's thought, but the second sentence talked her out of it.

Her gaze darted back to the three people at the counter. They hadn't looked this way yet, but that run of luck wouldn't hold much longer. Her mind continued to race, arranging plans, discarding plans, and then she sucked in her breath and held it.

"Go. Now. Right now. Chris has his back turned, drawing a Coke. Derek will see you, but he won't jump up and down and point at you."

Moose didn't move. Connie shoved. "Go!" she commanded in a loud whisper.

He turned and went. With his eyes cast down at the floor, he looked as guilty as any man could look. Connie shook her head. That man was not a good actor.

Fortunately, Chris was having difficulty with the machine's mechanism and Kevin moved to help him. Derek caught sight of Moose. His eyes flickered for an instant, but that was it. Moose got through the door without calling undue attention to himself, and Connie started breathing again.

Then Derek's eyes found her, and she realized she'd relaxed too soon. His face registered surprise, suspicion, and then downright anger. He wasted no time getting to her. "What's going on?"

She stared silently back.

"This better not have anything to do with that comic book."

There was no suitable answer. She couldn't even find an evasive one.

"Connie, dammit, what are you up to? Talk to me."

"Annie Connie!" Chris almost bowled her over. Clearly he

liked his aunt as much as he liked his uncle. Smiling, she knelt and returned his hug.

She looked up. "Hi, Kevin." She straightened but wouldn't meet Derek's eyes.

"You left almost two hours ago," Kevin said. "You should be long gone by now. Did you have car trouble?"

Too bad it wasn't that simple. "No. I ran into . . . an old friend. And we had lunch. He just left."

Kevin glanced at his brother. He probably thought that explained the dark look. He and Chris sat at the next table to await their food order. "No napkins?" He looked annoyed. A passing busboy stole napkins from another table, handed them over, and Kevin nodded his thanks.

"Well," Connie said, retrieving her purse from the booth, "I have a long drive—"

Derek took her hand. "I'll walk you to your car."

"That's not necessary. Your lunch is coming and your food will get cold." She tried to pull her hand free, but he held fast.

"Lunch is not the problem," he muttered. He led the way outside, pulling her with him. Having little choice, she stopped arguing and fell in step. Three teenaged girls at a front table gave him a once-over as he passed, but they didn't seem to recognize him; it was more of a *hmm* look. He wore a straight-hemmed shirt in emerald green over black trousers, and he'd always stood out in a crowd without even trying. One of the girls caught Connie's eye, gave her an apologetic smile, and then lowered her gaze. As she was dragged along in his wake, Connie wanted to shout *You can have him.*

He led her to a corner table with plenty of privacy, then stared at her until she sat down. A wind had sprung up, and only a few people were eating outside. He sat down across from her and then just watched her, saying nothing. She matched his stare and his silence and finally decided at least one of them should act like a grownup.

She managed a smile. "I hope you ordered French fries. They're good."

He didn't smile back. He folded his arms.

Her smile disappeared. "I don't like it when you do this, Derek. I never liked it."

"What am I doing?"

"Steamroller O'Reilly, at it again." She figured her eyes were snapping at him, just like her voice. "And then you act like a misunderstood innocent. That is one thing—two things—I have not missed these past two years."

Trying to hold on to her temper, she stared at a lemon tree in a square planter box, then wondered why she was trying to hold her temper. Her gaze shot back. "You are the most irritating, have-to-be-in-control man I've ever known. How I stayed married to you for four years, I'll never know."

"And you are the most irritating, stubborn woman I know. Those four years weren't exactly the most peaceful of my life. Now are you going to tell me what you're up to or not?"

"*Not.* I am my own boss, Derek. I don't owe you an explanation. I don't owe you a damned thing!"

Their gazes locked. From the look of him, he was working hard at holding on to his own temper. It was a long standoff, which he broke. Exhaling heavily, he looked at the sky. "And I'm not going to learn a damned thing this way, am I."

It wasn't even a question. He already knew the answer. She sat back, nodded. "Well. You may be slow, but you get there."

"Okay." He placed his hands palms down on the table, peered at them for the space of a long inhale and exhale, then looked at her. "Will you *please* give me an explanation of your meeting with Moose, as innocent or lacking in innocence as it may be, even though you don't owe it to me?"

She waited a beat but could think of no reason to continue

holding out on him, so she shrugged. "I ran into Moose. By accident. We had lunch, we talked, and he left."

"What did you talk about? Did Max and the comic book come up?"

"Of course they did."

"And?"

"And nothing. Stop it, Derek. You're doing it again."

"Would you prefer to go back inside and talk to Kevin instead of me?"

When she jerked to her feet, he did also, and she gave him a look that she hoped carried the steel she felt. "You take hold of my hand again, O'Reilly, and I promise you that I will make a loud and ugly scene."

Kevin and Chris appeared, carrying trays of foil-wrapped burgers, Cokes, and baskets of fries. They had father and son written all over them, from their tennis shoes to their tie-dyed tees in purple and blue. They set their burden on the table and took chairs. The battling pair remained standing.

"From the look of things," Kevin said mildly to his son, "we arrived just in time, partner." He unwrapped his hamburger.

Connie waited a long moment, but then finally she sat down, not wanting to pursue a fight in front of her nephew. Bickering was one thing; full-fledged warfare was another. Derek followed suit, but he was smart enough not to look victorious.

Kevin had included a Coke for Connie. She sipped it and shared Christopher's fries, while he explained his log-crossing technique to his dad with excited, disjointed phrases. As she listened, her mood eased. When she finished the Coke, she saw that Derek was through with his lunch, so she invited him to walk her to her car. If he was going to do it anyway, she figured it might as well be her idea. He appeared surprised, but Kevin looked smug, and Connie's ire again rose. She would dearly love to rub that pleased expression off her ex-brother-in-law's face.

"Take your time," Kevin told his brother. "Chris and I will head on into Sears. You know where to find us."

"I get a new fishing pole, Annie Connie."

She found a smile for Chris. "Wow, aren't you lucky." But she couldn't help wondering why, since he didn't like fishing.

She and Derek walked silently until they were out of sight and earshot. Then she said, in the kind of droning tone that a student who'd been called upon to recite boring facts might use, "Yes, the subject of the comic book came up. Hayworth keeps it at home, in a flimsy safe with an even flimsier combination lock. And I ran into Moose by accident, like I said. He works in that bank, right over there." She pointed. "His name is Ray Tidwell. And he's got a crush on someone named Darlene, and she's got an even bigger crush on him. Now is there anything else you want to know?"

"Uh-huh. Why did you mention the safe and how flimsy its lock is?"

She shrugged, making light of it. "It came up in conversation."

"Connie, don't ever play poker."

"Oh, for—"

"Come on, out with it. What are you thinking about Hayworth in regard to his safe and its flimsy lock?"

They'd arrived at her car. She leaned against it, sighed, and gave up on her acting skills. "You know exactly what I'm thinking."

His gaze left hers to wander the parking lot, and he uttered a long string of expletives under his breath. Then he looked back at her. "So help me, Connie, you scare the hell out of me."

She shrugged. What else could she do?

"Was this your idea," he asked, "or did it come from Moose?"

"Mine. He threatened to call Kevin and tell on me."

"Would that do any good?"

"No."

Though it was windy, she was hot in the full sun. But that wasn't the only reason she started searching her purse for car keys. Derek wanted to maneuver her into a corner, and she had no intention of going there.

He watched her. "Are you going home now, or is that wishful thinking on my part?"

"I'm not going home. It's late enough the freeway's already turned into a parking lot." For once she was grateful for traffic, because she didn't have to manufacture a reason to stick around.

"Will you come back to the house then?" he asked. "You can have the cot back."

"No, thanks."

"Then you can have the sofa, if you insist."

"I saw a Holiday Inn about two blocks ago. I'll get a room there." She looked up as if testing the atmosphere, in case it might give her directions. "I think it's south of here."

He smiled. "It's west. I saw it. That thoroughfare travels east and west."

"Oh. Okay. I'll spend the night there." She hesitated, looking at him. "You won't tell Kristy? I don't want to hurt her feelings."

"I don't know. Maybe that's what I need to do. Tell Kristy on you instead of Kevin."

She waited, holding his gaze. He appeared ready to stand there forever, right in front of the car door, so she said, "I promise not to do anything without talking to you first. I won't ask your permission, but I will talk to you. Okay?"

He studied her face, then nodded. "I believe you will. I'll settle for that."

"In some instances, apparently it's to my advantage I can't

play poker," she said dryly.

He grinned. "You learned my secret."

Then he sobered. An unfamiliar, almost sheepish expression crossed his face. "And, well, I guess I should apologize for acting the way I did back there. I was too, uh, well—"

"Overbearing?"

"Yeah. But only because I know you so well. And what I know both worries and scares me."

"Apology accepted. And I also apologize, for being so . . ."

"Bristly and stubborn?"

"Okay." She allowed a small smile. "And that was only because I know you so well, and I refuse to be led around by the hand."

He smiled back. Then he bent and, for the second time that day, lightly brushed his lips across hers. Again, the contact was short and powerful.

She took a deep breath, blinked, and worked on regaining her equilibrium.

"You haven't lost your touch," she whispered into those striking, blue-green eyes the television camera caught so well. Today, because of the color of his shirt, they were more green than blue.

"Neither have you," he whispered back.

Chapter Eighteen

"Julian Hayworth, please," Connie said precisely into the phone, trying to sound businesslike.

"This is he." Cultured voice, good grammar.

"Hello, Mr. Hayworth. I'm with ABC Security, and we have a fabulous deal for first-time clients. Your home isn't already covered with another company, is it, sir?"

"No, ma'am, and I'm not interested in your sales pitch. You can't offer me security better than what I can manage on my own. Goodnight."

The phone clicked in her ear. Connie grinned. "Oh, yeah?" she whispered into the quiet hotel room. "You don't say."

She replaced the receiver into its cradle, feeling proud of herself. That had been too easy. It'd taken an hour to work up the nerve to make that call, and then—

The phone rang. She jumped so high she slid off the chair and onto the floor. She scrambled to her feet, stared at the phone, and rubbed her rump through the red kimono.

But he couldn't have traced the call back to her that fast. Unless he'd used the star-69 feature? But why would he? And he wouldn't get her room anyway. He'd get the hotel's front desk, wouldn't he? Her heart was racing, her hands were shaking, and her blood pressure must be sky-high. She wasn't cut out for undercover work.

She picked up the phone on its fourth ring. "Yes?" Even her voice trembled.

"Hi," Derek said.

She closed her eyes and started breathing again. She sat back down.

"Checking up on me?" Having got past her scare, her voice was lighter, but he was so good at reading her, she was glad the telephone line was between them.

"Uh-huh, just making sure you're where you're supposed to be." He paused. "And wondering if you want company."

Settling back, she propped her feet on top of the bed. "Yes, I do," she answered honestly. "But if you show up, I won't let you in."

She could almost hear his answering smile, and then he said, "I believe you. On both counts."

"You can read me as well over the phone as you can in person?"

"Always could."

Well, in that case, hopefully Hayworth and his security system wouldn't come up. "That you could," she agreed. "Usually."

"Usually?" She heard his aroused interest.

Don't overdo it, she told herself. "Come on, Derek, you've got to leave me some mystique."

"That's what you call it?" His voice was smiling again. They allowed a comfortable silence, and then he asked, "What are your plans for tomorrow?"

She considered the question. The phone call to Hayworth weighed heavily and significantly, but she wasn't committed to anything, neither in mind nor actions.

"I don't know," she admitted. "But once I figure it out, I'll call you, as promised."

"I'll settle for that."

"But I won't be asking for your permission," she added.

"Guess I'll have to settle for that, too."

One of the babies complained in the background, and Connie smiled at the familiar sound. "Someone's unhappy."

"It's Abbie. That tooth just won't let up. Andy and Chris are sound asleep, but she won't cooperate with her mom or dad or me. The poor kid is miserable. Kristy just gave her a swig of liquid aspirin."

Connie saw the house in her mind's eye, the people in it, and she felt a strong flash of loneliness. She reconsidered inviting Derek to her room, but remained silent.

He asked quietly, "Are we still on for the charity benefit next month?"

She answered just as quietly, "Yes."

"I'm looking forward to it."

"So am I." Her voice was a mere whisper, but she knew he heard her.

Another silence, and then he said, voice soft, appealing, and tempting . . . oh, so tempting, "Goodnight, Connie."

"Goodnight," she whispered back, replaced the phone receiver in its cradle and stared at it. Then, with a brisk shake of her head, she picked up the remote and clicked the television on.

As she surfed channels, she caught the end of *Planet of the Apes*, the original. The movie was older than she was, but she loved the classic ending. Horse and riders traversed the surf and then the horse pulled up. The camera panned the crown's spikes before settling on the buried statue. Charlton Heston beat the sand with his fists, damned his countrymen, the screen grew black and the credits rolled. Connie wished she'd found the movie in an earlier stage. She continued surfing, found news and talk shows, and more news and more talk. She watched a weather channel, comparing the announcer to Derek, but became annoyed with herself. So she clicked off the set, pushed the slipper off each foot with the other one and shrugged out of the robe. Once she'd crawled into the big bed, she wished she'd requested two doubles. The huge king seemed even emptier and lonelier than the room was.

Next morning, with the clear light of dawn, also came the cold light of reason. Connie lay in bed, staring at the ceiling, glad no one besides herself knew she'd made a call to Hayworth last night. So what difference did it make if he was covered by a security system or not?

She rolled out of bed, showered and dressed, and as she ate breakfast in the hotel's coffee shop, she couldn't help wishing she were eating breakfast with Derek. She'd lived without him for two years. It had now only been—she paused and counted—eight days, and she couldn't think about anything but him.

Surprise, surprise.

Feeling dreamy, she drained her coffee cup. When she set it down, her pragmatic side intruded and warned her to be careful. Sure, they were still attracted to each other, but a second try could so easily become double disaster. She paid with a credit card, and while waiting for the transaction to be concluded, she worked on finding a balance between bewitchment and caution, which was a delicate and evasive state that didn't seem to exist.

Once she'd returned to her room, she headed for the phone. He'd be relieved to know she was going home and turning her back on whatever unlawful inclinations might've occurred to her. But then another thought struck, and she held the phone receiver in midair before hanging it up unused.

What harm could there be in telling Hayworth that others knew how sadly lacking his scruples were? He had no sense of fair play, but he was a businessman and should have a sense of self-preservation. She could threaten to write a letter to the local newspaper editor, explaining in detail how he'd acquired a particular comic book. And it wasn't an idle threat. She was already writing the letter in her mind.

She picked up the phone, then impatiently replaced it. She'd neglected to write the number down last night. Grabbing the phone book, she rifled its pages.

A woman answered. Was he married?

"Julian Hayworth, please," Connie said, forcing patience and pleasantness into her voice.

"He's away on business. He'll be returning Friday."

That took the wind out of her sails. "Is this Mrs. Hayworth?"

"No. I'm the maid. I come in on Tuesdays. Do you want to leave a message?"

"Is there a Mrs. Hayworth I could speak to?"

"He's not married. Do you want to leave a message?"

"No, thanks. I'll call back."

Connie hung up. Her mind was racing even before the phone receiver settled in its cradle.

To her credit, she tried to concentrate on packing, the new school year starting in the fall, the budding relationship with her ex-husband, but nothing worked.

Giving up, she again consulted the telephone directory, this time for the yellow pages. There was at least one question mark she could answer. But her fingers were as distracted as her mind was. The first number she jabbed into the phone was the wrong one; a doctor's exchange answered. She apologized, rechecked the number, and took more care punching it in the second time.

"Collectible Comics. Bob speaking." The voice was brusque. Either the place was busy, or Bob had no telephone manners.

"Hi. I'm hoping you can help me."

"I'll try to, lady, if you'll tell me what you want."

His rudeness grated on her. Connie considered hanging up, but she wanted the information. "I need to know how much a comic book is worth."

"You buying one or selling one?"

"Neither. I want to know how much it's worth."

A long pause, and then he said, "Okay." He sounded resigned, but at least he was humoring her. "What kind of book?"

"Kind?"

"Yeah. Spiderman? Batman? Wonder Woman?"

"Oh. SteelMan."

"Okay. Now what about SteelMan? Is a new character introduced? When was it first published? What kind of condition is it in? Can you tell me anything at all here to make my job a little easier?"

Connie drew in a deep, controlled breath and answered the only question she knew the answer to. "I understand it was published before the war."

"Before the war?" The tone of his voice changed.

"That's what he said."

"Which war?"

"Which war?" She frowned. Yes, there'd been multiple wars throughout the last century. And this one. "He said 1940. It'd have to be the Second World War."

"Uh-huh. Yeah, lady. Sure." The phone clicked in her ear.

Connie remained motionless for several seconds, then slammed the phone receiver into its cradle. "Were you born with that personality, Bob? Or did you have to work to acquire it?"

She took a deep breath. There were other places to try, but she was turned off and running short on time. The bedside clock told her she had a half-hour in which to check out of the hotel or request a stay over. She used the phone again to hold the room for another night, then grabbed her purse and left to walk the two blocks to Raymond Tidwell's bank.

He didn't appear pleased when he saw her. Darlene, dressed in a power-red pantsuit that looked sharp on her, was on her way back to her desk. She didn't appear happy at seeing Connie either but covered it up and turned her attention to her computer screen.

Connie walked to Moose's desk. Today's suit was brown tweed with a hint of gold thread running through it, the shirt was butter yellow and the tie had tiny gold checks in it.

"Nice suit," she said. "But you need more color in the tie."

He stared at her.

"Buy you a cup of coffee," she offered.

His stare didn't change.

She sat down. "Or we can talk here."

He stood and led the way out of the bank's back entrance, where there was a small patio, complete with a shady tree with benches built around its base. They sat there.

"Okay. What is it." His voice didn't end on a questioning note. He sounded fed up and had the look of one long suffering from trials and tribulations.

"Hear me out, Moose. Don't get up and walk away. Please hear me out."

He said nothing. He stared at the water fountain next to the bank's back door.

Now that she was here and had his attention, unwilling attention or not, she wasn't sure how to proceed. "I called Hayworth," she said, uncomfortably aware of how tentative her voice sounded.

No reaction.

"Last night. He doesn't have a security system." She'd expected him to react to this news as if she'd tossed him a live grenade, but he continued to stare at the water fountain, not even asking how she'd arrived at that conclusion.

"Then I called again this morning. He's away on business and isn't expected home until Friday."

Silence. Connie felt like she was talking to the air. She probably was. "The house is empty," she spelled out for him. "Until Friday."

Still nothing. She also stared at the water fountain. "Will you tell me how to listen to that dialing combination thing?"

That was the live grenade. He got to his feet and pulled her up with him. "Home," he said, his voice sounding carefully controlled. "Go home. Do not come back here again. I do not want to see you again. Go . . . home!"

He shook her as if she were a child, but used no more power than what was necessary to hold her in place. "Do you understand me, Aunt Connie?"

She didn't respond. His fingers tightened, and he shook her again. "Do you understand me?"

Still she said nothing. He let his air out forcefully, holding her gaze. Then he released her and stepped back. His expression was hard enough to scare a more timid soul. He stared at her for a long moment, then turned his back and stalked into the bank.

Connie was more unnerved than she wanted to admit. She sat back down and tried to look at the situation with a fresh eye. She couldn't do anything without Moose's help—if not his help, at least his input. But he was both adamant and formidable. She was out of her league.

Then she got to her feet, straightened her spine, raised her chin and reentered the bank.

No way Jose was she giving up.

A middle-aged couple sat at Moose's desk, so she took a seat in the waiting area. Darlene darted several looks between her coworker and Connie. Connie was also dressed in red: culottes, a simple cotton top, and sandals. But Darlene was taller, wore heels and a more striking outfit, and outshone Connie. Connie wished there was some way she could let the woman know that.

The couple at Moose's desk concluded their business and

left. Their chairs remained empty, but Connie stayed where she was. Moose looked up once and caught her eye. She stared steadily back.

Passive resistance. Passive aggression. Whatever one wanted to call it, the message should be clear that she wasn't backing off.

An hour passed. Darlene continued to direct glances her way, looking both concerned and puzzled, but Moose ignored Connie after that one look. He used the telephone, interviewed clients, got back on the phone, worked on the computer. Connie's rump got tired and she crossed her legs the other way.

When Derek walked through the front door, Connie wasn't surprised, but she did wonder how Moose had managed to procure the unlisted home phone number of the chief of police so quickly. Despite her preoccupation, Connie took a moment to check out her ex-husband. Neatly dressed in navy slacks and a casual open-necked shirt, he'd probably caught the eye of every other woman in the bank as well.

She and Moose stood at the same time, and she walked toward the back door. The corner of her eye caught the look of relief that crossed Darlene's face when Derek and Moose fell in step together. She suspected Darlene hadn't noticed anything besides Derek's gender and his apparent connection to Connie.

Outside, she sat on the bench, but the two men remained standing.

"I didn't break my promise," she told her ex-husband. "I haven't done anything. Once I decided what it was I was going to do, I would've called you before I did it."

Moose waited politely for her to finish. Then he told Derek, "She called Hayworth last night and found out he doesn't have a security system—don't ask me how she got that information—then she called again this morning and discovered he's away on business. And now she wants to know how to break into a safe.

Frankly, Uncle Dare . . ." He paused to breathe. "She scares the hell out of me."

Derek stared at the water fountain. "I know the feeling."

Connie crossed her legs and clasped her hands on the uppermost knee. "This is from a man who committed armed robbery three times? But you draw the line at burgling an empty house?"

"Could your brother put her in protective custody or something?"

"Or something," Derek mumbled.

"Would you guys sit down? You're giving me a crick in my neck."

"Just for a little while," Moose suggested. "Until she comes to her senses. Could be she's not thinking clearly. She seems . . . well, unhinged." Moose hesitated, doubt crossing his face. "Unless she's always like this?"

Connie could only see Derek's profile, but she caught his lips curving.

"I'm right here," she reminded them a little testily. "Talk to me. Not over me."

"You know her better than anyone else does," Moose continued, ignoring her. "What should we do?"

Her gaze traveled from one man to the other. This was turning into an extremely unproductive morning. "You could always invest in a piece of rope. Or maybe a set of handcuffs."

For the first time, Derek gave her a direct look. "That's the best suggestion I've heard so far."

"Yeah? You give it your best shot, O'Reilly." She jumped to her feet. She was through with diplomacy and coalition-building. Her gaze nailed both of them, and she hoped the spark of fire that fanned her temper showed in her eyes. "You two comedians can go help each other. I don't need you, or your permission. *I* will decide what *I* want to do, and then *I* will do it."

Her attention centered on Derek. "The deal's off. I might go home, and I might not. And I don't advise you to hold your breath waiting for that courtesy call."

She stomped away, relieved and surprised when neither man followed. She was angry because she hadn't been taken seriously, frustrated because she didn't know what she was going to do, and terrified because she knew exactly what it was she wanted to do.

Chapter Nineteen

Connie spent the rest of the morning in the stores. In light of the mood she was in, shopping could be considered therapy, but she had specific items in mind. She bought jeans, a cotton t-shirt, and a pair of sneakers, all in black.

When she returned to her hotel, she found Derek in the lobby.

"It's about time," he said. "I've been getting strange looks from the desk clerk, but he hasn't asked for my autograph. So I figured it was a tossup who'd show up first—you or hotel security."

She said nothing, barely pausing, but was aware that he followed her into the hall. If hotel security saw fit to stop him, she wouldn't come to his defense. But when she unlocked her door, he was still behind her. She left the door open and dropped her bags on the bed.

The maid had closed the drapes, so Connie opened them. Her room overlooked the pool, and she watched two school-aged kids splashing in the water, probably brother and sister. She turned.

Derek had taken the only armchair. Looking comfortable with one ankle resting across the other knee, he gave her a disarming smile. "Something tells me you're mad at me."

While she'd been shopping, it'd occurred to her that he and Moose had merely proved themselves wiser than she. Because it didn't seem fair to punish Derek for just being sensible, she relaxed her stance. She didn't exactly return his smile, but he must've caught her shift in mood.

"That's better," he said. "You're prettier that way."

She pulled the bench out from beneath the vanity and sat on it. "Don't push your luck."

He indicated the bags on the bed. "You've been busy."

She looked at the various bags but didn't comment.

"Have you had lunch yet?"

As if cued, her stomach growled.

He grinned. "Guess not. You still like spinach salad?"

"Umm."

"Good. I checked out the dining room's menu—there wasn't a whole lot to do while I was waiting for you—and that's the luncheon special. Shall we?"

"We shall. But give me a minute." She disappeared into the bathroom. When she reappeared, Derek was at the window, looking at the pool. She grabbed her purse. Using the vanity's mirror, she flicked a comb through her hair and freshened her lip gloss.

No longer hearing the kids, she glanced out the window at two bikini-clad women basking in the sun. She looked at Derek and grinned. He shrugged, giving her a half-smile.

She ordered the salad without looking at the menu, and Derek ordered a club sandwich. Though he liked to cook extravagantly, he ordered plain food when eating out. As simple as it was, the waitress took extra time with their order. When she called Derek by name, Connie understood why. Fortunately she was neither gushy nor star-struck, however, although Connie detected envy in the look the waitress gave her before leaving. So it wasn't just his celebrity status that had caught the woman's attention.

She buttered a piece of French bread. "Once you make prime time, it's going to be even harder for you to wander around in public."

"Once I make prime time? Do you know something I don't?"

"You'll make it. You must know that."

Turning somber, his gaze lowered, then again rose to meet hers. "Yes, I've got a shot at it, a good shot." She saw more vulnerability in him than she'd ever seen before. "It's scary, Connie. Sometimes, in soul-searching moments, I wonder which I fear the most—making it big, or not making it. There's adjustment either way."

She saw the man she'd fallen in love with and married, not the man she'd divorced, and her heart did a flip-flop. Fortunately, their food arrived, transporting her back to the present. Today's salad had yesterday's beat by a mile, and she dug in. Derek seemed satisfied with his sandwich but ate only half of it. He pushed the plate away and sipped from his water glass.

"Can we talk about you for a minute?" he asked.

She looked up, surprised. "What about me?"

"Were you planning on going out to Hayworth's house tonight or tomorrow night?"

With her gaze riveted on him, she slowly put her fork down.

He went on in the same mild tone. "When you were in the bathroom, I checked your purchases. They told a story, one I was hoping to avoid. Brand new black outfit. Black's a good color on you, but not that much of it. I repeat, when are you going out there?"

"You had no right to do that."

"I know I didn't. When are you going out there?"

Her response was a long time in coming, and it was honest. "I don't know."

"In that case, how about tomorrow night, or even Thursday? And I'm going with you. The extra day will give us a chance to work on Moose. Once he realizes you're not going to back down, he may join us as well."

"This is a drastic change from your attitude this morning."

Her posture was so stiff, she was becoming uncomfortable.

He nodded easily. "Uh-huh. But I know you mean it, and I know I can't stop you. And neither can I let you go by yourself."

When she didn't respond, his gaze dropped to the sandwich remnants on his plate. "You scare me, and you worry me. The whole situation does. Until you brought my attention to those women at the pool, I didn't even know they were there. That's how worried I was about your new black outfit. And they were, uh . . ."

"Well-endowed?" She managed a smile. "Not bad to look at?"

He grinned. "All of the above. And I wouldn't describe them as being overdressed."

Sobering, she looked down at her plate, and he signaled for the check. The waitress must've had her eye on him because it came quickly. Connie watched him put bills down to cover it, then his gaze rose to meet hers.

"What are you thinking?" he asked sharply, and she realized her doubt and suspicion showed.

Watching him carefully, she told him the truth. "I don't know if I can trust you. I'm afraid you're going to try to stop me."

"I can't, Connie. Other than talking you out of it, there's not a damned thing I can do. And so far I haven't had a lick of success talking you out of it."

She continued to study him, and he candidly returned her gaze. Though she couldn't read him as well as he could read her, neither was he a closed book. When she found no signs of unstated motives, she sat back with a decisive nod. "Okay. Tomorrow it is. Thursday might be too late. He could come home early, and we'd really be in trouble. And I suggest you talk to Moose. If I show up again, he's liable to call bank security."

"He probably would." When he chuckled, it seemed a weight

lifted from him. "I doubt he's looking forward to seeing me either," he said wryly. "But I'll let you know tonight how it went. Join me for dinner?"

"Uh-uh. If we have dinner together, we'll more than likely spend the night together, and I'm not ready for that yet."

"Well, at least you said 'yet,' " he muttered. Then his eyes turned quizzical. He squinted at her. "Did I hear you right? You're ready for burglary, but not—"

"Never mind." She pushed her chair back and stood. "I'll see you tomorrow."

She returned to her room, alone and frowning, as she pondered her use of the word *yet.*

Burglarizing plans were made by phone, with Derek initiating the calls. Connie didn't know how to prevaricate, and if she got Kristy or Kevin on the phone, she feared she'd spill the whole conspiracy.

After much discussion, their agenda remained amazingly simple. They would play it by ear. Master burglars, they weren't.

Moose agreed to help. Derek didn't say, and she didn't ask, how he'd managed to talk the big man into it. They'd be eating dinner at Moose's house Wednesday night. Derek was cooking lasagna, and then they'd proceed from there. It might've been the lasagna that had tipped the scales in their favor.

Her phone rang again as she was walking out the door of her room. She'd got more phone calls in two days at the hotel than she got in a whole week at home. She pushed the door shut and answered the phone.

"Good," said Derek's voice. "I was hoping I'd catch you. Moose's casserole is cracked, and I don't want to use it. Stop in that shopping center and buy one. In fact, buy two. You know the size I want."

She grinned. Her light mood was surprising, considering her

unusual plans for the evening. "Are you serious? No self-respecting burglar would go shopping for a casserole on her way to cracking open a safe."

"Uh-huh. If you want to eat, you bring the dish."

"He won't settle for extra crispy chicken?"

"Even if he would, I won't. Remember the directions? It's east of you, which means you turn right when you leave the hotel parking lot. The shopping center is also east, and it's on your way."

She nodded. "Yes, Derek. Thank you, Derek. I know where the shopping center is."

"Then, of course, turn right again when you leave the shopping center. Which means you have to use the same entrance slash exit that you used to turn in there."

"You're pushing it, Derek."

The housewares section wasn't crowded. Her purchase took two minutes. At the store's exit, she paused, then turned back around and found the hardware department, where she searched for flashlights and latex gloves. Directing several furtive glances around her, hoping no one was watching and wondering why she was interested in such things, she tested and then selected three slender flashlights that would fit nicely inside one's pocket, yet had good illumination.

On her second trip out of the store, a man who was entering held the door open for her. She looked up and stopped dead.

"Well, hi, Connie," Kevin said. "We hadn't expected you back so soon."

"Uhh."

"All in black? You look like you're trying out for a motorcycle club."

"Uhh."

"Is Kristy expecting you?"

She shook her head. Didn't the man ever shop anywhere

else? She realized how guilty and stupid she must seem, but for the life of her, she couldn't think of a thing to say.

They were blocking foot traffic, so he guided her away from the doors. When she risked another glance at him, he didn't seem puzzled or suspicious at her stupor. Instead, he was watching her with a knowing, smug smile.

"Derek said he had plans for tonight and would be late, but he wasn't very communicative beyond that. Now I see why. If he makes it home at all tonight, I'll be surprised." He bent and bestowed a kiss upon her forehead. "I couldn't be happier for the two of you. And Kristy feels the same way. Your marriage wasn't a mistake. The divorce was."

"Uhh."

He entered the store, leaving her standing there in her daze. Finally, she shook it off and made her way to the car. Apparently she was going to have overnight company tonight, whether she was ready or not.

She slipped behind the wheel, closed the door, and stared at the windshield. Slowly, she felt her expression smoothing out as stupefaction left her, and she guessed a dreamy smile was taking its place.

Then she shook that off as well and inserted the key in the ignition. First things first.

Moose's house was white with green trim, had a manicured lawn, a brick planter full of red zinnias, and a forest-green front door. When he opened the door for her, Connie cast a quick look behind her before she slipped inside.

"There's nothing illegal about entering my house," he said dryly.

"Very funny." She dug inside her bag and came up with gloves and a flashlight she handed to him.

"Oh." He blinked. "Yeah. Good idea. I guess."

Derek appeared at the other end of the room. "It's about time."

When she gave him his burglary supplies, he frowned at them, then her. "Just how much experience have you had with this kind of thing?"

"A couple of standup comedians," she muttered as she passed him. She found the kitchen by following her nose. Derek dried the two casseroles after she'd washed them. She watched him layer the first lasagna, and then heard John Denver come to life in the next room. She cut off a piece of Monterey Jack and went to join Moose.

As the big man rocked gently in an upholstered silvery green rocker, he motioned her toward the twin avocado armchairs that faced him. She sat down and they stared at each other. When he stretched long legs out and crossed his ankles, the chair stopped rocking. He clasped his hands over his ample stomach. "You've got balls, Aunt Connie."

She choked on the cheese, got it down, then gave him what she supposed was a wry smile. "I notice you didn't mention brains."

"No, I didn't. But if this caper works, Max will owe you, and so will I."

"And if it doesn't work?"

"I don't want to mention that, either."

Derek entered the room, munching on his own piece of cheese. "Thirty minutes."

"You made enough for leftovers, right?"

"Uh-huh, and there's an extra one in your freezer."

Moose's eyes lit up, and Connie smiled. She hoped Darlene was a good cook.

"I don't drink," Moose said, "but occasionally I get wine as a gift. I've got a good burgundy, if either of you would like some."

It took a while to uncork the wine, even with both men working on it—or perhaps because both men were working on it. Connie watched with amusement, offered to help, but neither man would let her near it. Uncorking wine was a manly thing.

When his guests had their drinks in hand, Moose saluted them with a bottle of Perrier. Derek sipped, then nodded. He liked burgundy, but Connie thought it was too heavy. She wished she'd asked for Perrier.

"Nice sound system," Derek commented, settling back in the other avocado armchair. "So you're a country fan."

Moose nodded. "I wasn't always. Max introduced me to it. Not everybody likes it, though. I can put something else on, if you wish."

Derek waved off the offer. "I like almost anything. And as far as Connie's concerned, if it isn't classical, it's noise. She's too hard to please, so don't even try."

When Connie gave him a pointed stare, his answering grin told her he'd said it solely to get a rise out of her. And he'd succeeded. Annoyed with herself instead of him, she broke eye contact.

Then Derek said offhandedly, "We need to decide on tonight's transportation." He rotated his glass and watched the gently swirling wine. "Taking three cars will turn Hayworth's street into a veritable parking lot, just begging for attention. We'll take my car."

Connie looked back with a frown. "You don't think that snazzy red convertible will draw attention? I have a dark-green sedan that no one will look at twice, so I should drive."

"I know the way," Moose said. "It only makes sense that I drive. I don't have a lot of legroom, but we'll manage if Uncle Dare rides in the front. Aunt Connie will fit anywhere."

"I've got plenty of leg room in the front and back," she countered. "And that classic Mustang is as much of an eye-catcher as Derek's convertible. I repeat, no one is going to look twice at a nondescript, green sedan. I'll drive."

"If you want room, I've got as much as you do," Derek said, his voice growing testy. "I repeat, we'll take my car."

"Think, Derek, think," Connie said. It was amazing how fast the art of argument came back to one. "For crying out loud, you might as well wave a flag from the aerial with our names and addresses on it."

His problem wasn't with which car they'd be using, she knew, but in who would be driving it. She could settle this quite simply by handing over her car keys, but she wasn't going to do that. Sure, he was a better driver than she—simply because he was the more experienced, simply because he always did the driving—but he was also too damned domineering.

"Uh, Uncle Dare, she may be right. If someone mentions having seen a red convertible around there when it all went down, don't you think your brother might become just a tad suspicious?"

Connie watched Derek struggling with the new odds and the logic. Then, in surrender, he merely stopped arguing and glared at his wine instead of her. He still didn't know how to lose graciously, but at least he recognized he'd lost.

Dinner was good; it might've been the best lasagna Derek had ever made. But it was over too soon, and it then seemed to take forever for night to fall. Moose was so antsy he gave up on playing host. He excused himself to do laundry, and then he cleaned out the refrigerator. Derek played solitaire at the dining room table. Connie paced.

As she neared him yet again, Derek put his cards down and gave her a hard stare. "So help me, if you pass by me one more time, I will forcibly put you in a chair. And I will not be gentle about it."

She stopped. "How can you be so . . . so . . . so calm?"

"I am not calm. I've got more butterflies in me now than I

ever get waiting for my camera cue." He picked up his cards. "If I had someone like you at the studio, I'd have gone bananas a long time ago."

She walked back to the front door. Her pacing path had been severely shortened.

But when she turned back around and found his gaze still on her, she sensed that he understood at least an inkling of what she was feeling. "Why don't you go help Moose fill ice cube trays or something?" he suggested.

"Because he's through with the ice cube trays," Moose said, appearing in the kitchen doorway. He walked to the table, rested his arms across the back of a chair and regarded Derek with envy. "It appears you've got something in common with Max, Uncle Dare. He was always the cool one. It was never yours truly."

Surprise crossed Derek's face, and then he said, "At first I wouldn't have considered that a compliment. But now I do."

Moose's gaze then flitted hesitantly between his guests. "At the risk of starting another argument, I'd still like to take my own wheels. You can follow me, I'll make the change into Aunt Connie's car just before Hayworth's house, and we can separate right after our getaway. We shouldn't be tied together any longer than we have to be. Uncle Dare can then come back for his car any time."

Derek executed an indifferent shrug. Apparently he'd accepted the fact he'd lost this round to his ex-wife. From her spot near the front door, Connie nodded.

"Settled." Moose straightened. "We should go. It'll take an hour to get there, and the sun has finally set."

Connie froze. She stared at her companions as if they were her executioners.

Both men watched her.

"We can call it off," Derek said hopefully.

Moose's expression was unreadable, but she doubted he'd complain if she backed down.

She closed her eyes and took in a deep breath. "No, we can't." She turned, opened the door, and led the way into their night of crime.

Chapter Twenty

The Hayworth house was in an affluent neighborhood and, in the view of tonight's visitors, conveniently set back from the road and out of sight of its neighbors. Connie parked a half-mile away among a copse of trees that surrounded a park, where the car wouldn't be readily seen. Nor should it arouse suspicion.

The sedan wasn't equipped with a keyless entry feature, which greatly annoyed Derek. He could unlock his convertible's doors in an instant from several feet away, as he told her more than once.

"Just how fast is a fast getaway going to be if one becomes necessary?" he asked, as if accusing her of something. The man was spoiling for a fight.

"If you're going to talk about getaways, you should keep your voice down," Connie said calmly, refusing to give him what he wanted because keeping her cool would irk him even more. "And the doors will open fast enough if we don't lock them."

"Once I get out of the car, I'll keep my voice down. And the doors will open just as fast for a car thief, won't they?"

Moose paused, half in and half out of the car. "Uh, Aunt Connie, in case you've got one of those hide-a-keys—"

"No hide-a-key."

"And no cell phone," Derek muttered. "She travels light."

They each took care to close their doors gently as they exited into the balmy night, and they cast furtive looks around the deserted park. Since there were no sidewalks, they walked the edge of the road and tried to look like three neighbors out for an innocent evening stroll.

After a few minutes, Derek glanced curiously at Moose. "You know the house and the neighborhood." His voice was midway between a whisper and normal. "But you didn't say how you knew it."

"Business. I handle his stock portfolio." His voice was also quiet, but closer to normal.

At his companions' surprised looks, Moose explained. "Pure coincidence. He has no idea I even know Max. He got my name from a satisfied client and invited me out here. More convenient for him if I made the trip, and with his kind of money, he gets what he wants."

He hesitated, then added, "I don't like working with him. He left his previous firm because he'd lost money, but it was because he didn't follow their advice. And he's not following mine either. He's a bully and needs someone to bully him back, but that's not the way I like to do business. He should be looking for another firm soon. If he doesn't, I'll suggest it."

Connie found herself walking faster and faster in order to keep up with her companions. She slowed them down, and, two minutes later, had to slow them down again. The second time, she wasn't as nice about it.

But once they approached the house, no one needed a reminder to slow down. They continued past the gated driveway into a row of dogwood trees before Moose came to a stop. A tall hedge on the other side of the road hid them from that house. A shorter hedge was behind the trees, between them and Hayworth's place. Distantly, a dog barked.

"So this is it," Derek murmured.

"Uh-huh," Moose answered.

"You're sure there are no dogs."

"No dogs."

"And no security system." Derek looked at Connie.

"That's what the man said. And he wouldn't let me sell him one, either."

Derek shook his head in disbelief. "A house like this, in an area like this, it doesn't make sense. He must be stupid."

"He is," Moose said. "But mostly just cheap. That's why he hasn't put money into security."

"And unscrupulous," Connie added. "I don't like him."

Derek looked at her. She thought his expression was on the condescending side.

"Well, he is," she said in response to his implied criticism. "And I don't."

"Remind me not to get on your bad side," Moose said. "Now shut up and help me find the break in this hedge. It should be . . ." He paused and pointed. "Right there." He'd no sooner pointed it out than he was through it. For a man his size, he moved fast.

Connie's gaze swept the area. Nothing moved. Derek motioned impatiently for her to follow Moose, then he followed her. They found themselves at the side of a driveway that appeared to meander through the grounds. The fastest route to the house from the road certainly wasn't the driveway.

"Okay," Moose said, slipping his gloves on. "You two stay here, just in case. I'll make a quick run around, then come back for you."

"Wait," Derek said. "Maybe—"

"Must we have an executive discussion over every move we make, just as we did over which car we'd use?" The big man sounded irritated.

Derek's motion for him to go ahead also held irritation. Moose disappeared. Connie watched the spot where he'd been, wrapping her arms around herself. Derek turned in a slow circle, looking everywhere. Then his gaze settled on Connie.

"Cold?" he asked.

She shook her head.

"Scared?"

She nodded.

She was surprised when he didn't step forward and put his arm around her. He must be waiting for her to make the first move, which meant that he was confident she would be making a move. That thought reminded her that although he didn't know it, he was going to be spending the night with her.

The thought alone provoked sensations.

"I think I'm more dumbfounded than scared," he said, his words bringing her back to the mild night air. He drew his gloves out of his back pocket and pulled them on, motioning for her to do the same. "Here we are, decked out in black and dutifully wearing our skintight gloves, waiting patiently for our cohort, who is casing the house we intend to burglarize. I don't believe we're doing this."

"This isn't what your brother thought we'd be doing tonight either."

His head tilted in a quizzical attitude. "Pardon me?"

"Nothing." She rubbed her gloved hands together, familiarizing herself to the feeling. Then Moose loomed before them so suddenly that she leaped at Derek and knocked him back a step.

"It's clear," the big man said. "Let's go."

For an instant, Connie was frozen in place. Derek watched her, possibly wondering, or most likely hoping, that she'd back out after all. Then she forced her feet to move, and he fell in step behind her.

"It's safe," Moose said as he led the way. "Or at least it's empty. I don't know how safe it is. I rang the doorbell and knocked. And checked the downstairs windows and doors, hoping we'd get lucky, but everything is locked up tight. There's an open window on the second floor, though, that's near a tree and a wall trellis. We can boost Connie up into the tree and she can check it out."

"No," Derek said. "I'll do it. If I can't, we'll jimmy open a door or something."

"Back off, Derek. I didn't come along for the ride. I'll try the window."

"No, you won't."

When he was serious about something, he brought every inch and pound he had into bearing. If they were alone, Connie knew she'd never get near that window. But they weren't alone. She dropped the argument, waiting until they were next to the tree and beneath the partially opened window.

The lowest branch was still quite high, but it was thick enough to stand upon and go on from there. She hoped she wouldn't need the help of both men, since one of them wasn't favorably minded, but that limb was a long way up there.

"The trellis isn't sturdy enough," Moose said. "Probably won't even hold her. The tree is our best shot."

"Then we'll break in another way," Derek said. He'd been studying the tree and the trellis and was looking more and more dubious. "I don't want Connie up there on her own."

She said nothing, which might've tipped him off, but it didn't. She waited until he started toward the other end of the house, showing them his back, and she motioned to Moose. Quickly, one foot was in his hands and she was boosted up, but she couldn't reach the branch. She held on to his head for balance, got one foot onto his shoulder, and reached again for the limb.

"Oh, for . . . *Shit!* Dammit, Connie, don't you have even a lick of sense?"

"Help us, Uncle Dare, before she goes sprawling."

His long line of cussing didn't stop, but she felt Derek's steadying hand on her leg and rump. Then she had both feet on

Moose's shoulders and got her arms around the branch. One foot found a knothole in the tree's broad trunk, her other foot found another one, and then she was on her own.

She walked vertically up the trunk until she could wrap one leg around the branch and wrestle her way onto it. Then, finally, she was safely sitting astride it. She blew her breath out, and Derek finally stopped cussing. The two men were intense in their silence.

She took a long moment to get her breathing back to normal, and another moment to relocate her courage, then she got both feet under her, gripped an overhanging limb for balance, and walked the branch to the house.

The window wasn't held in place by a locking guard. Neither man had mentioned that possibility, but it had occurred to Connie. Getting back down, if she couldn't get the window open, would've been more interesting than getting up here in the first place.

The window rasped as she pushed it, resisted for an instant, then slid all the way open. She stuck her head inside. The crisp scent of a lemony cleaner hung in the air. It was a bathroom, and the space she was in was a tub and shower combination. If she fell, the porcelain wouldn't be kind to her.

"Most accidents happen in the bathroom," she muttered, as she gripped the towel bar and pulled herself halfway in. It didn't feel sturdy, but it held, and she reached for the shower rod to get herself the rest of the way in

Once she got her feet and legs under her where they belonged, she took time for an easier breath, then pulled out the flashlight. After the narrow beam showed her the doorway, she slipped the light back into her pocket. She got one foot on the tile floor—and then froze with one foot still inside the tub. Her gaze flew back up to the window. A spotlight wavered, passed, then returned and held.

Her heart beat wildly as she bounded for the doorway, and she came close to losing her balance before the leg inside the tub caught up to the rest of her. There was cover down there in the yard for Derek and Moose. Wasn't there?

Then she pulled up short when the spotlight moved on. She stood in the connecting doorway between bathroom and bedroom. The light traveled slowly over the bedroom window, then went on its way.

Was the spotlight only a routine check?

There wasn't a part of her that wasn't trembling. If that light had been thirty seconds sooner, it would've caught half of her hanging outside the window.

She returned to the bathroom, knees shaky, and stepped up onto the edge of the bathtub to look outside the window to check on Moose and Derek. She heard their sibilant whispers but couldn't catch the words. She wanted to yell at them to shut up.

Then she realized that Derek was in the tree. She stepped down into the depth of the tub and threw her hands up. "Of all the stupid, numbskull, idiotic . . ."

"Connie?"

"For crying out loud, you couldn't wait two minutes for me to get downstairs and open the door?"

"That spotlight scared me. I didn't like you up here on your own."

"Watch out. You don't want to tumble in here headfirst." She guided his hand to the shower curtain rod. His baseball cap was knocked off his head and she picked it up. She wanted to get out of the tub to give him room, but her way was blocked by a vanity on this end and by Derek at the other end.

"Can't say this is the smartest move you ever made," she grumbled, working to get him upright. "Be tough to think of a stupider one."

After some tricky maneuvering, he was finally on his feet. She replaced his cap where it belonged. One arm had gone around her as he'd searched for balance, and now his other one joined it. She twisted. "That way," she said, and motioned for him to precede her out of the tub.

"Umm." He didn't move. "Been a long time since we shared a shower." He rested his chin on top of her head. "Although we've never before been fully clothed in one."

"Uh-huh." Twisting impatiently, she pushed at him. "Move, Derek. That way." She pointed again, but his hands moved up and down her back, then slipped beneath the hem of her t-shirt.

She stamped her foot. "What do you think you're doing!"

"Not the best time or place, I know, but do you realize how long it's been since I held you like this?" He nuzzled the top of her head. "You feel good. You've been so careful these past weeks, not even letting me within touching distance. Now that I've got you, I don't think I want to let you go."

She gritted her teeth. "I don't believe this."

"Ouch!"

"Be grateful it was only your shin I kicked. Now let me out of here."

At the end of some more tricky maneuvering, she'd managed to push her way past him and was out of the tub. "Where's Moose waiting?"

"The back door. In the kitchen," he said. "Ow!"

She turned. "Now what?"

"Vanity has a sharp edge on it," he mumbled. "Just like you."

"Then use your flashlight. That's what it's for."

The kitchen's outside door had three locks on it. She thought she'd never get it open.

"It's about time," Moose said, crowding through. He closed the door and pressed his back against it. His gaze was directed upward and his breathing was rapid. "I'm not cut out for this," he said to the ceiling.

Connie had no time for sympathy. The kitchen had the outside door they stood in front of, then another one that probably led to a garage, and her flashlight picked out two hall entrances. The richer a person was, the more complicated his kitchen had to be? "You said the safe is in his study. Where's that?"

His head turned as he tried to get his bearings. "I'm not very familiar with this part of the house. But I think . . ." He paused, then pointed. "Through there."

Derek was the first one into the hall, stumbled over something, caught his balance and came up swearing.

"Derek, use your light. Please?"

Moose moved around them to take the lead. He had enough sense to snap his flashlight on. It illuminated a hardwood floor that Connie already knew was there because of the noise it was making.

The third door Moose opened, he stepped through. "This is it." The light played over a royal blue carpet as he walked across the room and then behind an oversized desk. Connie and Derek followed. At least they weren't making as much noise in here.

"And there it is," Moose said, as if he'd discovered Aladdin's lamp. A small safe sat on the lowest shelf of a standing bookshelf, and he knelt in front of it, knees popping. "Looks the same as I remember. Let's hope he didn't get smart and take that book out of there and put it in safekeeping where it belongs."

Now that she was faced with the night's objective, Connie's mind seemed to freeze. Her heart was thundering, and her nerves were in overdrive. It was difficult drawing an even breath.

Moose didn't move for a long moment. Then, swallowing audibly, he put a hand on the combination wheel. "Now both of you are going to have to be quiet. Back off and don't breathe."

They became so still and so quiet, they could've been part of the furniture. The only sound was a clock ticking somewhere, getting louder and louder, and an occasional grunt from Moose. Straining her ears, Connie discerned the muted whir of the combination wheel as Moose rotated it, but no telltale clicks.

Apparently, he heard no clicks either. He kept spinning, and Connie started fidgeting. Even Derek shifted his weight from one foot to the other.

"Uh, Moose?" she murmured.

"Shh," the big man said, and didn't look up from what seemed to be his intense scrutiny of the floor. It appeared that his ear was connected to the safe.

Derek's hand enclosed hers, as if he thought that might help to keep her quiet. She forced herself to count to twenty-five, but then could contain herself no longer. "Maybe he changed safes."

"It's the same safe," Moose said. "Please . . . shut . . . up."

This time, she got all the way to fifteen. "What's the problem? You said your buddy told you how to do that."

"I also told you he was my drinking buddy. Our powers of communication may have been somewhat impaired." His dark shape moved as he looked in her direction. "Aunt Connie, could you maybe find something else to do somewhere else? Something quiet?"

Connie closed her eyes and tightened her fists. Derek's fingers squeezed hers back. She pushed her tongue against her teeth and didn't try to stop herself. This time, she was determined to make it all the way to a hundred. The clock ticked louder. Her body was so tense that her legs hurt. She shifted her weight to one foot, then the other.

Fifty. She had to make it at least to fifty.

"All right!"

Connie's eyes flew open at the same instant the safe's door swung back. Moose's penlight came to life, illuminating a plastic-wrapped, thin magazine with a brightly colored cover resting on top of various envelopes and stacks of papers. Connie recognized the silver and black colors of SteelMan, but a small baggie of crushed leaves hid the super hero's face.

She and Derek stepped closer, barely daring to breathe.

"I actually broke into a safe," Moose said. He rocked back on his heels. "Damn, I'm good."

Then his head twisted around. "But now that we've got it, what are we going to do with it? I'm afraid to touch it."

"Me, too," Connie breathed.

"It's so valuable, it must require special handling."

"Yeah," Connie agreed. Fine group of crooks they were. If they'd robbed a bank, they would've forgotten a bag to put the money in.

Derek unfastened the top buttons of his shirt, pulled out a manila envelope and gave it to Moose. "Put it in that."

Connie glanced sideways. "You are one cool crook. I am impressed."

She caught the quick flash of his teeth in his brief smile.

Moose pushed aside the plastic baggie, then paused. "I wonder if he's got a prescription for that."

"Purely recreational would be my guess," Connie said.

Sensing Derek's frown, she glanced at him. "What?"

He continued to stare at her, and she grinned, realizing how casual she'd sounded. It was her turn to read his mind. "Well, it's been two years. You'll never know, will you."

He smiled back, then gave her a decisive nod of his head. "I'd know."

Reverently, Moose slipped the magazine into the envelope, then handed it to Derek, who folded the flap and secured the clasp. He slipped the envelope inside his shirt, redid the buttons, and smoothed the ends of the garment inside his belt. Then he motioned to Moose, who still knelt in front of the safe.

"Close that thing and let's get out of here."

At Derek's words, Moose shifted position, but only to reach into his back pocket. He withdrew his wallet, pulled out a bill, and bent again to place it in the safe approximately where the comic book had rested. Using both hands, he elaborately smoothed out the bill.

"What . . ." Connie murmured in puzzlement along with Derek, and then she broke into a grin. "Perfect!" she said, and exuberantly smacked one palm against the other. "Is that, uh . . ." She squinted up at Derek. "Who's on a ten dollar bill?"

"Hamilton," he said absently, frowning down at Moose. Then he said, "Nice gesture, Moose, though don't you think it's a little juvenile?"

"Nope," Moose said, unabashed. "He paid ten bucks. Money returned. Transaction cancelled." His voice held a fastidious note that was incongruent with his position in front of a burgled safe. "Max will love it," he added.

"Yes," Connie said precisely. "Very fitting."

Derek exhaled heavily. "If you two children are finished, can Moose please close the safe so we can get out of here?"

This time Moose complied. And the same instant the safe clicked shut, three heads snapped toward the window, and every gaze fastened on the set of rolling, bright lights.

"No," Connie whispered. "No."

Moose had been in the process of standing. He knelt again, as if to hide from the lights. "It's closer now. They're on the grounds."

"Those are headlights," Derek whispered. "Not the spotlight. And I don't think the police would announce themselves with headlights." He glanced at Connie. "Someone's home early."

"But the maid said Friday." The window was now dark, but her attention hadn't moved from it. "For crying out loud, is it too much to expect her to get her dates straight?"

Derek grabbed Connie's hand and headed for the study door, pulling her with him. "No," Moose said. "He'll come in through the garage, and he'll see you before you can get to the front door. Hell, I don't even know if there are any other outside doors."

Derek hesitated, then pushed the door closed. He turned back to Moose and threw his arms wide, releasing Connie's hand. "Then what?" he snapped.

Moose still knelt, with only his arms and shoulders visible above the desk. He ducked, disappearing behind it, and then said, "You got a better idea?"

A distant door was opened, closed, and footsteps sounded in the hall. Derek moved toward the desk, but Connie stayed put, searching the darkness for a better place to hide than behind the desk. Then she remembered her flashlight and clicked it on. Another door was right in front of her. She headed for it.

"No!" Derek commanded in a guttural whisper. He grabbed for her but came up with empty air. "Connie, get over here!" He started after her, but Moose grabbed his belt and yanked him down.

The door to the study opened.

Chapter Twenty-One

Connie had made it through the doorway but didn't have time to securely close the door. She held off, not even breathing, fearing the click of the latch would alert Hayworth.

When he switched the light on in the study, she got a sketchy look at him through the crack between the door and its frame. He looked tired, not suspicious, and she allowed a slow, cautious breath. He also appeared ordinary, which surprised her, then she felt silly in her surprise. He was a middle-aged, respectable looking man who wore his years well. Because she'd heard nothing good about him, she'd expected to see . . . what? An ugly person?

Then as he crossed to his desk—where else would he go?—Connie's spirits took a nosedive, and in the next instant her anger shot up. The maid couldn't get her dates straight, Hayworth couldn't be trusted to stay where he belonged, and her partners in crime should've had enough sense not to try to hide behind the stupid desk.

The pair of men would have the upper hand, but Hayworth would recognize Moose, and possibly Derek as well. A happy ending to this scenario wasn't possible.

Hayworth stopped at the outside, non-business end of the desk, thumbed through the mail he'd brought in with him, then put the stack atop the desk's blotter. He rolled his shoulders, massaged his forehead with the fingers of both hands, and then turned. He crossed the room, switched the light off, went out and pulled the door closed behind him.

Connie suddenly felt as limp as an old piece of lettuce. She leaned her forehead against the doorframe and tried to realign her brain with her muscles, but Derek pushed the door open and sent her reeling.

"Just what the devil did you think you were doing?" His voice was the barest of whispers and held barely controlled anger.

"Me?" she shot back, once she caught her balance. She stalked back to get in his face. "You could search forever and not find a worse place to hide than behind his desk. That's where his computer is, and his safe, and his . . . his letter opener. Of all the—"

"Shut up!" Moose loomed between them, his voice a growling whisper, and put a huge hand on the back of each of their necks as though he wanted to knock their heads together. They shut up.

They listened to receding footsteps, then another door opened somewhere.

Moose's hands fell to his sides. He said, his voice low, very controlled, "Any minute now, he's going back to the kitchen for a snack, and no way is he going to twice miss the unlocked door that should be locked. Now just what do you two escapees from the debating club think we should do about that?"

"Unscrew the light bulbs," Connie said without hesitation.

"Huh?" blurted two voices. She sensed the decreasing strain in each man as bewilderment replaced his tension. And she also picked up on their shared suspicion she'd lost her mind.

Patience was difficult to find, but she came up with some. "We can't get out of here without dealing with him, so let's do it on our terms." Her tone was similar to the one she used when explaining a lesson to first-graders. "He's bound to recognize Moose, if not both of you. But if he can't turn the light on, he can't see you. Right?"

They stared at her for a fraction of a second longer—just like primary school students when faced with a new concept—then they parted to start locating and unscrewing light bulbs. Connie squinted into the dark, trying to remember the layout of the room she'd seen in the brief time the lights had been on. How many lamps? Where were they? She hoped there wasn't an overhead fixture.

Distantly, a toilet flushed. If they'd known that was where he was, they would've already been out of here. Now if the man would just go upstairs and go to bed, their problems would be over. But that wasn't going to happen. His next stop would undoubtedly be the kitchen, as Moose had predicted.

Another thought occurred to her. "Your voices might give you away, too, either one of you. So if we have to talk, let me do it."

From opposite ends of the room, their heads turned toward her. Derek whispered, "Maybe. But maybe it wouldn't be a good idea to let him know one of us is a woman, either."

Moose's head turned toward Derek. "Might be hard to keep that a secret. She's a bit on the small side." He paused, then added, "And she's also got a fuller head of hair than you and me."

Derek removed his baseball cap, came to her and set it on her head. She tucked her hair under it. "Remember the John Wayne impression I used to do?" he asked. "If we have to talk, I'll do that. Agreed?" His head swiveled questioningly from her to Moose.

The big man's shoulders lifted in an elaborate shrug.

"Agreed," Connie said. Then the most obvious escape route struck her, and she squeezed her eyes closed in disgust. *Oh, for crying out loud.* She was stunned with her own stupidity. And the fact that she shared this particular obtuseness with her companions only made them dense times three.

She raced to the window and yanked the blinds up. With eyes and hands she searched for the locking mechanism, becoming almost frantic when she found nothing, then her body sagged. She released the blinds and let them fall back into place. "Picture window. Doesn't open."

"Could've told you that if you'd asked," Moose said.

Though their eyes had adjusted to the dark, she doubted he could see the scathing look she sent his way. He may have sensed it, however, because he turned away from it. She remained at the window. With thumb and forefinger, she separated the slats and stared yearningly outside at freedom.

Behind her, Derek whispered, "How about in there?" His clothing rustled as he moved toward Connie's hiding place of choice. "Let's check out those windows. Might have better luck."

"I don't think so," Connie said tonelessly, and turned to look at him. "Our luck just ran out." With a tilt of her head, she indicated the peephole she'd made in the window blinds.

He stared back, then came to stand beside her. He stooped and peered through the slats with her at the man approaching the house on foot. The figure stopped. His head tilted at an upward angle as he most likely looked at the opened window on the second floor. Then his head lowered and turned toward the other end of the house, his attention supposedly on the lighted section where Hayworth was.

Moose came to stand next to them, and Derek moved aside so the big man could see. Moose almost had to bend in two to look out, but he didn't attempt to make his own peephole. "Oh, golly, it just keeps getting better and better. Is that who I think it is?"

She gently removed her hand, and the two slats moved back into place. She and Derek exchanged a long look. The phone rang, shattering the stillness, and all three of them jumped. Full of dread and guilt and a looming sense of defeat, just as she suspected her fellow conspirators were, Connie stared at her companions.

The shrill sound was cut off in the middle of the third ring. After Hayworth's almost inaudible murmur, his voice rose in surprise. Then footsteps sounded in the hallway, passing them, heading toward the front of the house. The click of a deadbolt reached them, and a door opened.

"Chief O'Reilly?"

Connie's head dropped. She rested her forehead on Derek's chest.

More murmuring, then the noise of the door's chain being released.

But why the chief and why alone? She quickly dropped that thought, however, because she knew the answer and didn't want to dwell on it.

"Next door," Moose whispered. "Whatever room that is, it's got to be better than this one. It doesn't have the safe in it."

They crowded through the door, and Moose risked a quick flashlight search of the room, keeping the light away from the hall door. It appeared to be a library and was smaller than the study. Moose clicked his light off and pushed the connecting door almost closed, leaving it open by a sliver as Connie had.

She wanted to go to the hall door to listen to the conversation between Hayworth and Kevin but was afraid to continue moving for fear she'd trip over something. Then once they became still, the muted voices at the front door became clearer.

". . . don't understand." The voice sounded peevish. "All I requested is a routine check, just like every time I go out of town."

"As I was trying to explain," Kevin said, "it was noted during the last drive-by—routine drive-by—that an upstairs window was open. We didn't know you were home, so that aroused our suspicion. But I see now there's no cause for alarm. Sorry I bothered you."

Connie crossed her fingers. Maybe their luck hadn't run out.

"I haven't been upstairs, so it must've been the maid. She's done that before." Irritation replaced the complaining note. "I'm going to have to fire her and start interviewing again. Do you realize how difficult it is to get decent help?"

Kevin's silence was eloquent regarding this age-old malady of the wealthy. The situation held little room for levity, but Connie felt a weak smile forming.

"Since you haven't been upstairs," Kevin said, "it might be wise to check the whole house. As long as I'm already here."

Connie closed her eyes, not wanting to look at either companion.

Hayworth said, with an almost audible shrug, "Sure. Why not? Like you said, as long as you're here. And of course there's no charge." The front door closed, and their footsteps sounded in the hall. "We can start in the study, where my safe is." The steps stopped, and the study door opened.

Connie's head turned toward the library's other exit, wondering if they could make it down the hall and outside before Kevin was aware of them. But they'd heard every door Hayworth had opened, so the opening of their door would be just as audible, and that hardwood floor announced everything that made contact with it. Unless they could remove their shoes and run out of here in stocking feet? Except Kevin and Hayworth were already on the other side of the partially open door between the library and study. Just how much noise would she and Derek and Moose make knocking things over with their elbows while getting their shoes off?

"That's funny," Hayworth said. "I was just in here, and the light worked fine then." After a short pause, the room brightened. "Bulb was loose." There was a longer pause. "It was really loose. I wonder how—"

"I don't see a safe. Where did you say it was?"

"Over there, behind the—"

Squeezed in front of the two men, Connie had a clear view of Hayworth, but she couldn't see Kevin. Hayworth had grown still, one hand still pointing to the desk, then the hand dropped to his side. He said, "Nothing seems amiss in here. No need to check the safe after all."

Connie drew her eyebrows together. The light bulb had been so loose it might've fallen out of its socket, yet he'd found nothing amiss? Then she remembered the safe's contents, and a glimmer of light appeared at the end of the tunnel. Hayworth had something else on his mind besides a loose light bulb. Deliverance had been presented to them, in the form of a plastic bag containing a substance its owner didn't want to display to the chief of police.

When Kevin didn't respond readily, Connie wished she could see him so she could gauge his manner. Then he said evenly, "As we'd agreed, as long as I'm here, Mr. Hayworth . . ."

"Thank you, but it's not necessary. I've been home long enough that if anything was wrong, I'd have noticed it. And we don't need to check upstairs either." He stopped, and when he spoke again, his voice sounded stilted. "I apologize that my maid's carelessness caused you to waste your valuable time tonight." He massaged his forehead. He didn't have to feign weariness; the man was tired, but the movement was too elaborate. He looked back up. "Now, if you don't mind, I'm exhausted. I need a sandwich and a good night's sleep."

Stepping aside, Hayworth motioned toward the door. The gesture held confidence, yet there was an underlying sense of nervousness in it.

After a long silence, with no discernible movement in the study, Kevin asked, "What's in the safe, Mr. Hayworth?"

Despite the severity of the circumstances, Connie was

impressed. But she hoped this was a clash her brother-in-law would be losing.

Hayworth's confidence seemed to take a harder hit. His effort to regain control was evident. Then he straightened, his body appeared to grow rigid, and he drew upon what was probably ingrained arrogance. "I assure you that there is nothing within my safe that would be of interest to you. Now, if you don't mind . . ."

Again he motioned toward the door, this time superciliously.

At the end of a long silence, in which Hayworth lost another degree of hauteur, Kevin said mildly, "Yes, sir. And you're welcome."

Clearly taking his time, he passed in front of Hayworth and entered the hall, and their unwitting host took an instant to steal an easier, deeper breath before switching off the light. He then followed the chief of police, and the study door was pulled closed behind them.

Absolute silence, stillness, and disbelief reigned at the connecting door to the library.

Footsteps receded down the hallway. The front door opened and closed.

"Ai . . . yi . . . yi," Connie breathed.

"Never thought I'd be grateful for that man's failings," Moose whispered. He backed up. She hadn't realized how cramped she was until he moved.

"We're not out of here yet," Derek reminded them. His voice was as quiet as his manner was grim. "Hayworth must be on his way to the kitchen by now, and Kevin needs time to get all the way gone. He was on foot. Who knows how far away he left his car."

Connie came to life. Once Hayworth discovered the unlocked door in the kitchen, he'd undoubtedly grab the phone to call for help, so she had to beat him to the draw. She pulled the door open and headed for the desk. On her way she motioned toward the window. "Check on Kevin's progress." Her voice was clipped, tight with tension. "If he's still hanging around out there, we're out of luck and options."

Derek inched the blinds apart. Connie picked up the phone receiver and gratefully noted the dial tone, which signified that Hayworth wasn't already on it. Then she racked her memory for the number of the time-recording operator before realizing the service had been discontinued. *Damn!* Just when you needed something, it was gone. Who could she call to jam up the phone line without leaving a clue to her identity? And whoever she called had to have automated twenty-four-hour service.

Then abruptly she aimed her penlight at the phone pad and chose numbers by their letters. She'd recently changed phone companies because it'd grown impossible to speak to a live person when she'd called with a question or problem, and the automated choices were endless. She could kill thirty minutes if she had to, and the number was the company's name. Super easy!

"If you had a gun, where would you keep it?" she asked of the room in general.

"In my bedroom or study," Derek answered without hesitation.

"Thank you for your call." Connie jumped at the recorded voice. It seemed unduly loud.

"If he heads upstairs, we're out of here," she said. "If he comes in here . . ." Instead of finishing the sentence, she threw her head back and stared at the ceiling.

"Okay, Kevin's out of sight," Derek said. "And hopefully out of hearing distance."

"If you're calling regarding your telephone service, please press one. If you're calling regarding your cable service, please press . . ."

Connie punched a number without looking at it.

"What's taking him so long?" Moose asked. He was actually wringing his hands. "Is he not even going to notice the—"

"Moose, get that light bulb, the one at the door," Connie said, her hand over the mouthpiece. "And put the thing in your pocket this time. I don't want—"

She jerked the receiver away as the punched numbers resounded in her ear. Each man must've caught her action because their heads snapped toward her. With lips pressed together and hands clenched, she waited for Hayworth to figure out what was happening. She'd counted three beeps and wished she could also dial nine-one-one and hand this emergency over to a professional. Then she scrunched up her face. The lawful professional had just left. She wanted the other kind?

After Hayworth's multiple beeping, the recorded voice started all over again.

"What the hell?" Hayworth said. He sounded more angry than scared.

"Your call is very important to us," the voice droned on. *"Please listen carefully to your choices because the menu has changed."*

Then he must've caught on, because he asked, overriding the recording, "Who is this?" His voice held no alarm that she could hear. The situation couldn't look good from his end, yet he sounded like he was in control of it. If he headed out the front door after Kevin, the kitchen would be open for their escape, or at least for an attempt at it.

The operator was on choice number four, which told Connie that Hayworth wasn't in a hurry. She knew he was still there because she heard him breathing. Then he asked, voice again overriding the droning, "Where are you?"

At the same moment Connie was invited to press number five if she had a question concerning billing, the phone clicked in her ear. She held the receiver against her chest, muffling the sound.

"We're on," she whispered into the darkness.

Chapter Twenty-Two

Cell phone, Connie's mind suddenly screamed at her, and her muscles tensed so tightly she felt like a block of stone. Unless Hayworth was too cheap to have one? She understood minutes cost a fortune on those things. Or if he had one, he might've left it in his car like Derek did.

Then quietly, slowly, the door to the study opened.

If their host had a cell phone at hand, he'd already used it. When the light switch again didn't produce light, the form at the door reached for the lamp, but this time he would find no bulb in the socket. Straightening, he remained still, facing into the room. His guests were at an advantage because they were accustomed to the dark.

"Who are you?" he asked, exhibiting no sign of being intimidated.

She wondered how they were going to handle Mr. Julian Hayworth.

"What do you want?" Then he added dryly, "As if I didn't know."

He didn't seem alarmed by his intruders, so he probably thought they were the Maxwell brothers. Since he'd won all the encounters so far, he'd be thinking he'd win this one, too.

"Come all the way in, pilgrim. Don't be shy."

Despite the intensity of the moment, or perhaps because of it, Connie wanted to giggle. Derek's impersonation skills had never been good, and he hadn't improved with lack of practice.

John Wayne would've winced.

Derek stood near the window. He flicked his flashlight on, directing it at Hayworth, and it picked out the gun in their host's hand. The weapon was directed at Connie, who stood in front of the desk and still held the noisy phone receiver.

The gun changed direction, pointing toward Derek's light. Connie replaced the phone receiver in its cradle and clicked her light on. At the same instant, Moose clicked his on. He stood at the opposite side of the room from Derek, and Hayworth's gun hand wavered. He had a dilemma.

Connie felt a sense of satisfaction. The man had been too cool; he'd needed to be brought down a peg. Then the gun returned to cover her, in the center of the room. She nodded, her satisfaction taking a back seat. That was his wisest choice, but it still didn't feel good. Derek's light rose and caught Hayworth full in the face.

His head jerked away from the blinding glare. "All right!" he snapped, allowing force to his anger, but the gun lowered to his side. "Okay."

The tension in the room, at least among the three uninvited guests, eased a bit.

"You got hold of your shooting iron in record time there, pilgrim," John Wayne said conversationally. Derek also knew how to be cool. "Where do you keep it?"

Connie was reminded of a joke about men and their preoccupation with guns, all kinds of guns, and it was harder containing her giggle this time.

"What do you want?" Hayworth repeated, ignoring the question. He still wasn't cowed, not by a long shot. And he still had the weapon.

"Just to ride off into the sunset," John said reasonably. "Our movie, our script. Now you mosey on over here to your desk and sit yourself down. We'll tuck you in all secure-like and take our leave. And on your way, you can deposit your iron on that table there with the useless lamp on it."

"Which one of you is Max? The one with the poor impersonation skills? Who is that supposed to be, anyway? Elvis?"

Connie clamped her lips together, hard. She feared she wasn't going to get out of here tonight without cackling out loud.

"I see the big guy over there," Hayworth added. "But where's the dummy? The one in the middle is too short. But he was still stupid enough to hold on to the phone, telling me exactly where he was."

In retaliation, Connie raised her light, shining it in his eyes. He evidently didn't like that, and he'd had time to regain confidence. His gun hand rose.

"Watch it!" Derek made a quick move forward, and Connie put her arm out to stop him.

The gun lowered again. "You're not Max," Hayworth said thoughtfully.

Connie dug her fingernails into Derek's arm, then pulled at his collar to get his head down so she could whisper into his ear. "You're letting him play you. Get back to where you belong and stop being stupid."

He took his time but stepped back. Connie set her flashlight on the desk, pointed toward Hayworth, and without hesitation walked toward him. As she approached their unwilling host, she gratefully noted that his gun hand remained down, probably because he was trying to figure out what the "dummy" was up to. The moves from her self-defense class sprang immediately to mind and hand. Not allowing him—or herself—time to think, she grabbed the wrist of his gun hand with her left and reached for the weapon with her right.

She heard Derek's sharp intake of breath and was aware of scrambled movement behind her. But he must've thought better of interfering because he remained where he was.

Expecting Hayworth's resistance, she jabbed her right elbow into his ribs before he could react. He grunted, hunching to protect his stomach. With the edge of her right hand, she gave him a sharp blow on the wrist of his gun hand—and then she had the gun. It was almost comically easy. The instructor had said that in physical confrontation, surprise was one's greatest ally, and she was right.

Quickly, Connie stepped back. If Hayworth figured out he was dealing with a woman and got the gun back, he'd be writing his own script.

But then Moose was there, and Hayworth was propelled toward his desk and chair and was in it before Connie had time to blink. He grunted, possibly more in surprise than pain, as his backside collided with the chair.

Then his voice, cold and hateful, grated into the darkness. "You are not getting that book back, damn you! I will not, under any circumstances, open that safe. Do you understand me?"

His speech was ignored.

There was nothing to tie him up with, so Derek manhandled the man's shirt off him. "Silk," John Wayne said. "Fancy duds."

The man's miserliness evidently didn't extend to his wardrobe. Derek wrapped the garment around man and chair, then tied the arms of the shirt together in three knots at the back, leaving their host's hands free.

"So, how does it feel to be going home empty-handed, pilgrim? *Again.*" Hayworth's voice oozed spite. Tied up in his desk chair in his t-shirt hadn't dampened his antagonism.

Moose had exhibited no respect for the man, calling him an ineffectual bully, but Connie thought Hayworth was a touch more formidable than Moose had given him credit for. She didn't want to take the man on.

Then she faltered, not breathing for an instant. She had taken him on; she'd disarmed him. A sudden tremor threatened to overtake her.

As if cued to her weakening state, Moose took the gun from her, fiddled with it, then stuck it inside his belt. She was glad to be rid of it. That was the second time she'd held a gun in her hands, and she fervently hoped there wouldn't be a third time.

Derek stepped back, surveyed his handiwork with the aid of his flashlight, and then directed the light toward the telephone. It was out of Hayworth's reach, but the desk's chair had wheels. Derek tested the length of the cord, then carried the phone to the table at the door that held the useless lamp. The time it would take the man to maneuver the chair over the rug all the way to the door would allow them at least to get off the grounds. Moose removed two of the desk's drawers and lined them up on either side of the chair, which should give them a couple more minutes.

The men joined Connie at the hall door. Hayworth's voice, choked with enmity, followed them. "So you won this round. But you can tell Max for me he'll never get that damned book back. There is nothing—absolutely *nothing* he can do—that will make me give up that magazine."

Turning, they gave him a long look.

"We left you your stash," John Wayne said.

They sprinted down the middle of the road, the men pulling Connie along between them, and fortunately encountered no traffic. Derek and Moose had started out with each of them holding on to one of her hands, but their collective holds had quickly moved to her elbows. There were moments during which both her feet left the ground at the same time.

Then they were at the car and inside it. Three doors closed in unison, noisily enough that she winced. Drawing attention to themselves at this stage was too stupid to think about.

She was so shaky, she couldn't get the keys out of her pocket. She had to get out of the car, dig into her pocket, and then get back in again. Moose was silent, but Derek maintained a long string of expletives, more than enough for both men. Finally, the key was in the ignition, the car was in gear, and she got it moving. And Derek got quiet.

She drove carefully, concentrating on not making a wrong move. They'd come so close to disaster, and now were so close to pulling it off that she was terrified of doing something stupid and blowing the whole thing. She studied every intersection, and every stoplight was a potential trap. She even slowed for green because it was eventually going to turn to yellow.

"Connie," Derek said through his teeth, "let . . . me . . . drive."

If she could find a place to pull over, she'd gladly give up the wheel. Then at long last there was the parking lot and the Mustang. Connie pulled into it and found an empty slot next to the vintage Ford.

The lot belonged to a theater. Plenty of cars, but thankfully no people wandering around. They sat, still and quiet, for a long time.

Moose broke the silence. "One more piece of business, then we're through with this. Hopefully for forever." He blew his breath out in a rush. "Hayworth's gun. Max and I dismantled ours and threw the pieces away in different garbage cans across two counties. And I'm thinking that's an excellent destiny for this one."

"Go for it," Derek said.

Connie twisted in the seat to give the big man a look that she figured carried her relief. "Thanks."

He opened the rear door and exited the vehicle. Derek and Connie followed suit.

Derek gave her a hard look over the top of the car. "On the

subject of guns, I couldn't believe what I was seeing when you went after Hayworth and his gun. I was tempted to kill you myself." He waited a beat, expression not easing. "I still am."

She shrugged; what else could she do? "Seemed like the right thing to do at the time." Then she added, remembering his aborted move, "I was surprised you let me get away with it."

"He didn't," Moose said. "Not exactly. I had to hold on to him." He gave Derek a cautious look. "Sorry about that, Uncle Dare, but she was playing him just right. If you'd rushed him, he might've shot in self-defense."

Derek might not have liked it, but he let it go. "He sure came up with that gun fast," he said musingly. "I'm still wondering where he kept it."

At his words, the silly joke about men and their guns again cropped up, and Connie grinned, then giggled, then lost it. The evening had been too full of tension, and she'd held herself in check for too long. She leaned against the car and let the laughter roll while tears of mirth streamed down her face.

"What the . . ."

The men had spoken in unison. Then Derek asked, almost worriedly, "Connie?"

The joke itself wasn't that funny. But a story is in the telling, and the image of the substitute teacher who'd told this one—a middle-aged matron with a strong resemblance to Mrs. Doubtfire—stuck in Connie's mind. The woman had been so primly deadpan that she was hilarious.

Regaining her breath, Connie wiped her eyes and carefully avoided looking at either man. "It's okay. I'm okay. Delayed reaction, hysteria. Whatever you want to call it. I—" Another giggle threatened, and she caught it just in time. "I'm okay. Honest."

She concentrated on the theater marquee. Derek watched her for a short moment, but she wouldn't return his gaze. No way was she even going to try to explain. So he then looked at Moose, lifted his shoulders and shook his head. Apparently giving up on her, Derek pulled the manila envelope from beneath his shirt and handed it to Moose.

The big man accepted it, and then just held it.

Mirth left Connie as she stared at the envelope, as if mesmerized. Every moment of this evening had been worth it. They hadn't committed a crime tonight. They'd corrected one.

"We did it," Moose murmured. "We really did."

Opening the door of the Mustang, he reverently placed the envelope on the passenger's seat, then closed the car door and turned back to his cohorts.

He appeared uncomfortable, and Connie recognized the awkward social stage of *where do we go from here?* They stood next to a parking island surrounded by a planter box filled with pink and purple petunias. Stepping up onto the platform, giving herself some extra inches, she threw her arms around Moose, startling him.

"I love you, you big moose. And I don't even know if I'll ever see you again." She planted a big kiss on his cheek. "You tell Max and Petey that I love them, too. Okay?"

His return hug was as tight as hers. With an arm still around her, he extended his other hand to Derek. Then, with a smile, he clasped that arm around his shoulders as well. "Wouldn't mind taking on a couple pen pals." His voice was slightly choked. "I doubt this divorce of yours is going to take, and I'd like to know what happens with you two."

He released them and stepped back. "And I wouldn't mind getting some pictures every now and then of Abbie and Andy and Chris. Those kids stole my heart."

"You got it," Connie said. "And I'd like to be kept up to date on you and Darlene. It's way past time you and she started cooking. Get a move on, big guy."

He grinned, nodded, then got into his car. Connie couldn't help but wonder how he fit into it.

She and Derek watched the Mustang until it was out of sight. Connie had the comfortable, satisfied feeling of a job well done. Still standing on the planter, she looked at her ex-husband.

"Hey, pilgrim," she said. When he turned to her, her eyes were almost on a level with his. "If you were to put your arms around me again, I promise not to kick you in the shin this time."

She still wore his baseball cap. He removed it and put it on his own head, turning it backwards. The effect made him appear as young as he'd been when she'd first met him. But the gleam in his eyes was a mature one.

Returning his hands to her hair, he fluffed it. His fingertips on her scalp made her toes tingle. The massage was slow and sensual, and clearly affected him as strongly as it moved her. Their gazes held. His hands traveled down her back, creating a prickly sensation even through the shirt, and came to rest at her waist. Her arms encircled his neck.

"Beautiful," he whispered. He pulled her forward until she rested against him. Without his support she would've tumbled face first off the platform. "You're beautiful," he repeated.

"You're not too bad-looking, yourself, O'Reilly."

They engaged in an unhurried kiss that kept building, at times heating up, then pleasantly leveling off, and then going back to hot. It felt so right to be so close that they were almost one again, wrapped so securely in each other's arms. She wasn't sure which of them broke contact when they finally pulled apart, but it was just in time. She had no more strength than a bowl of Jell-O.

"It's been a long time," she whispered.

"Too long." He swallowed audibly, then squinted, as if having trouble with his vision.

"We'd best move this to another location," she said breathily.

"Agreed." He kissed her nose, then drew back to meet her eyes. "The sooner, the better. Do you have any suggestions as to where? Right about now, I'd settle for the back seat of a nondescript, green sedan."

Umm, she thought, but didn't say it. "I've got a better idea." She tilted her head. "I know where there's a really nice room. It's not far, and it's got a view of the swimming pool."

"Hmm. Tell me more about this room."

"Got a TV with a really neat station that plays old movies. Classics."

"Anything else?"

"A *Do Not Disturb* sign one could hang on the outside doorknob if one had a mind to put it there."

He nodded soberly. "Good point. One could watch classic movies for as long as one desired without being interrupted. My interest is piqued. Does this room have any other furniture in it?"

"If I remember right, there's a king-size bed. Big and luxurious and roomy."

He paused, as if thinking that one over, and looking doubtful. "Isn't that more room than we'll need?"

She nodded with emphasis. "Yep."

Chapter Twenty-Three

At the parking lot's exit, Connie took longer than necessary to check traffic. She wasn't sure which way to turn to get to the hotel, didn't want to admit it, and was hoping to spy a landmark that might give her a hint.

"It's left, Connie," Derek said mildly.

After executing the turn, she sneaked a sideways glance at him. "Thanks."

The corners of his mouth turned up, but he didn't give her a direct look.

She hadn't made two whole blocks when she became aware of flashing red and blue lights behind her. "Uhh," she said, attention riveted on the rearview mirror. She looked at Derek. "What did I do wrong? I hope to hell I did something wrong."

"I don't know." He'd twisted toward the center of the car and was looking over his shoulder. "I didn't catch a mistake. Maybe he just wants to get around you in order to go after someone else. But you have to pull over, regardless."

Yes, that she did. No options. She pulled off the road and braked, and the lights behind her followed suit. "Oh, crap," she said to the mirror. She set the gear in park and turned off the ignition. "Kevin would recognize my car, but he wouldn't be in a patrol car . . . would he? Does he even know my license number?"

His gaze remained on the back window. "Doesn't have to know it. Just has to ask for it. And whoever this is, he just opened his door."

While her pulse threatened to run away with itself, Connie watched her side mirror. A tall figure exited the patrol car and approached on the driver's side. She pressed the window release button, nothing happened, and she pressed it again. Meanwhile the man arrived and knocked gently on the window.

"Auxiliary," Derek said, and she gave him a look that must've carried her incomprehension. He pointed at the ignition. "Key has to be in auxiliary to roll the window down."

"Oh. Yeah." She fumbled with the key, then the window release, and finally got it rolled down. *Good going,* she thought, *now get hold of yourself before you blurt out how guilty you are.*

It wasn't Kevin who stooped to peer inside, but she wasn't sure if that circumstance should be positive or negative. "Yes, officer?" she asked in a voice so shaky that if he didn't already know what she'd been up to, he might start wondering.

"Good evening, ma'am," he said without pulling out his handcuffs. That much was positive. Then she realized that her driver's license was buried in the pocket of her jeans, so she was going to have to ask him to back up so she could get out of the car to get it. *Oh, gee whiz.*

But he didn't ask for her license. He looked across her at Derek. "Hello, Mr. O'Reilly. It's nice to meet you. I watch the news every morning and would've recognized you anywhere."

Connie blinked. He'd pulled them over to get an autograph?

Derek nodded politely. "Nice to meet you, too. Is there a problem, officer?"

Connie began to feel like a third wheel as she sat in the middle of the two people and their nice conversation. Now that it didn't appear she was going to be arrested, her wits were making a comeback.

"No, sir," the policeman said. "No problem. Your brother simply requested that if anyone saw your car—"

"It's my car," Connie pointed out.

His attention returned to her. He was young, freckled, and redheaded. His eyes were brown and confused. "Excuse me, ma'am?"

"It's my car. As you can see, I was driving it. Thank you for telling my passenger there wasn't a problem with my driving."

"Oh. Yes, ma'am. I'd been given the description and license of this car as well as Mr. O'Reilly's convertible. And, as I said, you didn't do anything wrong." He waited a beat, brow furrowing, then his face cleared and his gaze again skimmed past her. "Your brother requested that you and your wife—"

"Ex."

"Er, excuse me?"

"I'm his ex-wife. I mean that *he* is *my* ex-husband."

There was a long pause. "Yes, ma'am. Of course, ma'am." She could tell that he was adding up reasons for their divorce. Then again he looked beyond her, again dismissed her. "Would you, and, er . . ."

"Robertson." Her voice was tired and pained. "My name is Connie Robertson."

After taking a deep breath, he started all over again. "Mr. O'Reilly, your brother requested that you and Ms. Robertson stop by his house tonight. As soon as possible. Can you do that, sir?"

"Yes," Derek said evenly. "We will."

The officer nodded. "I'll radio it in. Thank you, sir."

"You're welcome," Connie said.

When she spoke, the man halted for an instant in his move to stand upright, then he straightened and left. She faced front as he walked back to the patrol car, and she continued to stare straight ahead as he pulled out and passed them.

Derek's gaze never left her. "I was wondering if you were going to produce a pair of boxing gloves, Ms. Robertson. Was all that necessary?"

"He was talking over me and around me, and was too insensitive even to know it. Excuse me. Insensitive? May I change that to stupid?"

"You want to fight with me now, or do you want to save it for Kevin?"

"Oh, hell." She rested her forehead on the steering wheel.

"I don't suggest you get in his face like you did with that cop."

"Go up against your brother?" She sat back and looked across at him as if to plead. "Derek, there's no way I can go up against your brother."

"You did it once." He'd already eased up, it appeared. Apparently he'd dismissed the interlude with the redheaded cop as easily as the cop had dismissed Connie. "You held your own then, and you will again."

Then he added, "It could be worse, you know. What if that cop had stopped us before we let Moose off? We'd have still had him, the comic book, and Hayworth's gun."

She collapsed, folding her arms across the steering wheel and laying her forehead on them. "Oh, crap," she breathed, silently thanking Moose for his foresight in insisting upon his own car. And wondering how she was going to handle herself once school started in September. Her vocabulary needed attention. With her head on her arms, she slanted a look at Derek. "I don't like this. I don't like it at all."

"Can't say I'm exactly thrilled with it." Slouching in his seat, Derek tilted his head back and stared at the visor. He drew in a breath and let it out noisily. "He shouldn't have even been out there tonight. This is his day off. And the chief wouldn't respond to calls like that anyway. So he must've specifically requested to be informed of anything going on at the Hayworth house."

"Yeah, I'd already figured that out. He was expecting

something and was suspicious of us." She scrunched her face up. "With good cause."

Now she leaned her head back and stared at her own visor. To a passerby, they might've looked like tired travelers taking a nap. "I'm sorry, Derek. For getting you into this."

"I'm not. I did nothing wrong tonight, and I'm not sorry for any of it." He frowned, staring into space. "I'm surprised I did it," he said slowly, as if just now examining his feelings and being surprised all over again. "But not sorry."

A long silence followed. Then Connie asked, voice dull, "What are we going to do?"

"Face him. What else? He can't prove anything. And hopefully, he doesn't want to. He probably just wants to push a little bit. If I were in his shoes, I'd want to push a whole lot."

She straightened up and pressed her hands against the steering wheel, bracing herself for the coming ordeal as much as repositioning herself in the driver's seat. She had to work for a second or two until she was able to swallow, and then she turned the key in the ignition.

Kristy let them in, appearing friendly, but it looked like she was working hard for neutrality. She'd been doing a lot of that lately, Connie realized. The strain was showing in everyone. Kevin was on the phone, and his wife motioned for their guests to sit. She was barefoot and wore a different robe. This one was a knee-length, candy-striped duster, buttoned demurely to the neck. Connie figured it had to be new. It would've been a better choice for her to borrow if she could've found it.

"Tied up with his own shirt," Kevin said, supposedly repeating what he'd just been told over the phone line. One elbow was propped on the arm of the chair as he held the receiver to his ear. His other hand lay loosely in his lap. He had the look of a weary man, and he didn't even glance at Connie and Derek.

His attention seemed to be on the ceiling.

Connie took one end of the sofa, and Derek took the other.

Kristy questioningly raised her coffee cup, gaze traveling between them. "It's decaf," she assured them. They shook their heads. She sat in the armchair near Connie's end of the couch, tucking her feet under her. She smoothed the robe over her knees, sipped her coffee, and along with her guests watched and listened to her husband's end of the phone conversation.

". . . yeah, changed his story a couple of times. Doubt that we've got the whole thing yet, and we may never get it. Keep me posted." He hung up.

He closed his eyes, leaned forward to rest his elbows on his knees, and massaged his forehead with both hands. "How tall are you, Connie?"

"Huh?" She'd wanted to keep a low profile and let Derek deal with his brother, but that snapped her head up.

"You heard me."

"Five-two and a half," she answered guardedly.

"She's stretching that," Derek said.

Kevin snapped his eyes open and nailed them both with a hard stare. He'd lost the weary look. "I have never known anybody as *stupid. And* as reckless. *And* as incredibly lucky, as the two of you."

Connie couldn't hold the flinch back.

"Please note that I am not going to be asking you anything else," he went on. "I don't want either of you to tell me anything. Not a damned thing. I do the talking. You do the listening." He waited a beat. He looked like a firecracker in human form, one with a very short fuse. "Can you handle that?"

The two people on the sofa didn't respond. Derek didn't appear intimidated but seemed to have lost his flippancy. Connie folded her hands in her lap and returned her ex-brother-in-law's stare. She was back in the principal's office, but as Derek had told her she would, she was handling it.

Kevin rested his elbows on the arms of the recliner and made a tent with his fingers. "Okay, here goes. About thirty minutes ago, three people with a gun broke into Julian Hayworth's house—"

At the look that crossed Connie's face, Kevin stopped and stared at her. So did his brother. If he'd been close enough, she believed Derek would've kicked her.

Closing his eyes, Kevin shook his head. "Oh, Connie, please don't enter a life of crime. You'd never make a living at it."

When he again looked at them, it appeared he'd lost some of his heat. Then he went on. "So that part of it wasn't true. It was *his* gun, he held *you* at gunpoint, and somehow you got it away from him. That makes more sense. I couldn't see either one of you entering with a gun and waving it around."

Again he closed his eyes and shook his head. "I just heard what I said. I'd accepted the fact you'd broken into that house, but not that you did it with a gun. I don't believe this. I don't believe this whole, stupid night."

Connie stared at the rug. From the corner of her eye, she saw Derek pick up Andy's favorite toy that had been peeking out from under the sofa, a cloth turtle. He ran his thumb over the speckled green and black back.

"Okay. His gun." Wearily, Kevin nodded to himself as he supposedly put the pieces together to make sure they fit. "He probably doesn't have a permit for it, so didn't want to admit ownership."

Then, his attention returning to the two people who sat on the sofa, he resumed his narrative. "Judging by Hayworth's description, one of the three was undoubtedly Moose, but we still have no more information on him than we had before. Hayworth was certain, however, that neither of the Maxwell brothers was part of the group. Although one man was near Max's build, the resemblance stopped there. Whoever he was, he communicated by speaking in an irritatingly poor imitation of John Wayne."

His eyes rested pointedly on his brother. Derek didn't look up from the turtle.

Kevin's gaze fixed on Connie. "The most interesting character, however, was the third guy. According to Hayworth this . . . *man* . . . was about five-five or so and was built sparingly, but was exceptionally strong. He's convinced he was a jockey, a very well-conditioned one. And this guy was the most gutsy and nervy of the trio. At one point, Hayworth was able to get hold of the gun—he wasn't at all clear on how this came about, but he was quite clear on the fact that the jockey had then manhandled him and wrested it away by force."

Kristy's face grew pale. She sipped coffee and stared at the slate blue carpet.

Relentlessly Kevin continued. "However, my dear Connie, unlike the guns the Maxwell brothers used, this one was undoubtedly loaded."

The following silence was almost deafening. Connie guessed she'd also paled. She was having difficulty believing she'd done what she'd done and was carefully avoiding Derek's eyes. Everybody's eyes.

"That's the one thing that's going to save you, and I'm going to wonder for the rest of my life how you pulled it off. But because of the gun incident, he's convinced the short one was male, so the two of you will never be suspected." Kevin's expression hardened. "But this evening's caper could've had any number of lasting—and tragic—consequences." When he spoke next, his voice rose and his words rushed together. "And that makes me so damned mad, and so damned scared, that I'd like to knock your idiotic heads together."

He took several deep breaths, clearly reining himself in, and ran his hands down his face. "Right now you're sitting across from me. And I can vent. But we came close. That close . . ." He paused and held up thumb and forefinger, no space showing between them. ". . . to all three of you being arrested by me. That would've broken my spirit. And my heart. And Kristy's and Christopher's."

He stood and crossed to the fireplace. It appeared he was too tense to sit. The fire screen hung at a slant, and he jerked it to close it. It promptly opened again. "Got to fix that," he mumbled.

With his gaze remaining on the fireplace, Kevin said, "That loose light bulb bothered me. A lot. But I thought I'd missed you. Maybe only by a hair, but I figured you were already out of there. But then Hayworth said the next time he entered the study, the bulb was gone."

He looked across at them. "He had something in his safe he didn't want me to see, so he ushered me out. That saved your necks, and mine. But I have to have your word, right now, that you're through with this. Under no circumstances will *either* of you *ever* go after that comic book again. And you're not leaving this house tonight until I have that promise."

This time, Derek was no better than Connie at hiding his surprise. Their heads jerked toward each other.

"What?" Kevin's eyes narrowed, gaze flitting from one person to the other. "He lied about that, too?"

Connie sneaked a look at him. He'd sounded almost pleased.

"He didn't want to lose face." Kevin's tone took on a musing quality as he stared into space. "Couldn't admit he'd lost." Then his eyes and voice sharpened as he looked back at them. "But you got it? You really got it?"

His gaze continued to move between the two people on the sofa, as if seeking confirmation, then he caught himself. "No," he said quickly. "I didn't ask that. Don't answer that."

He crossed back to the recliner and sat down.

Yes, Connie thought. The man was pleased. But no way was she going to comment on that.

"So it's over," Kevin said, as if test-driving the statement. He glanced at his guests. It appeared the statement passed the test, though evidently some of his ire remained. "But I'd still like to wring both your necks," he said in an undertone.

Then he looked at his wife. "But I admit I've also got this ridiculous, equally strong desire to hug them."

"Then you hug them. I'll strangle them." Kristy's feet landed on the floor with a thump, and her empty coffee cup hit the table with a clatter. Her glare nailed Connie. "It's my turn. He may be done, but I'm just getting started." Her stare was so brittle, Connie dropped her gaze. It had been easier when Kevin was mad at her.

"So help me, Connie Louise Robertson, you scared me so badly tonight I don't know if I can ever forgive you." Her gaze left her friend to sweep the room while she wagged her head. Clearly she'd been holding in a lot of emotion for a long time.

"And to think I used to envy you." She seemed as disgusted with herself as with Connie. "You set a course and stayed with it, regardless of the consequences, exactly like you did tonight, while I berated myself for being too straitlaced. You had all the fun, and I was little Miss Goody Two-Shoes."

She looked back, eyes still intent, but Connie saw more concern than anger, and she also saw hurt. "Marriage tempered you," Kristy went on, "but didn't tame you, and I was glad. But then divorce left you wounded, and I missed the old Connie. Even though she'd too often had more spirit than common sense."

Leaning toward the sofa, she placed her hand atop her friend's. "Looks like you're back, kid, in no uncertain terms. But, honey, you went too far tonight. You were lucky, incredibly lucky, and even successful. But it so easily could've gone the other way. Like Kevin said, you're sitting here now. But I had visions of visiting you behind bars, in a hospital bed with a bullet in you, even—"

When her voice cracked, she grew quiet and looked at the floor.

For the first time that night, a sense of guilt was born within Connie. Her fingers tightened around Kristy's. An apology wouldn't cut it, and she wasn't sorry for stealing back the comic book anyway. But she was responsible for the strain on her best friend's face, and that she regretted.

Kristy said softly, without looking up, "I'm afraid, Connie, really afraid that if you ever pull anything like this again, I won't be able to forgive you."

Connie swallowed past a lump. Lightly she squeezed her friend's hand. "I understand. But if you can find it in your heart to forgive me this one last time, I promise in the future to stick to teaching school and leave crime to the criminals."

"Can I have that in writing?" Derek asked.

"That's *not* funny." In the same instant, she dropped Kristy's hand and snapped her head around toward her ex-husband. "I'm serious."

He stared back, unmoved. "So am I."

"A show of support wouldn't exactly be amiss here, O'Reilly."

Hearing Kristy's laugh, Connie looked back, her eyes squinting with surprise.

"Well, that's one good note." Kristy leaned her head back and grinned at the ceiling. "You're a couple again. Breaking into a house and committing robbery must've cemented something somewhere."

Kevin snorted. "That's all it took?"

"Yep. Doesn't make much sense, but that's them," she said dryly. "And I love them both." She stretched her arms above her head, and with the action, she visibly let the tension go. She added, "Oh, what a night this has been. I am so totally looking forward to putting it behind me."

Then she sat up straight, clasped her hands in her lap, and her gaze swept over each person in turn. It ended on Kevin, stayed there, and she wet her lips. "Goodnight, Connie. Goodnight, Derek," she said without looking at them.

When there was no immediate movement, she glanced at the people on the sofa. "I just realized how I want to bring this night to a close," she explained patiently. "But I really shouldn't go sit in his lap until the two of you are out of here."

Kevin looked at her, their guests, again at her. "Er, what?"

"You heard me. But if you really don't understand, I'll explain in a minute." She made shooing motions at the couch. "Go."

Again Connie squinted. She'd held her own against Kevin, but Kristy was throwing more curves than her husband. "Uh, what?"

Derek grinned. He stood, got Connie's hand and pulled her to her feet. "It's that straitlaced manner of yours, Kris. When you step out of it, you throw them both."

Chapter Twenty-Four

As she drove away from the O'Reilly house, Connie's heart, mind, and every other part of her was focused on the room with the oversized bed and the *do not disturb* sign. She figured the same went for Derek. But, although her foot remained steady on the accelerator, the car was slowing. As she frowned and pumped the pedal, she was aware of a familiar, sinking feeling forming in her gut. Anxiously she checked the fuel gauge.

"Pull over," Derek said, but she was already guiding the car into the right lane. Then she pulled onto the shoulder, barely making it before the sputtering started, and then abruptly ceased. She turned the key off, wondering why she bothered. The car wasn't going anywhere.

She rested her forehead on the steering wheel. Traffic whizzed by. "No," she muttered. "I don't believe this." All she needed now was for the redheaded cop to come by and ask her passenger what the problem was.

"You don't even have a stuck gauge to blame it on," her passenger said. "What's the matter, don't you ever check on how much gas you've got? It's that little window, right there."

"Don't start with me," she warned. She didn't lift her head from the steering wheel.

"Oh, I want to start with you, all right, but it's not an argument I've got in mind." The seat creaked as he changed position. "Talk about frustration. Are we ever going to get around to starting something, anything, besides an argument?"

She felt a slow grin crease her face. Well, it had been his idea in the first place. She looked sideways without lifting her head. When his eyes met hers, she raised her head, twisted around and looked pointedly into the back seat.

His response started out as a light chuckle, then developed into a full-throated belly laugh. "I'd love to call your bluff—if it is a bluff—but since I've waited this long, I can wait a little longer. And I can guarantee it's going to take more than a back seat tumble to satisfy me anyway."

Their gazes held. "But you tempt me, Mrs. O'Reilly. You really tempt me."

"It's Robertson."

"For now, maybe. Not for much longer."

"Oh, yeah? You sound pretty sure of yoursel—"

"Now's not the best time to get into it—we're out of gas and parked on the shoulder of the freeway in the middle of the night. I promise you, without doubt, that we will pick this up later, but right now we need a can of gas." He opened his car door. "And I'm wasting no more breath trying to talk you into a cell phone. You're getting one at my first opportunity. Period."

She didn't bother telling him that was also at the top of her agenda. She opened her door.

"Uh, Connie." Half in and half out of the car, he looked across at her. "If I asked you to lock the doors and wait here, you'd want to go with me. But if I asked you to go, you'd wait. Right?"

"I'm going." She withdrew the keys from the ignition and got out of the car.

He directed a shrug toward the chain fence lining the freeway. "She's going."

An exit was less than a quarter mile away, and from there it was a block to a gas station. Neither of them minded the walk. Connie felt like she was still on an adventure, an unending one that had started two weeks ago. She enjoyed her ex-husband's company, their banter, and her hand in his. And she still had that marvelous, euphoric sense of a job well done.

Arriving back at the car, he poured a small amount of gas into the carburetor, and then emptied the can into the tank. They drove to the station and filled the tank, but when Connie exited the station's lot, she pulled off onto the side of the road instead of heading back to the freeway.

Derek gave her a questioning look. She stared at the road sign at the corner of the intersection. "If I'm not mistaken, a couple of miles in from here there's a small farmhouse where we recently spent some time." She looked across at him. "Right? Or do I have my directions mixed up again?"

"Nope." He chuckled. "You're right on that one."

Her gaze returned to the sign. "We started something there one morning we never got to finish. Somehow, it only seems fitting we return there tonight." She gave him another sideways glance. "What do you think?"

"I think the owner would have us arrested for trespassing."

"He's just jealous because he can't do John Wayne like you can. Where's your sense of adventure?"

"You haven't had enough adventure for one night? After the risks we've already taken, you want to take one more?"

She grinned. "Uh-huh. And tomorrow morning, we could walk out to the stream. I've even got a blanket in the trunk we could take with us."

He continued to watch her. He was tempted, she could tell.

"I know where there's a key," she coaxed.

"So do I. Under a pink flower in the back yard."

"More precisely, under a rock next to a pink flower. An azalea."

Obviously he was still thinking and still tempted, so she gave him time.

"Okay," he said finally. "But there's a condition."

"A condition?"

He laughed, probably because her surprise showed on her face. She hadn't gotten instant surrender, but, as he'd pointed out, the farmhouse was an off-the-wall destination and riskier than the Holiday Inn. But she hadn't expected him to attach strings.

She watched his expression smooth out and slowly grow sober. Then he reached over, put his hand on her knee and squeezed. "Yes. A condition. You have to promise we'll talk about when—not if—you'll be changing your name from Robertson back to O'Reilly."

It wasn't going to be all or nothing with him this time, she could tell. No more push from him other than that slight pressure on her knee. She could pull away from the curb and drive straight ahead, get back on the freeway and proceed to the Holiday Inn. Safe, no risk. Or she could turn around, go back and take another shot at something that had been started—and interrupted—a long time ago.

The second wedding of television's most eligible bachelor—to his first wife—drew more media attention than either of the principals was comfortable with. The simple ceremony they'd envisioned quickly mushroomed into a small extravaganza.

They found a way around it, however.

The ballroom at a prestigious downtown hotel was booked for the reception, and the penthouse bridal suite had also been reserved. But, known to only a select few, it was the best man and matron of honor who would be using it.

After the ceremony, the bride and groom dutifully sipped champagne, partook of their wedding feast, led the first dance, and cut the huge wedding cake. Then a friend of Derek's, a celebrity in his own right, appeared and drew a sizable amount of attention.

Mr. and Mrs. Derek O'Reilly were there—and then they weren't.

They changed clothing in back bathrooms, near housekeeping. With the kids in their grandparents' care, Kevin and Kristy stood guard in the hallway outside the respective restrooms. Dressed in jeans, t-shirts, sneakers and baseball caps, the bride and groom met in the corridor, feeling and looking like runaways.

Derek's headgear swore his allegiance to his beloved San Diego Padres, but Connie's expensive hairdo was now tucked inside a cap bearing the San Francisco Giants logo. Derek took a double take.

"Huh?"

"Never mind. I wasn't paying attention. I just bought the first one I saw."

"You need helmets instead of those caps," Kevin said with a grin. "And boots. And you could escape on motorcycles."

Kristy tried to swallow a giggle, but it got away from her. She quickly looked around, as though fearing that one laugh might alert the whole reception to their whereabouts. "Whatever your mode of transportation is, you best get to it," she warned.

She looked exquisite in a mint-green gown that left her shoulders bare, emphasized her waist, and flowed to her feet. Her hair was stacked on top of her head, curling tendrils teased her forehead and neck, and tiny gold buttons adorned her ears. Kevin had seldom taken his eyes off her. When she spoke, he looked her way, and the look of a man smitten once more appeared on his face.

"I don't know how much longer your luck is going to hold," she added, and the four people exchanged quick goodbyes. "I can understand your not wanting to tell anyone where you're going," Kristy told Connie with her hug. "But I hope you'll at least tell us where you've been when you get back."

Connie and Derek exchanged secretive smiles.

Derek and Kevin traded car keys. Derek looked dubious when relinquishing his. "Don't worry about it," his brother said airily. "You take care of my van; I'll take care of your convertible."

The snazzy red convertible was a sharper-looking honeymoon vehicle, but the nondescript green sedan was a better getaway car and had won hands down. It was packed and waiting three miles away in a supermarket's parking lot. The van would get them to it, and its owners could then pick up their vehicle at their leisure.

Kevin walked with them to the service door leading into the parking lot, then clasped an arm around each of them and drew them close. The hug was a tight one. "It better take this time," he whispered, sounding both gruff and choked. "I've gotten dressed up twice for you guys, and I don't intend to do it again."

Then his gaze strayed to his wife, and he again checked her out with the eyes of a hungry man. Abruptly he shook himself, as if forcing himself back to the present, released the two people and pointed at the door. "Now get the hell out of here. Go. And for Pete's sake, at least *try* to stay out of trouble."

One week later, in red cotton shorts and a halter, Connie was stretched out on her back on a padded lounge. If she were any more relaxed, she'd be snoring. Derek, wearing khaki shorts and an open sport shirt in vivid orange and green, stirred on the lounge beside hers.

The day was balmy, the crash of waves thunderous and soporific. In the background, in one of the guesthouses behind them, Willie Nelson was on the road again. She heard Derek slip his shirt off. "Whew. I need a cold beer. How about you?"

"Umm." She barely managed a negative gesture.

"Anything?"

"Umm." She managed one more shake of her head.

"You've got a serious control problem there. You need to learn to channel all that energy."

When he returned, he sat and stared at the ocean while sipping his beer. She remained dreamily comatose. Voices grew near, and then chairs scraped as their neighbors joined them on the community terrace.

"Could really go for a root beer," said one voice.

"Bring me back some ice water," said another.

"I miss Chris," said a plaintive voice near Connie's elbow.

She couldn't count the number of times Petey had said that since they'd arrived. He was a grown-up living in a lonely child's world, and Connie's determination to engineer a play-date between those two kids before Christopher got much older was again reinforced.

Opening her eyes, she gave him a lazy but commiserative glance. Wearing his Bart Simpson t-shirt, well-worn jeans and scruffy sneakers, he looked like the kid that he was.

"Yeah, I know what you mean," Moose said. He stared wistfully at the ocean. "Wouldn't mind having a baby or two on my lap right about now. I could take them wading, and maybe build sand castles and stuff."

Max laughed as he returned with the drinks. It still seemed strange to hear him laugh, but they'd found that he was a lot more relaxed at his new home on the Mexican coast. "Somehow, it's hard to imagine a honeymooning couple dragging along three kids." He handed a glass of water and ice to Moose. "But I am glad they chose to spend some time with old friends."

"Perfect wedding gift," Derek said. He sounded like a man at peace with the world and his place in it. "A honeymoon to die for. Beautiful location, great neighbors, cozy cottage. Thanks, Max."

"Umm," Connie agreed.

"Moose, may I have that glass for a minute?" Derek asked.

Warned by a sixth sense, Connie sat up—but not fast enough. Half the glass of ice and water splashed across her bare midriff. She yelped, swiped her arm across her stomach, and glared at her husband.

He handed the glass back to Moose. "Thanks. Left you a little bit."

"That'll wake you up in a hurry." Max grinned at her. He wore an oversized sleeveless undershirt which showed off tanned skin, baggy beige shorts, and brown sandals with wide straps.

He added, his gaze taking in the two of them, "And that cottage is yours any time you want it. Just let me know, and I'll keep it free. Made the same invitation to my old buddy over there. If he ever gets around to needing a private little place for two."

Moose was silent.

Connie was still glaring at Derek. But once she became aware of the big man's silence, she turned toward him and drew her sunglasses down onto the bridge of her nose. His Hawaiian shirt had splashes of orange, green and gold, similar to Derek's, and he wore it over khaki shorts the same style as Derek's, but each garment was several sizes larger.

"Well?" she asked pointedly.

Not meeting anyone's eyes, Moose smiled self-consciously at his diminished drink. Then he blushed.

"All right!" Connie brought her open palm down onto Derek's bare leg below the hem of his shorts, just sharp enough to sting.

"Ow!" He jumped, and then gave her a steady stare.

She put sweet insincerity in her smile. "Sorry. Got this serious control problem. My enthusiasm sometimes gets away from me."

She looked back at Moose. "When?"

But he still wasn't meeting anyone's eyes. Sounding and looking ridiculously shy, he mumbled, "We're working on arrangements. Or at least she is. I'll be happy with anything." Awkwardly, he glanced at Max. "But I told her I want to arrange the honeymoon. And I'd like to take you up on that offer, Max. Thanks."

Max looked like a proud parent. Regarding Moose with a happy half smile, he sat back in his chair, crossed his ankles and folded his hands across his stomach. "Any time, old buddy. You name it."

Connie was sitting directly opposite Moose. She waited, biding her time, and watched his gaze light everywhere but on her. "Well, big guy," she drawled, really dragging it out, "you must know by now. Can she, er . . . uh, cook?"

He turned pink. He directed his gaze at the sky. He asked plaintively, miserably, "Uncle Dare, can you shut her up? Muzzle her . . . something . . . anything?"

Her grin grew. "I take it the answer is affirmative?"

Fortunately for her victim, her stomach rumbled. It sounded as loud as a wave crashing on the beach. She made a face, placed her hand on her midriff, and glanced sideways at Derek.

His face split into a grin. "Time for dinner, Mrs. O'Reilly?"

"Evidently. How long? And what is it?"

"Depends. What do you want?"

"Been eyeing that eggplant for two days."

Max gave her a curious look. "What's that?"

"That purple thing," Moose said. It didn't appear that he even tried to repress his shudder.

"Give it a chance," Connie told him with a smile. "The way he does it, it's all tomato-ey and cheesy. You might like it."

Petey stood up. He didn't appear any more interested in dinner plans than he'd been in wedding plans. "Max, can I go watch TV? It's time for the comics."

"Sure. Did you practice saying your Spanish words today?"

"Three times. They're getting easy." He hesitated, looking pained. "You can give me some more if you want to."

"Tomorrow's soon enough. Go watch your comics. You're learning a lot just through TV."

"That reminds me," Moose said as Petey left. "The comics. That's something I wanted to talk to you about, Max. *Again.* There's got to be a better place for SteelMan than in your underwear drawer."

Max shrugged off his friend's concern. "No one around here even knows I've got the thing. If I initiated security measures, then they'd guess I've got something valuable. SteelMan's got a good home. He'll be just fine right where he is."

Derek excused himself and went inside to work on the eggplant but returned so quickly Connie guessed he'd prepared it earlier and had simply put it in the oven. She wondered what he would've done if she'd said she wanted hamburgers.

She also became aware of the change in Max's mood. His expression seemed strained as he stared at the ocean, glancing occasionally at Moose, then her and Derek, then back at the surf. She wondered what was bothering him, and how long it would take for him to spill it.

She apparently wasn't the only one who'd noticed. The atmosphere on the deck became quietly expectant. Then it seemed that Max caught it, too, because he said, carefully avoiding everybody's eyes, "About SteelMan. I'm thinking I might have to sell him. And it's only right to let you guys know, considering the risk you went to in stealing him back for me in the first place."

Three gazes fixed on him, in various degrees of surprise and disapproval. Connie was the first to speak. "Sell SteelMan? Why?"

He squirmed, still not meeting anyone's eyes. "Well, Moose is getting married, and he lent me a lot of money to buy this place. I don't—"

"Shut up, Max." Moose looked relieved. "Like I told you, I follow my own investment advice, and I'm good at my job. I'm fine. This place is paying for itself, just like you figured, and you can continue paying me back in installments. Don't even think about selling SteelMan to pay me back."

"I can't speak for my partners in crime," Derek said. "But I went to too much trouble to get that book back. I'd rather lend you the money than see you sell it. SteelMan is . . . is . . . well, family."

"That he is," Connie agreed in her schoolteacher voice. "Derek and I broke the law that night." She glanced at Moose. "With family." She paused and looked at Max. "And for family, whether we're related or not. Every time I think about it I still have difficulty believing we got away with everything we got away with. It's just not right to sell that comic book. Please don't."

Max studied his feet inside the aged pair of brown beach shoes. "Well, okay, I guess. What can I say? Seems I'm seriously outnumbered here." Looking up, he gave them an exaggerated shrug. "So it looks like SteelMan stays where he is. Right there in my undershorts."

A brief, pained silence followed, during which no one looked directly at anyone else. Squinting, Derek stared at the cobblestone floor. Connie swallowed hard, pushed her tongue against her teeth, and looked at the patio doors. Moose watched the ocean, his face going through contortions. He lost it first, guffaws exploding out of him, and the newly married couple followed suit. Whoops of laughter rang across the terrace.

"What?" Max said, gaze traveling from one person to another. "What did I miss?" Then his face reddened. "Oh." His eyes closed, and his face scrunched up. "Oh."

Removing the sunglasses, Connie wiped her streaming eyes with the back of her hand. "Oh, for crying out loud. Never have I laughed so hard, fought so hard, or been so scared until the day SteelMan entered my life."

She drew in a long breath. "Talk about the good old days. Life certainly has calmed down since then." She caught Derek's eyes, and added with sweet mischief, "Lately, one might even say it's become downright tame."

"You think?" Derek leaned toward Moose. "May I have that glass of water back, please?"

Connie jumped to her feet with more haste than grace. At the sliding glass door, she paused and turned back. The glass had changed hands, but she thought she was out of range. "Uh, Max, you do understand you don't have to sell the book in order to find out its value? I tried checking once, didn't get anywhere, but it's gotta be worth more than five thousand bucks."

Max nodded soberly. "Yep, it is. I thank my lucky stars every day that Hayworth didn't take me up on that ridiculous price tag I put on it. When I finally got around to looking into it, I double-checked, then triple-checked, and I still can't believe it."

He said nothing more. Three gazes remained on him.

"Well?" Connie asked. "Do we have to beg?"

"Max," Moose said patiently.

Derek settled back into his chair. "Mr. Maxwell, any minute now, you're going to get the rest of this glass of ice cubes in your lap. Now, just how much is that book worth?"

After taking a long slug of root beer, Max said mildly, "Around a hundred and eighty grand."

Silence.

Moose broke into a slow smile. "It just keeps getting better and better. We didn't steal a measly five thousand bucks. We stole a hundred and eighty big ones." He made a loud smacking sound. "Damn, we're good."

Connie stepped inside the cottage and stood aside for Derek to enter. The key was proving difficult to pull out of the lock. He got it, pushed the door closed, and crossed the room ahead of her. Watching him, she leaned her back against the door, remembering the day she'd married this man for the second time.

Exiting the van, they'd headed for the green sedan, hand in hand, and then his arm encircled her shoulders and pulled her close. "It's not legal yet," he whispered.

Twisting her head around and up, she gave him a look that was probably quizzical.

"Not until it's consummated," he explained.

"Oh." Those blue-green eyes were again mesmerizing her. "In that case, I vote for legal," she whispered. His gaze, and the legal state of their marriage, chased everything else right out of her mind. They stood at the side of the green sedan for a long while before she remembered they needed keys and she had them.

As he watched her search the voluminous bag she called a purse, he said, "When you start braking for green lights, it's my turn to drive."

Coming up with the keys, she squinted questioningly at the sun, as if it might have arrows pointing out directions. "Which way is south?"

His chuckle was fast and deep. He snagged the keys. "Get in the car. That side."

Their marriage had been legal for several days now. Putting the room key on the nightstand next to the bed, he faced her.

"Well," she said.

"Well," he agreed.

"You realize that it's already been a week, and we haven't had a fight yet?"

"Don't let it bother you. We'll get around to it."

He slipped his feet out of the thongs. Connie checked out the feet, the bowed and hairy legs, and the flat stomach and hard chest exposed by the unbuttoned shirt. When her eyes finally met his, his mouth quirked.

"Umm," she said, "you look good."

"Dear wife. That goes both ways."

"SteelMan earned my life-long gratitude by bringing you back to me."

"I'd say that goes both ways as well."

Television's one-time most eligible bachelor, and he was all hers. And she was his. "Would you accuse me of understatement again if I said he'd forever won me as a fan with that feat?"

He just stood there with that smile.

She walked toward him, taking her time. "You know, in some ways, the second time around is better than the first."

He tilted his head. "Hmm?"

"Maybe because we're older and wiser, and know just how precious our love is?"

"Hmm."

"I've noticed you're giving me a lot of space." She continued her slow journey. "Have you noticed that the more you give me, the less I seem to need?"

"Hmm."

There was one step left. She took it, but didn't touch him. Instead she looked up at the curve of his lips, the light of anticipation in his eyes, the ardency in the set of his face and heard his quickened breathing, all of which were as potent as foreplay. "Hmm," she echoed, voice also a little on the breathy side. "Got quite a limited vocabulary there. Does it denote limited energy and enthusiasm as well?"

"Uh-uh." He put his arms around her, one at her back, stooped to get the other under her knees, and then he lifted her up only to turn around and put her down on the bed.

He was short on neither energy nor enthusiasm.

ABOUT THE AUTHOR

Bobbie O'Keefe enjoys reading so much that she tried writing her own novel. And she even got published. She and her husband live in the San Francisco Bay Area, where she visits the ocean as often as possible, and she *always* has to go wading. www.bobbieokeefe.com.